FRENCH CONNECTION

CLUB PRIVÉ 5

M. S. PARKER

BELMONTE PUBLISHING, LLC

Copyright © 2016 Belmonte Publishing LLC

Published by Belmonte Publishing LLC

FREE BOOK

Get a book for FREE! Click Here to subscribe to my weekly newsletter and start reading the exclusive 200 pages stand-alone Erotic romance, *The Billionaire's Sub*.

READING ORDER

Thank you so much for reading the Club Privé series. If you'd like to read the complete series, I recommend reading them in this order:

ONE
CARRIE

I leaned back in my chair and stretched my arms above my head. My elbows popped, a sensation filled with both tension and release. I rolled my head, trying to loosen the tight muscles in my neck and shoulders. When I'd been a paralegal at Webster and Steinberg, I thought I knew what it was like to have to sit at a desk for hours at a time. Now, after almost a year of running my own pro bono law office, specializing in sexual harassment and sex trafficking cases, I knew just how naïve I'd been. I looked back longingly at eight-hour days.

Not that I was really complaining. I loved my job. I'd been good at divorce law, and there had been a few times when I'd been able to see the good I was doing. But with this, being able to select my own cases and experience the difference I was making in people's lives, I felt like my years of hard work were finally paying off.

Like now, I had this pet project going on. A few months back, a soft-spoken woman came into my Manhattan office and told me her daughter had been tricked into the sex trade. Once

I'd gotten the name, I'd known why she'd come to me rather than the cops. Client confidentiality would prevent me from sharing the fact that Robyn Leeds, daughter of the governor, had chosen to trade her body for money. Since my office was just me and my assistant, Zoe Masters, Mrs. Leeds felt she could trust us to be discreet.

I'd found Robyn through a source in the police department when the fifteen-year-old had been picked up in a sting. She hadn't been happy when I'd come to get her, but I'd managed to make her see reason and agree to testify against her "boyfriend," Little Tino.

Or so I'd thought.

For the past month, I'd kept tabs on Robyn, calling to check in every couple days to see how she was doing. Her parents were notorious for leaving her by herself while they took business trips to the Bahamas. Usually, Robyn was good about answering my calls or at least getting back to me right away if I had to leave a voicemail. This week, however, I called three times and hadn't heard from her at all. I was starting to get worried.

Part of the reason Robyn had let Little Tino talk her into having sex with his friends, and then with strangers, was that she craved being taken care of. With her parents on another of their trips and no one except the housekeeper around, I had a bad feeling she'd gone back to her pimp who was out on bail.

I pressed the intercom. "Zoe, I need to you to keep calling Robyn every hour and tell her to call me. Tell her if I don't hear from her by the end of the day, I'm involving the cops." I waited for my assistant to agree, but there was only silence. I frowned and tried again. "Zoe?"

When I still didn't get a response, I stood and walked out of my office. Zoe wasn't at her desk. I glanced into the conference room next to my office and found it empty too. There weren't many other places Zoe could be. My office was nice, but not very big. I checked the restroom, wondering if she'd just forgotten to tell me she was taking a break, but she wasn't there either. It wasn't until I glanced at the clock as I headed back to my office that I realized it was almost noon and the morning had rushed by like a speeding train.

I frowned at myself. Zoe always took her lunch from eleven-thirty to twelve-thirty, and I never asked her to let me know when she was going since she always went at the same time. I just usually paid better attention than this.

Just as I reached my office door, I heard the lobby buzzer. I scowled, wondering what idiot couldn't read the hours posted on our lobby sign. I was tempted to ignore it, but that would mean I'd either have to get back to someone or track down a package. I wasn't in the mood to do either.

I walked over to Zoe's desk and hit the front desk intercom. "Yes?"

"UPS delivery, ma'am," the desk manager said. "He needs a signature."

"Send him up." I sighed and closed my eyes.

I was exhausted. Between worrying about Robyn and working on a proposal for Congressman White, as well as trying to sort through the cases that came across my desk, I hadn't slept more than a few hours a night in a couple of months. And it wasn't like anything I was doing could be put aside. It was all too important. Every case had the potential of saving a life. Robyn could be in trouble. And the proposal for the congressman was key in the fight against sex trafficking.

I'd first met Joshua White about six months ago when I'd

attended a fund-raiser for sex trafficking awareness. He'd been passionate about the subject and after learning what I did, had asked me to work on a proposal detailing all of the areas in which the law was negligent. I'd finished the document but was still working on the polish. I had a meeting with his assistant tomorrow to present my case, and she would decide if what I had was good enough to pass on to the congressman. It had to be perfect.

The front door opened and I straightened, fixing my best disapproving expression on my face. It wasn't difficult. The man who entered was just a bit above average height, with broad shoulders, but I couldn't see any of his features. They were hidden under the brim of his hat and a pair of dark sunglasses. He kept his head down, so my stern glare was lost on him.

I took the package and scrawled my name on the receipt.

"Thanks," I said tersely as I handed the clipboard back and tossed the box onto Zoe's desk. I turned to walk into my office when the delivery man spoke.

"Aren't you going to open it?"

I froze. I'd know that voice anywhere. My pulse quickened. There was only one reason I could think of why my boyfriend would be delivering a package while dressed like a UPS man. Desire flared deep inside me. It had been a while since Gavin and I had role-played, and never at my work. I wasn't quite sure what my role was supposed to be, but I knew Gavin would make sure I understood where we were going.

"Do you want me to open it now?" I asked, turning around.

He pulled off the hat and tousled his dark hair. Next came the sunglasses, revealing those deep blue eyes that made me weak in my knees. "Ms. Summers, I think you need to check your package and make sure it's not damaged."

"Certainly, Mr. Delivery Boy." I gave him a polite smile and carefully unwrapped the package. I caught my breath as I opened the box, revealing its contents.

Two tiny pieces of rich purple silk were inside. I held up the bra as if inspecting it, and then the panties. They were both easily half the size of what I was wearing at the moment.

"They look fine," I said with a casual lift to my shoulder.

He took a step toward me. "I think you should try them on, just to be sure."

"Oh really?" I raised an eyebrow.

He nodded and I saw a hint of a dimple as he tried to keep from smiling. "And, I'll have to carefully examine them to ensure everything's in order."

"I don't think so."

The quirk of his lips told me I'd given the right response.

"Ms. Summers, if I delivered a defective package, I could lose my job." His face went puppy dog, his voice just shy of pleading. "You wouldn't want to be responsible for that, would you?"

I tapped my toe and sighed, then picked up the package and motioned for him to follow me. "You can wait in my office while I change in my private bathroom."

Gavin followed me, closing the door behind us. He stopped partway into the room and waited.

I made my voice as firm as possible. "Don't touch anything. I'll be right back."

Once in the bathroom, I quickly stripped off my work clothes and underwear, leaving them in a neat little pile on the edge of the sink. My skin was flushed with arousal as I slid into the tiny panties and then fastened on the bra. Once I was finished, I took a step back to get the full effect in the mirror. I was grateful I'd shaved this morning.

I owned far more lingerie now than I had before I'd met Gavin, and this was definitely one of the sexiest things I'd ever worn. The panties were sheer, leaving practically nothing to the imagination. The bra was not only equally as transparent, but was so low cut that I was pretty sure, if I breathed too hard, my nipples would pop out. It hooked in front and the clasps were covered with a cute little ribbon that fell all the way to my bellybutton.

Just one more thing needed to be done. I usually pinned my hair back at work because many people thought I was younger than twenty-five and, for a lawyer, looking youthful wasn't always a good thing. Now, I pulled the pins out and let my golden curls fall around my shoulders. Gavin liked my hair down.

With a final smile at my reflection, I headed back into my office. Gavin was standing right where I'd left him. I gave myself a moment to appreciate the way the uniform hugged his body, and then I walked out of the bathroom.

His eyes lit up when he saw me, and then darkened with desire, but he didn't break character. "What do you think, Ms. Summers?"

"I think you might need to take a closer look and make sure I didn't miss anything."

He closed the distance between us in two quick strides, but stopped before our bodies touched. He looked down at me for a moment and I thought he'd give in and kiss me, but he didn't. Instead, he reached out and cupped my breasts, his expression almost clinical. "It appears to contour nicely to your body."

He ran his thumbs across my nipples, back and forth again and again until I couldn't quite stop myself from moaning.

"Seems the material doesn't detract from sensitivity," he said matter-of-factly. His palms were hot as they slid down over my ribcage to my hips. "But I better check the panties too, just to be sure."

His index finger ran along the elastic and I shivered. Goosebumps rose on my skin and he slid his hand around to my ass. The only fabric there was a thin strip that didn't actually cover anything, so it was all skin-on-skin as he squeezed and rubbed, all the while making his way to where the material disappeared between my cheeks. His fingers teased at the crack, then slid further down so that his hand was moving between my legs.

Despite the awkward angle, his fingers managed to brush against the now-soaked crotch of my panties and I swallowed hard.

"Hmm," he said. His forehead furrowed as a thoughtful expression crossed his face. He removed his hand.

"Is there a problem?" I was trying for innocent, but couldn't deny the breathless quality in my voice.

"Your panties appear to be wet, Ms. Summers." He circled around me until he was out of my line of sight. An arm snaked around my waist and his fingers danced across my lower abdomen, then dropped lower.

I drew in a sharp breath as his fingers pressed against me through the thin material. He ran them up and down, thoroughly wetting the fabric before pushing it aside. I moaned as his index finger slipped between my lips and I spread my legs, giving him the room he needed to work.

"Why, Ms. Summers." His breath was hot against my ear. "I believe I may have found the problem." The tip of his finger circled my entrance, teasing but not penetrating. "There seems to be a leak. I may need to plug it up. What do you think?"

I smiled and nodded mutely, my eyes closing as I silently willed him to touch me where I needed it. All of the tension of the day was a giant ball inside me and I knew if he could make me come, it'd all fade away.

Fingers lightly pinched my nipple and I cried out as a jolt of pleasure went through me.

"I asked you a question." Gavin's voice was low, taking on the authoritative tone that brought another rush of juices flooding south. He hadn't used that tone in a long time. "Do you think I should do something about this little problem we have?"

"Yes, please."

The words were barely out of my mouth before his finger was sliding into me.

"Shit," I breathed. I pressed down on his hand, desperate for friction on my throbbing clit.

Gavin's arm wrapped around my waist, holding me still. He made a disapproving sound. "No, Ms. Summers. You need to stay put."

Stay put? How in the world did he expect me to be still when his finger moved so slowly? I was certain I'd go crazy before I could orgasm. Before I could ask, or even think of how to say the words, his hand shifted and a second finger joined the first. He wasn't exactly being rough, but he wasn't gentle either as he thrust his fingers into me over and over. Then his heel pressed against my clit and I grabbed onto his arm, my nails digging into his flesh.

"Yes!" I cried out as his hand moved, pushing against all the right places. My body was on fire, burning from the inside out, and I could feel my climax approaching.

"Come on, baby," he said. His teeth scraped over the shell of my ear. "Come for me. Make those panties even wetter."

He pressed his lips against the spot where my shoulder and neck met, then bit down. Not hard enough to hurt, but enough to push me over the edge.

I pressed my lips together to hold in a scream as I came. I'd never been a screamer until I'd started fucking Gavin. Now, my body shook as pleasure coursed through me as well as from the effort to keep my love noises inside. It had been weeks, maybe months, since I'd come that hard. He held me upright, his fingers working me as high as I could go and then beyond, almost until pleasure became pain, and then he stopped. His hand slid out from between my legs and he turned me so that I was facing my desk.

"Now, Ms. Summers, look what you've done."

My chest was heaving as I drew in deep breaths, each one threatening to make my breasts burst free of their silken confines. Gavin put his hand on my back and applied pressure, telling me without words what he wanted me to do. I complied, leaning over my desk, resting on my elbows.

"I think you owe me for pleasuring you," he said. He ran his hands over my back and sides, then underneath me to squeeze my breasts. "What do you think?"

I wasn't sure I could speak, but I managed a single word. "Yes."

"And what do you think you should give me to show your gratitude for a job well done?" Gavin's fingers teased my nipples, the fabric between them almost chafing on the sensitive flesh.

"Anything," I gasped. Nobody knew my body the way he did. "Anything you want."

His fingers pulled my panties to one side, dragging across my still wet skin. I moaned but didn't move from where Gavin wanted me. The moan turned into a surprised yelp as he roughly shoved his fingers inside me. My head fell forward as he thrust at least two of them into me.

"Fuck." I closed my eyes. He hadn't been that forceful with me in months. I hadn't realized how much I'd missed it.

"Fuck? Is that what you want?" His free hand managed to unsnap the clasp on my bra, freeing my breasts.

"Yes," I answered immediately. I pushed back against his hand. "Please."

"Please what?"

He loved making me say what I wanted, tell him how it felt having him inside me. I understood it. He could say anything and it would make me wet.

"Please fuck me," I begged.

"If you insist, Ms. Summers."

His fingers slipped out, leaving me empty and wanting. I heard the sound of a zipper and then, he was pushing into my pussy. My muscles trembled as my body stretched to accommodate him. Even with foreplay, it was a tight fit, and his cock filled me completely, reaching places no one but him had ever reached before.

He buried himself with a groan, his hands sliding under me to cup my breasts. He gave me a moment, waiting for the muscles surrounding him to stop their fluttering. No matter how many times we did this, that first penetration never got old. And then he began to move, pulling back until he was nearly out and then slamming forward, sending near-painful pleasure coursing through me as his cock sank deeply to the root.

When I'd first seen him naked, I hadn't been sure it was

possible for him to fit inside me, and it wasn't a naivety thing of not understanding how biology worked. He was huge. But it wasn't size alone that made him a magnificent lover. He knew what he was doing and, from moment one, I'd known we'd been made for each other.

I cried out as he drove into me and it was all I could do to brace myself on the desk. His hands squeezed my breasts, then began to play with my nipples. His long fingers were talented, knowing just the right way to roll and pull. He'd once made me climax from my nipples alone, something I hadn't thought was possible until he'd taken me to bed. Now, it added to the other sensations I was feeling until my entire body was like a single live nerve.

His hands moved to my hips, gripping me tight as he fucked me, each thrust hard enough to push me onto my toes. I'd have bruises later and, if the pressure bubbling inside me was any indication, it'd be worth every one. I felt his rhythm falter and knew he was close. I shifted my weight onto one arm and slid my other one beneath me. I half-expected him to stop me from touching myself, remembering one of our first encounters where he'd done just that. He'd told me then that I was his, that he would be the one to bring me pleasure. This time, however, my fingers reached that spot between my legs without interference.

I felt him pulse inside me as I started to rub my clit. A few passes was all I needed and then I was coming too, my pussy contracting around his cock as it emptied into me. I heard him groan my name and his arms slid around my waist as he slumped over me for a moment.

Before my pulse had returned to normal, Gavin pulled out, causing another shudder to run through me. Even soft, he was big enough to get a reaction. After a moment, I straightened.

"Thank you," I said as I fixed my bra and panties. I'd change back into my other underwear in a moment, but I was suddenly aware that I was in my office and almost naked. My thighs were slick with our cum and I was glad I had my own bathroom. Clean-up would've been a bitch otherwise.

He grinned at me as he tucked himself back into his pants. "You've been working so hard and I figured since we hadn't done it here, now was as good a time as any."

I glanced at the clock and swore. "Zoe will be back—"

"No, she won't," Gavin interrupted. "I arranged for her to take a two hour lunch. You still have plenty of time to get cleaned up and presentable before it's back to work." He took my hands and leaned forward to kiss my forehead.

I leaned against him. The tension I'd had before was gone, melted away. I'd missed this. I wasn't the only one who'd been working hard. Lately, it seemed like the only time we saw each other was when one of us was sleeping. I'd thought moving in together would bring us closer, and I supposed we would've seen less of each other if we'd been living apart, but it didn't make things easier.

"So," he said. "I got a call a couple hours ago and have a dinner meeting with a potential new client tonight. What do you say? Dinner, dancing, some wine, then we spend some quality time together?"

I wanted so badly to say yes. A night with him was what I needed, but I sighed and straightened. The moment was gone. "I can't tonight. I have to finish my presentation for Congressman White. If I can get his assistant interested, there's a good chance the congressman will use some of my ideas for a bill against sex-trafficking."

Gavin smiled, but I could see the disappointment in his

eyes. I hated putting it there, but I was doing important work. There were thousands of young women out there being held against their will, forced into sexual slavery, and I had to do everything in my power to free them.

"I understand," he said as he released my hands. "But tomorrow night, you and I are having dinner at La Petite." He gave me a cocky smile. "It took me a month to get those reservations."

I smiled back. "It's a date." I glanced at the clock again. "But now, I really need to get dressed." I winked at him. "Unless you think I should see clients like this?"

His eyes narrowed and he grabbed me, pulling me against his chest. His mouth came down hard on mine and I could feel the fire there as his tongue pushed past my lips. He plundered my mouth, all teeth and tongue, until I was gasping for air.

"No one sees you like this but me," he all but growled as he finally released my mouth.

"Never," I agreed. I let myself have a moment, then sighed. "But you really do need to go."

I could feel the reluctance in his arms as he released me, but he knew as well as I did that I had work to do. The door to my office was swinging closed behind him as I disappeared into the bathroom. It was time to return to reality.

TWO
GAVIN

My little tryst with Carrie had taken more time out of my day than I'd planned, but it had been worth it. She did great work, and I knew it was important, but I could tell things between us were suffering. Today had been the first day in over a week that we'd had sex. For some people, that would've been about average, but when you considered that nine or ten months ago, we'd had sex almost every night, this was a bit of a dry spell. Our time together had been slowly decreasing over the months. When we'd first gotten together, we hadn't been able to get enough of each other. Now, it was same old, same old.

I was late as I rushed down to the streets of Manhattan. I groaned in frustration and ran my hand through my hair as my cab pulled up to the curb. The hat I'd worn had given me hat-hair, but again, worth it. I could still feel Carrie's smooth skin under my hands, feel her tight channel squeezing every last drop from my cock.

Dammit. Just thinking about her was getting me hard again.

As I walked into Abruzzi's Italian Dining, I forced myself to think of things of a less appetizing nature. I was already running behind for my dinner with Vincent Paoli. I doubted greeting him with an obvious erection would help make a better impression.

Paoli had contacted me a few days ago and said he had a business proposition for me. He hadn't given details over the phone, only said that he was interested in investing in a European expansion for Club Privé. I'd spent the last year remodeling my club physically as well as changing its reputation from a sex club into a dance club. I'd even sold my software company, with a hefty profit, so I could focus completely on the club. I'd been getting bored with writing software and designing apps anyway. It was time to branch out, and Paoli seemed like he had the right kind of connections to make something like this fly.

I scanned the restaurant as I entered and spotted Paoli right away. In his early fifties, he dressed like Don Johnson... from the eighties. White suit jacket with a t-shirt underneath it and he even had his salt-and-pepper hair styled like Crockett in Miami Vice. In the right light, he actually kind of resembled Johnson. If I hadn't done my homework and knew he was an extremely successful businessman, I might've thought twice about going through with the meeting based on looks alone.

I made my way through the tables, nodding a greeting when Paoli looked up. As I took my seat across from him, I spoke, "Sorry I'm late. Traffic was a bitch."

Paoli waved his hand in a dismissive gesture. "I took the liberty of ordering us some scotch."

I didn't try to hide my surprise. "I wasn't aware they served scotch here."

"For me, they do." He grinned at me and drained his glass. "Drink up." He motioned toward the glass in front of me.

"Thank you, Mr. Paoli," I said as I took a sip of the alcohol. My eyebrows went up. This was expensive stuff.

"You're welcome. And call me Vincent."

"Vincent." I nodded.

He leaned back in his chair as a waiter came over with another drink. I'd been here often enough to know at least a few things on the menu so we both ordered. Once the waiter was on his way back to the kitchen, the talk turned to business.

"I don't know if you recall," Vincent began. "But I visited your club twice last year during the first few weeks it was open. I was here on a business trip and looking to have a bit of fun. I've never forgotten it."

"Thank you." I tried not to shift uncomfortably. If he hadn't been back since then, he probably didn't know the club had gone through some changes.

"It got me thinking and I couldn't get this idea out of my head. I want to open a club like Privé in the French Riviera. A legit private club for the rich and famous." He regarded me with a serious expression. "I could hire someone already in Cannes, but I love the way Privé is designed. Creative. Elaborate. And that's what I want for my club. I'd like to make this an extension of your club here, with the two of us as equal partners."

I forced a smile and took a drink to avoid having to say anything. Somehow, I doubted Vincent would be quite as enthused when he found out that Club Privé was just another dance club now. Granted, it was still one of the most elaborately designed clubs in the city, but I'd had a lot of it redone to suit its new purpose.

"I'd like you to come to Cannes to take a look at the site and go over the building plans with my architect." Vincent emptied another glass. "Bring a lady friend, if you like." He grinned. "Or don't. I'm sure a man like you doesn't lack female attention."

I was torn. In all honesty, the club wasn't doing nearly as well as a dance club as it had as a sex club. I wasn't quite losing money, but it was close. If I hadn't had the money I'd earned before and what I'd gotten from the sale of my software company, I'd be hurting financially. As it was, if I kept having to spend on remodeling and putting out money to fund Carrie's pro bono law office, I was going to run out eventually, and what little I was bringing in from Club Privé wasn't enough for both Carrie and me to live on, even if I downsized my spending. And it certainly wouldn't be enough to keep Carrie's office afloat.

If I did this for Vincent and he was an equal partner, I wouldn't exactly be responsible for it being a sex club. I could make sure he was aware of my stance on bringing in escorts, but I wouldn't have to feel like I needed to police things since I'd be here in New York.

I could go to Cannes with Carrie, give him all of the suggestions and business tips that he'd need to get things started, and spend the rest of my time on vacation with my girlfriend.

That idea was appealing on so many levels. Financially it made sense and personally, it was the best thing I'd heard in a long time. Carrie and I had both been working so hard, we hadn't been able to get away. In fact, we rarely had more than a single day off at the same time, and most of those had been holidays, so we'd spent them with my daughter. Not that Carrie ever complained about that. Carrie adored Skylar and vice versa. It would just be nice to have some time for just the two of us. As loathe as I was to admit it, the spark between us had been flickering dangerously low as of late.

"I'd love to expand Club Privé to the French Riviera," I said, smiling at Vincent. "And I'm sure my girlfriend would love a chance to see Cannes."

"Excellent." Vincent rubbed his hands together. "Now, what do you say after we eat, we make a little stop at your club for some dessert?"

It didn't take a genius to know that he wasn't talking about some apple pie. I managed a tight smile and felt a wave of relief that I had a good excuse to refuse. "I'm sorry. The timing's awful. The club's closed right now. Renovations."

Vincent looked a bit disappointed but didn't force the issue. I was glad for that. I'd eventually make sure he knew that I was concerned about the club in France being used as a thoroughfare for the sex trade, but I really didn't want to explain the whole reasoning behind what I'd done to Club Privé here. Telling a new partner that my former partner had been selling girls and women to the highest bidder, and I hadn't noticed until it was almost too late, didn't exactly make me sound like an intelligent businessman.

The waiter returned with our meals and Vincent turned the talk to general things. We talked sports and family, where we'd grown up, the basics of conversation. He didn't ask anything too personal or even about how the club was doing now, for which I was grateful. Once we finished, it was handshakes and a promise to be in contact within the next couple days with details about the trip.

I waited until I was climbing into a cab before calling Carrie.

"Hey, babe!" I could barely contain my excitement. "I've got some great news, but I want to tell you in person. See you in a few?" I glanced at my watch. It wasn't too late, which meant I could share my news and we'd still have time for some celebratory sex. My cock stirred at the thought of being back inside her for the second time today. It had been more than six months since we'd gone more than once in a day.

Then she sighed and I knew my fantasy of making slow, lazy love to her was just that.

"I'm sorry, hon. I'm still at the office, working on my proposal. It has to be perfect, and I'm already exhausted. I'll probably fall asleep at my desk."

I could hear her trying to put a bit of humor into her words, but there was more fatigue there than anything else. I tried not to be too disappointed. She was busy and it was for a good reason. It wasn't like I was getting brushed off for something like clothing design or, I smiled wryly, running a club.

"That's fine," I said. I hoped the cheerful note in my voice didn't sound as forced to her as it did to me. "Focus on your proposal and after you nail it tomorrow, we'll celebrate at La Petite."

"Sounds great." She sounded distracted and I knew she was already back into her work. If she came home at all, I'd probably already be asleep and I usually left before she did, which meant I mostly likely wouldn't see her until we met at the restaurant.

I pocketed my phone and stared out the window as I rode back to our place. I'd lived here longer alone than I had with Carrie, but it had never truly felt like home until she'd moved in. When she wasn't here, it seemed like too much space for just one person and I wondered how I'd ever stood it before.

I rubbed my chin and tried to remember if we still had a bottle of wine. I was suddenly in the mood for a glass or two. Everything good I'd been feeling about today faded behind a maudlin mood that I knew was here for the rest of the night.

I had to admit, Carrie and I needed this business trip slash vacation more than I'd originally thought.

THREE
CARRIE

I was practically bouncing as I walked into La Petite. Things had gone better than I'd ever dreamed and I couldn't wait to share my news with Gavin. We'd both been working so hard lately that it seemed like we hardly ever got to see each other. He'd been sleeping when I'd gotten home and was gone when I'd woken up, but that was about par for the course these days. I'd actually completely forgotten about the reservations he'd made here until he'd reminded me yesterday.

"I'm here with Gavin Manning," I told the hostess as she approached me. The jealous glint in her eyes told me that either Gavin was already here or she'd met him before.

"Right this way, Miss." She gave me a professionally polite smile that didn't reach her eyes, and walked toward the far side of the restaurant.

While I'd eaten La Petite's food before, I'd never been inside the restaurant and I tried not to gawk as I followed the hostess. Sparkling chandeliers, expensive carpeting, furnishings that looked like they cost more than I used to make in a year. The place was almost overwhelming. If I hadn't known personally that the food was insanely good, I'd have thought they were trying to make up for the quality of their meals with the ambiance.

I saw Gavin a moment before he saw me and wondered what had him looking so serious. Then he raised his head and his entire face lit up. My stomach clenched. I wondered if there would ever be a point when my body didn't react to seeing that smile. I certainly hoped not.

"Hey, babe." He stood and reached out his hand.

I caught another flash of jealousy from the hostess as Gavin kissed my cheek in greeting. We took our seats and a waiter immediately came to the table. Gavin ordered another of whatever he'd been drinking before I'd arrived while I skimmed the wine list. I was no connoisseur, but I did know what I liked. I ordered a glass and the young man hurried off to bring us our drinks.

My news was on the tip of my tongue, but I didn't blurt it out. I wanted to savor it a moment longer, wait until the drinks arrived so I could offer a toast. The waiter returned in record time and then told us to signal as soon as we were ready to order.

We both raised our glasses at the same time.

"I have great news," I said.

Simultaneously, Gavin said, "I've been waiting to tell you this." We both smiled and Gavin nodded at me. "You go first."

The polite thing probably would've been to say the same to him, but I was too excited. "Congressman White's assistant loved my proposal and called him right there! He's going to meet with me next Thursday."

Gavin tapped his glass against mine and we both took a drink. The alcohol helped take the edge off of my buzzing nerves. I'd want to be careful, though, until the food arrived. I'd forgotten to eat lunch today and alcohol on an empty stomach with this much excitement wouldn't end well.

"That's so great, babe," Gavin said sincerely. "So Thursday's your big day? That's really fast. I'm so happy for you."

I shook my head. "No sorry, not this Thursday. The following week.

"Oh." His face fell and I knew something was wrong.

"What?" I asked.

"It's fine," he said stiffly. "Don't worry."

I frowned a little, but decided the best way to get that smile back was to let him share his news. "What was it you wanted to tell me?"

The smile he gave me was polite, but it didn't touch his eyes. Whatever my news had triggered wasn't going to be easily chased away. He took another sip of his drink and I tried not to press him to share what was bothering him.

"Last night, I had that business dinner," he said.

I remembered him asking if I could go with him.

"This man, Vincent Paoli, wants a Club Privé in Europe, the French Riviera to be exact. A legit, private club for the rich and famous, particularly the Americans who visit, which is why he came to me. He needs a partner, and he wants me."

"That's wonderful!" I interrupted.

His smile tightened. "He wants to discuss further plans on site. In France." He sighed. "Since we've never gone anywhere together and we've both been working so hard, I wanted to take you to France, but it's the same week you'll be going to DC."

And now I understood the problem. I reached across the

table and squeezed his hand. "That's great news. And I'd love to spend a week in France with you." I released his hand and leaned back in my seat. "Is there any way it can be put off until after my trip? I mean, will a couple days make that much of a difference to the club?"

"I can try to reschedule."

Gavin's good humor seemed to be back and I relaxed a bit. Both of us having good news and being together to celebrate it was rare. I didn't want to spend all night with him being moody because our schedules conflicted.

"I don't know about you," I said. "But I'm starving."

Gavin signaled for the waiter who'd been hovering in the wings. It hadn't taken me long with Gavin to realize how many people waited around to do things for him. Not in a bad way, and he didn't take advantage of it, but he was definitely used to it, which was funny since he hadn't been born into it. I wondered if I'd ever get used to having money, but then I remembered that the money keeping my business afloat and paying all of the bills wasn't actually mine to begin with.

When we'd discussed him supporting my law practice, and us moving in together, we'd gone round and round about the financial situation. Technically, I was listed as a partner at Club Privé, but I'd had little time to do any real work on the business. Gavin had wanted to just put my name on his accounts and let me do what I wanted, but I hadn't been comfortable with that. I loved Gavin, and even though neither of us had said it, I knew we both saw our future together. Still, we'd only been together a little over a year and we'd been through hell at the beginning. We'd finally managed to compromise, but I was always aware that the money in my account came from a paycheck I received from my boyfriend for a business I barely thought about anymore. Sometimes, the money thing bothered me, but if I got the congressman to help get this bill passed, it'd be well-worth the sting to my pride.

FOUR
GAVIN

I had to admit, I was a bit surprised when Carrie suggested we get dessert at home, our not-so-original or subtle code for 'let's get out of here so we can have hot, sweaty sex'. I'd planned on making a move, but I'd already prepared myself for a preemptive excuse about how hard she'd been working and how glad she'd be to get some sleep. Granted, that was the truth and I knew she wasn't using it as an excuse not to be with me, but it was getting harder not to feel like that. And, of course, that was followed by guilt since I knew everything Carrie did was to rescue exploited girls, boys, men and women. It wasn't just about the sex though. Sure, I missed making love to her, of having the time to indulge our desires, but I missed the connection more.

I hoped that her sultry smile when she'd mentioned dessert was the beginning of us getting back on track. When we'd first gotten together, she'd enjoyed having me coax her out of her comfort zone and had even asked me to teach her more about the things I'd liked, the things that had led me to create Club

Privé in the first place. But then she'd begun to throw herself into her work and, lately, I'd been wondering if she'd ever really wanted that in the first place or if she'd just said it to make me happy. It was the kind of thing a couple should talk about, but we had such little time together anymore, I didn't want to waste it bringing up such a heavy subject. I could survive without a lot of the things I enjoyed in the bedroom. I was more worried about if I'd survive losing her.

"You're thinking awfully hard," Carrie said as the cab took us home.

"It's nothing," I said. I slid my arm around her waist and smiled. I was disappointed that I hadn't been able to surprise her with this vacation to Cannes, but I refused to let it spoil our evening. I was excited for the opportunity she had and I was proud of her for all of the work she was doing.

She leaned against me and sighed. "I've missed this," she said softly, pulling my arm more tightly around her.

"Me too," I said. I pressed my lips against the top of her head. While I loved the sparks and electricity that came with us touching, there was something to be said for a slow burn as well.

I paid the cabbie and gave him a nice tip as a thank you for not trying to make chit-chat and just letting us relax in silence on the ride. Some taxi drivers felt the need to fill silence, but he hadn't, letting Carrie and me maintain the anticipation between us. As we headed toward the doors, I reached out and took her hand, threading my fingers through hers. My skin hummed where it touched hers and the sensation traveled up my arm. I'd forgotten how such a simple gesture could make me want her so much.

Neither one of us spoke as we rode up in the elevator, but

the moment the door to our loft closed behind us, I pulled her into my arms.

"I've been thinking about this all day," I said before lowering my mouth to hers.

The moment our lips touched, heat flooded through me. She moaned as I slid my tongue into her mouth and I felt her hands clutch at my shirt. I kissed her slowly, thoroughly exploring her mouth as if for the first time. My hands slid down to the small of her back and rested there, hovering just above her ass. As her tongue curled around mine, I dropped my hands lower, squeezing the firm muscles as I pulled her even more tightly against me, letting her feel my erection pressing against her stomach.

"Bedroom," she gasped, tearing her mouth away from mine. "Now."

We shed our clothes as we went, my desire to take it slow replaced by her contagious urgency. By the time we reached the bed, both of us were naked. I reached for her, loving the feel of her silky skin beneath my palms. I cupped her breasts, my cock stiffening even more at the weight of them. I loved her body, every dip and curve, every flaw and imperfection. It was all her. I brushed my thumbs over her nipples and they hardened under my touch. I never tired of how her body responded to me. The flush of her skin. How wet I knew she would be when I finally reached her pussy.

She slid her hand down my chest and I sucked in a breath as she raked her nails across my skin. Damn. I loved when she did that. When her hand closed around my cock, I groaned. She stroked me expertly, knowing exactly how I liked to be touched. I shifted away from her grasp, not wanting this to end too quickly, and bent my head to take one of her nipples into my mouth.

She moaned as I sucked on the hardened bit of flesh. I alternated suction with tongue and teeth, teasing at it until I felt her hands in my hair. I released it and started to move toward the other one, but a hand on my chest stopped me. Carrie gave me a little shove, just hard enough to let me know what she wanted. My eyes met hers and she smiled.

If she wanted to drive for a while tonight, that was fine. I threw back the covers and situated myself on the bed. My heart thudded in my chest as she climbed onto the bed and straddled my legs. The heat inside me grew. It ~~had~~ been a while since she'd been on top and I'd missed the sight of those beautiful breasts bouncing while she rode me.

I swallowed hard as she positioned herself above my cock. Things were moving much faster than I'd wanted them to go, but with her rubbing the tip of my aching dick against her wet pussy lips, how the hell was I supposed to tell her to wait? I grabbed onto her hips, wanting to drag this out, but Carrie had other ideas. She lowered herself onto me, her pace slow but not teasing. Without any prep, she was impossibly tight, squeezing me almost to the point of pain, and I could only imagine how it felt for her.

I grabbed onto the sheets and gritted my teeth, using every ounce of my self-control not to lose it right there. I squeezed my eyes closed as wet heat enveloped me and I could feel the muscles in her thighs trembling with the intensity of being filled so completely. It didn't matter how many times we did this or how well I prepared her, the initial penetration was always like this, a nearly overwhelming sensation as our bodies fit together in a way that we never had with anyone else.

She sighed as she came to rest, her fingers flexing against my chest as her body adapted to my size. I opened my eyes, and studied her face, tracing every inch of it. Her eyes were closed, her brow furrowed in what looked like concentration. Her lips were parted slightly, her no-smudge lipstick earning its name after our earlier kiss.

When her eyes opened, she saw me looking and smiled. She shifted her hips, angling herself until her clit rubbed against the base of my cock. I knew she'd hit it right when she shuddered and then began to move. I waited for her to get her rhythm before following, raising my hips to meet her downward thrusts with upward ones of my own, driving myself deeper into her.

"Fuck, yes..." she hissed as we clashed together.

I let her control her movements and busied my hands at her breasts. If we weren't going to take things slow, I wasn't going to be as gentle as I usually tried to be. I cupped her breasts, then squeezed, drawing a moan from her. I took her nipples between my fingers and began to roll and tug on them, increasing pressure as she arched her back, pushing her breasts at me. I had the sudden image of putting clamps on that tender flesh, hearing Carrie's cries of pleasure as I taught her to enjoy the new sensations, soothing them after removing the clamps, leaving them swollen and tender...

I shook my head. I didn't need that. This was enough. I gave her nipples a twist, not enough to cause real pain, but enough to give her a jolt. Carrie's body jerked and her nails dug into my chest. I hissed, enjoying the pinpricks of pain from where she was marking me.

Her breathing was coming more rapidly now and I dropped one of my hands, still using the other to manipulate her nipple. I slipped my hand between us, my fingers quickly finding her swollen clit. Two passes over that little bundle of nerves and her body was tensing as she came. Her pussy tightened around me and I swore. I was getting close but I didn't want this to end yet. I wanted to flip us over and drive into her until she came again and again, screaming my name. I wanted to bury my cock deep inside her and lose myself in her body.

Before I could do any of that, Carrie was rolling off of me and taking my cock in her mouth. One hand massaged my balls as the other gripped the base of me, taking care of what she couldn't get into her mouth. She bobbed her head, the suction just this side of painful.

"Carrie." I put my hand on her head. "Please, babe. I'm too close."

She dropped her head further down, taking me all the way to the back of her throat, something that had taken a lot of practice for her to accomplish and something that was always guaranteed to make me come.

I cried out, my fingers twisting in her curls as I came. She drew back as my cock spurted into her mouth, letting the last bit catch her chin. She grinned at me as she wiped it off, then climbed off of the bed and headed into the bathroom. I watched her go as I tried to catch my breath. Not that I had an issue with getting an amazing blow job from my girlfriend, but what the hell had that been? Even with the smile at the end, it didn't feel like she'd done it because she thought I'd wanted it, but rather because it had been the quickest way to get me to finish.

When she came out of the bathroom a few minutes later, she handed me a warm washcloth, then pulled on one of my t-shirts and climbed back into bed. I waited for her to say something as I cleaned myself up, but she rolled onto her side, her back to me, and didn't say a word. I tossed the washcloth into the hamper and pulled the covers over us both. I moved up next to her, curling my body around her from behind, and brushed back some of her hair. I pressed my lips against the spot under her ear that always turned her on.

"I love you, babe," she murmured. "But no more tonight. I'm exhausted."

She already sounded half-asleep, so I knew she wasn't lying, but it stung. Had that been the reason for what had happened? Carrie rarely took control of things like that in the bedroom, and the few times she had, it had always been to tease me, to prolong the sexual experience. Never to have a quickie. Not that I was opposed to quickies, but they were usually because we had some place to be at a specific time or we were in a position where we could be caught by other people. Not in our bed at nine o'clock at night. If she'd said she was too tired for sex, I would've understood. If she'd said she wanted a quickie because she was tired, that would've been fine too, but something about that had been off.

I frowned, tempted to roll over and stay on my side of the bed. I couldn't help but wonder if Carrie had fucked me tonight as much as a consolation prize because she hadn't been able to agree to the trip to France right away. Was that what our relationship had become? Pity fucks and just getting off? If all I'd wanted was an orgasm, I could've taken care of that myself.

I tightened my arm around Carrie as a stab of fear went through me. Was this the beginning of the end? I was already feeling like my sexual needs were being put on the back burner, and I was willing to give up the kinks that I liked, but if I lost the rest of the connection we had, I didn't think I could handle it. Falling in love with Carrie had been the best and hardest thing I'd ever done, and I couldn't lose her.

I was more determined than ever to get us to France. We needed this. We had to get the fire back. I rested my cheek against the top of Carrie's head and concentrated on the sound of her slow, steady breathing, letting it lull me into a restless sleep.

FIVE

GAVIN

When I woke up, Carrie's side of the bed was empty, save for a note on her pillow. She'd gone into the office to work on polishing her proposal for her meeting with the congressman and to try to track down the governor's daughter. I frowned as I read the note. I remembered Robyn Leeds from when Carrie had been asked to help find her. She'd asked me if I'd thought it'd be a good idea since she was a lawyer, not a PI. The last I'd heard from Carrie, Robyn had been doing fine and was ready to testify against her pimp. Had Carrie told me that something else had happened and I didn't remember?

I sighed as I climbed out of bed. That seemed like the sort of thing I should know. I'd planned on spending the day with Carrie, the two of us doing some things around the apartment. Maybe going out for normal couple stuff like grocery shopping. Granted, we rarely ate anything at home anymore, but maybe buying specific things would make us more likely to want to start. Now that she was at work, I found myself alone in the apartment with nothing to do.

Before I'd met Carrie, these were the kinds of days I'd have used for networking, mingling at the club, meeting new people who could benefit from the software I designed, or ones who were just important people to know. People like Vincent Paoli.

Since Carrie was gone, maybe this was a good time to start coming up with ideas for the European club. I could've worked from home, but there wasn't really a point if I was the only one here. For a moment, I let myself think about what it would be like to have the kind of life where Carrie and I were sitting together in the living room, working from home. The distracting glances. Little flirtatious touches that turned into more as we both said we should be working.

I had to admit, that had been more of what I'd envisioned when we'd moved in together. I'd thought, with us being partners at Club Privé, we'd spend weekends and evenings working together here, cuddled together while we shared a laptop. Maybe separate laptops, but sitting next to each other, involved in the other's work.

"Dammit." I raked my hand through my hair. I had to get out of the house and I needed to convince Vincent to postpone the trip to France.

My driver was waiting by the time I got downstairs. Carrie and I alternated using cabs and a private car service, but right now, I didn't feel like flagging someone down or having to deal with someone who might be chatty. Despite the business opportunity of a lifetime, I wasn't in the best of moods.

When I arrived at Club Privé, the construction crew was hard at work. That was good. I'd never worked with these guys before and I hadn't been sure what to expect. After the whole thing with Howard, I'd ended contracts with every company he'd personally hired. Most of them had probably been clean, but I refused to take a risk that I was working with anyone who'd contributed to Howard's "other" business.

I nodded at the foreman as I passed on my way to the elevator. The soundproofing on the second floor muffled the noise from downstairs as soon as I stepped into the hall. My office would take care of the rest. All of the rooms up here had been given the best soundproofing available. Two people could stand on either side of the door and scream at the top of their lungs and would never hear each other.

As I swiped my access card, I found myself glancing toward the end of the hall. The door there led to a room I hadn't been in for nearly a year. Carrie had suggested we keep it and had teased that she and I could use it for me to introduce her to more of the BDSM lifestyle I enjoyed. Instead, the door had remained closed. I'd only been in there once since the police had cleared it as a crime scene, and that had been to let in the cleaning crew.

Part of me never wanted to step foot in there again. My memories of the place were torn. On one hand, it had been the first place Carrie and I had ever had sex, an encounter that had shaken me to the core. I'd known right then that she was the one, even if I hadn't wanted to admit it at the time. On the other hand, however, it was also where Howard had assaulted and nearly raped Carrie before trying to kill us both.

I entered my office and closed the door behind me, shutting out the rest of the world. Not for the first time, I wondered if I should've just sold the whole building and started over from scratch. A new place, one without memories. A new start.

I sat at my desk and tried to focus. France could be my way

of seeing if that'd be possible. If I could design another amazing club, I could prove to myself that I could do it again here.

Before I could start sketching out any ideas, a buzzing sound told me I had a visitor. My heart thudded at the thought of it being Carrie coming to see me, but when the door opened, it was Daniel, my foreman.

"Mr. Manning," he said as he stood at the edge of my office. He was a large man, solidly muscled, the kind of guy I'd look for to run security.

"I told you before, Daniel, you can call me Gavin." I smiled even though I wasn't really feeling it. I didn't have anything against Daniel, but I wanted to be alone right now. "Now, what can I do for you?"

"The construction's taking longer than anticipated." He got straight to the point. "We've run into some shoddy workmanship when we got down to the bones."

I scowled. Damn Howard. "How far back is this going to set things?" Daniel grimaced and I almost said that I didn't want to know.

"At least three weeks."

I closed my eyes and resisted the urge to massage my temples. Three fucking weeks because Howard had hired a company that did a half-assed job. The least the perverted fuck could've done was get this right.

"And, Sir? There's something else." Daniel sounded downright nervous now.

I opened my eyes. "What is it?"

"The custom-made chrome and glass finish that you wanted for all of the walls has been delayed. The manager of the company called me this morning and said that they'd gotten in a rush order from another customer, and since we hadn't put a rush on the finish..."

"Our order gets delayed," I finished the statement. This day just kept getting better and better. Only the expression on Daniel's face kept me from blowing up. Rich men in positions of power often shot the messenger and I could tell that Daniel was afraid he and his crew were about to get fired for things they had no control over.

"I can call around, see if I can find someone else who can do it," Daniel offered.

I shook my head. "It's not your fault. I'm pissed, but not at you." I pinched the bridge of my nose as I thought. "Figure out the date you'd need it. Call the manager back and tell him to have it ready on that day or he'll lose my business for good. If he names a price, haggle a bit, but pay whatever we need to pay to get it here on time."

"Yes, Sir," Daniel said. He turned to go, then paused. "And, Mr. Manning, if I were you, I'd get someone to take a look at the wiring up here too. If it's as much of a mess as it is in your walls downstairs, you're going to need to have some work done. I don't know how that got past inspection."

"Unfortunately, I do," I said. I didn't want him thinking I'd bribed anyone. "My former business partner dealt with the inspectors, as well as hiring the electrician and construction crews."

Daniel nodded in understanding and left without another word. It was too bad I couldn't hire him to do the construction in Cannes, I thought, as I looked down at the empty sheet of paper on my desk. But, if I decided to change things up here, he was definitely first on my list of hires.

And speaking of France, I had a phone call to make. I hated

the thought of asking Vincent to change the date of an all-expenses paid trip to France, but it was for Carrie and she was one of the only two people in the world I would do anything for. The very least I could do here was ask.

I picked up the phone and made the call. Vincent answered on the second ring.

"Gavin!"

At least he sounded thrilled to hear from me, I thought. That was a good start. "Hope I didn't wake you, Vincent," I said as I glanced at the clock. "I wasn't sure if you were out enjoying the night life."

"I was," he said. "But I've been up for hours. You know how it is. Men like us never sleep."

I chuckled, then waited the appropriate number of seconds to transition from small talk to business. "I was actually calling about your invite to the Riviera."

"Great," he said. "Do you need one ticket or two?"

"Actually," I said. "I was wondering if it'd be possible to postpone the trip a week, or at least a few days. My... business partner has a previous engagement that Thursday." That was true. Carrie was technically my business partner.

"Your 'business partner'?"

I could hear the air quotes and knew I needed to be honest. "Yes, Carrie is my girlfriend, but she is also a partner at the club. She came on after my previous partner... left."

"But you are the controlling partner, correct?" Vincent asked.

"Yes," I said.

"I'd like to help you," Vincent said with a sigh. "But it can't wait. I already have an appointment set up to check out the site. It's a hot property and that was as long as I could delay it. If I don't have an answer for them by the end of that week, they're going to move on to another buyer."

"I understand." And I did. Business was like that. Time was money and things sometimes moved fast. "I'll double-check to see if there's anything that can be done from this end." Even as I said it, I knew it wouldn't be possible. A congressman wasn't going to change his schedule so I could take my girlfriend to France to open a sex club.

"Just let me know soon how many tickets to book," Vincent said. "And best of luck."

"Thanks." I was barely listening as I hung up the phone.

I put my head in my hands. What was I going to do? I couldn't ask Carrie to miss the meeting with Congressman White. Aside from it being a great connection for her to have, this bill was important. What was my business compared to the lives of people in sex slavery? And my only other option was to go without her. It was a business trip, but I had no doubt that me going, alone, to France for a week to open a sex club wouldn't be healthy for our relationship. She trusted me, but we were already growing apart. My gut told me this could break us.

I stood abruptly. It was too quiet in here. I couldn't think. I opened the door and the sounds from downstairs, though muffled, were loud enough to tell me that I wouldn't be able to work down there either. I scowled. Why couldn't we just go now? Drop everything and get on a plane tonight. No empty beds and notes. No dealing with this construction shit and what it could mean for the club. Just me and Carrie.

I went out the back way, not wanting to risk Daniel stopping me to talk about something else going wrong. I pulled out my phone, ready to call for a driver, but as I stepped out into the warm spring day, I changed my mind. A walk might be exactly what I needed to clear my head.

Before I'd gone two blocks, I'd come to at least one decision. This was an opportunity I couldn't pass up. With or without Carrie, I was going to France.

SIX

CARRIE

I should've known, when my weekend ended with Gavin saying he couldn't get the dates of the France trip changed but that he was going anyway, that things were going to keep getting worse. Monday consisted of more fruitless attempts to reach Robyn, a call from the DA saying that they couldn't find her either and if she didn't testify, Little Tino was going to walk. Oh, and getting threatening calls from two different pimps had been fun. I'd ended that day grinding my teeth until my face hurt.

Then there was Tuesday, when I spilled my morning coffee on my favorite work blouse, staining it and leaving me without caffeine until I could get a new cup. And, of course, there was the tension at home, even when we barely saw each other. It hung around us like a shroud.

By the time I was sitting at my desk on Wednesday afternoon, trying to call Robyn for what felt like the thousandth time, I'd pretty much written off the entire week as a loss. I'd decided to forget this week and focus on the next, my excitement about meeting with Congressman White next Thursday the only thing keeping me sane.

"Yes?"

A familiar surly voice came across my phone.

"Robyn?"

A half-hearted curse answered my question and told me that I didn't need to bother identifying myself.

"What do you want, Carrie?"

I pushed down my urge to snap at her and reminded myself that no matter how grown-up she pretended to be, Robyn was a kid and the victim in this situation. She thought she was making her own choices, but I knew she was being manipulated by Little Tino.

"I've been worried about you, Robyn. You haven't answered your phone for over a week."

"Yeah, well, no one asked you to be worried about me, did they? I know it sure as hell wasn't my parents."

I closed my eyes. This was bad. "I have been worried, I care about what happens to you." I needed to say something to rebuild our trust. Plus, it wasn't a lie. I really did care for this girl.

"Right. All you care about is my testimony. You don't give a shit about me."

I took a deep breath. "That's not true, Robyn. I hope you don't really believe it."

She scoffed, a keep exhale of breath. "Well, you don't have to worry anymore. I am safe."

Worry thrilled through me. "What do you mean? Where are you?"

"I'm with the one person in the world who really cares me. I'm with Little T."

If I hadn't been sitting down, I would have fallen to the floor. Surely not, surely this girl couldn't be that stupid.

"Robyn," I breathed. "Please tell me where you are, I'll come get you. You have to get away from him."

She scoffed again. "I'm not going anywhere. This is where I belong."

"But, the court case..." I started.

"Yeah, no. I'm not doing it."

I cursed silently and fought to keep my voice calm. "What do you mean you're not doing it?"

"I'm not testifying against Little Tino. He's the only person who really cares about me."

"That's not true." I knew I was repeating myself but she needed to hear it again.

"Bullshit," she snapped. "He's here when I need him. He takes care of me. He loves me."

"He doesn't love you, Robyn–" I started to say.

"What the hell do you know?" she interrupted.

My hand tightened around the phone. The only time I'd ever heard Robyn get that belligerent with anyone but her parents was when she was on drugs. Before I could ask her if she was using again, she went on.

"You're so busy worrying about everyone else's life that you don't have one of your own. Probably haven't had a man in years and wouldn't know what to do with one if you did. You don't know what love is, because if you did, you wouldn't be after me like this."

I swallowed hard, trying not to let my voice show how much her words fed into my fears about Gavin and me. "Let me help you, Robyn. I can get you into rehab. Get you off the drugs and you'll be able to think more clearly then."

"Fuck that," Robyn snapped, and then her voice softened. "Look, I know you think you're doing good, but it's pointless. My parents are pissed and won't pay for rehab. I go in some state one and Little Tino makes a couple calls to his buddies. You know what it's like, doing a train of thugs and addicts? It's not pretty. I'll pass on the rehab, the testifying and the parents who don't give a shit."

"Please, let me..."

"Please nothing. Leave me alone."

Click.

The call ended before I could finish processing what she'd just said or even begin to consider a response. I set my phone down and stared at it, myriad emotions coursing through me. At first, I was furious with Robyn. I'd worked my ass off getting her clean and running interference for her. Then my anger shifted to the appropriate people. Little Tino for seducing her and then turning her out. Her parents for not realizing that their daughter was more important than anything else.

I picked up the phone and dialed her father's office. He'd told me more than once to never call him at the office or on his landline. He had a special burner phone he used for everything relating to Robyn. He had to try to keep her out of the press as much as possible. If it had been for her sake, I would've applauded the gesture and followed protocol, but I knew better. He didn't want the media finding out what kind of a mess Robyn was and saying, however much truth there was to it, that it was all his fault.

"Governor Leeds's office," a professional-sounding woman answered after just a couple rings.

"Hi, this is Carrie Summers. I've been working with the governor's daughter. I need to speak with him."

There was a long pause, as if the woman knew I wasn't supposed to be calling this number. "I'm sorry, the governor is out of the office for the rest of the week. Good-bye."

For the second time in under two minutes, I was hung up on. I was half-tempted to call her back, but I tried the burner number instead. The number was out of service. Well, I supposed that was one way to make it clear you'd disowned your daughter or gave up on her at least. I called the home, but got the answering machine. I didn't trust myself to leave a civil message, so I hung up without one and then debated calling the DA to give him a head's up about Robyn.

"Carrie?" Zoe knocked and then poked her head in my office. The bright smile on her face gave me hope that something good was going to happen today. "Congressman White is on line two for you."

My eyebrows went up. The congressman was calling me directly? "Thanks, Zoe."

She grinned at me, gave me a thumbs up and went back to her desk. I took a deep breath and reminded myself that I'd be face-to-face with this man in a week. A phone call should be nothing. I wasn't sure if I believed it, but it did settle my nerves a bit.

I picked up the phone. "Hello?"

"Miss Summers." A rich, deep voice came over the line. There was a smoothness and intentional cadence to it and I wondered how many speech coaches he'd had to get that sound.

"Congressman White," I said. "It's a pleasure to hear from you."

"I'm afraid you might not say that in a moment." He laughed, but it was the kind of laugh that people did to let you know that they're actually half-serious. "I'm afraid I have some bad news."

Of course he did. I sank back in my seat.

"First let me tell how much we appreciate everything you have done for this cause. I still want to talk to you about the bill, and human trafficking is very much an issue I care about."

I could hear the 'but' coming.

"But due to the upcoming mid-term election, my advisors have suggested I wait until after the election to start touting new pieces of legislation."

I closed my eyes, seeing all of my hard work going straight into the garbage bin.

"I don't want you to worry though. When I'm re-elected, this will be the first thing on next year's agenda."

"Thank you, Congressman," I forced myself to say it even though I wanted to tell him how pissed I was, how I felt he was putting politics over human lives. If he did get re-elected, burning a bridge now in a fit of temper wouldn't help anyone.

"Needless to say," he continued. "We'll want to reschedule our meeting for a later time. No use talking over things now when it'll be a while before we can do anything about it."

"I understand." My voice was polite, but I could hear the hollow note in it. I didn't understand, not really. I'd put everything in my life on hold for this and he wasn't willing to take a chance on it? It wasn't like this was something controversial like abortion or same-sex marriage. It wasn't as if a big contingent of voters would be picketing to keep the sex slave trade going.

"I look forward to speaking with you in the future, Miss Summer," he said. "And I hope I can count on your vote come fall."

"Thank you for your time, Congressman," I said automatically.

I slumped in my chair, any hope I'd had for salvaging this week gone. The one thing that had kept me going for the past few weeks had been knowing that what I was doing would be placed into the hands of someone who could make a difference. Now, it was just words and pieces of paper. Although I'd spent days poring over them, perfecting them down to the last sentence... now, they would be read by no one.

I lay my head on my desk and could have cried, but I was so depressed that I couldn't even muster up anything other than a mild annoyance.

My cell phone dinged and I considered not even looking at it, but it hadn't been Gavin's ringtone, which meant it could be from anyone else. I picked up my phone and almost smiled. It was from Leslie.

Leslie and Dena had worked with my former roommate, Krissy, and me at Webster and Steinberg. The four of us had been inseparable, but since Krissy had moved to LA and I wasn't working in the same law circles as Leslie and Dena, we hadn't seen each other as much as I wished we had.

I read Leslie's text and then actually did smile. Hey, stranger. Want to meet Dena and I for drinks at Huggins? They're having a special mid-week happy hour tonight.

I didn't even have to think about it. Absolutely. I needed a girls' night out.

Being at Huggins Bar & Grill with Dena and Leslie brought back so many memories, not the least of which was this this had been the place I'd seen Gavin for the first time. Krissy had bet me I wouldn't get the phone number of the hottest man I'd ever seen. I had, and that had started it all. Huggins wasn't only about meeting Gavin though. My friends and I had come here all the time after work to kick off the weekend. Most of the time, it had been my only social interaction before going back to the apartment I'd shared with Krissy and shoving my nose in a book or writing a paper for school. The other three had always been the more social ones.

Leslie was the most out-going out of all of us. Bubbly and flirtatious, she loved being the center of attention, but managed to not be obnoxious while doing it. Surprisingly, she and Krissy had rarely butted heads even though Krissy was just as head-strong. I always assumed it was because they usually had the same goals: find hot guys, fuck hot guys and move on.

I smiled wistfully. Things had changed. Krissy had found

her hot guy in Los Angeles, fucked him, but hadn't moved on. I was happy that Krissy had found love with DeVon, but it still made me sad that she was on the other side of the country. We talked, but not as often as we once had. I loved my other friends, but she was the closest thing to a sister I had. No matter how much Krissy and Leslie were alike, it wasn't the same.

Then there was Dena. She was the quietest one of the three of us, but in a ruthless kind of way. She was the sort of lawyer everyone underestimated because she looked like she was twelve even though she was twenty-six. She'd walk into a court room looking like a school girl then massacre her opponent with an organized, brutal argument. I was always thankful she was on my side.

Unlike Leslie, with her brilliant red curls and enviable curves, Dena was a quiet kind of beauty. She kept her white blond hair in a short pixie cut and, with her pale gray eyes and fair skin, she looked like she should be the poster child for some sort of snow fairy. Not that I'd ever say something like that to her. She was kind of scary sometimes.

They were both there when I arrived ten minutes late. Since they were still working their way through Webster and Steinberg, they would've left work together, just like the four of us used to do. I felt another stab of nostalgia as I made my way over to the table. I sat across from them and tried not to look sad at the empty chair next to me.

It must not have worked because the first thing Leslie said after we exchanged greetings was about Krissy.

"She called a couple days ago to tell me how well things were going with DeVon and the business. Apparently, it's getting really serious between the two of them." Leslie narrowed her bright green eyes at me. "She also said she'd tried to call you but kept getting voicemail."

I felt a stab of guilt. I'd been working on my proposal for the congressman pretty much every waking moment and hadn't had a chance to call Krissy back yet. "It's been a busy week."

Dena and Leslie exchanged one of those glances that Krissy and I used to have, the kind that doesn't need any sort of explanation because two minds are in sync.

"I've been working my ass off on this proposal for Congressman White." I hated how defensive I sounded.

"How's that going?" Dena asked, deflecting the conversation.

I gave a frustrated sigh and took a gulp of the Lemon Drop that had just been put in front of me. Usually I loved the things, but tonight, they just made me sad. No matter what we'd ended up drinking at the end of the night, Krissy and I had always started off with Lemon Drops.

"That well?" Leslie asked.

"I put so much time into it and I get a call this afternoon from the congressman saying he wants to table any discussion about it until after the election in November."

"Seriously?" Leslie tossed her curls over her shoulder. "This isn't exactly the kind of issue that divides people. You'd think he'd want to be showing that he's taking a firm stance against human trafficking."

"You'd think," I agreed dryly, draining my drink. "I just feel like I wasted all this time, sacrificed so much, to get this done and it's all been for nothing."

"Sacrificed?" Dena's voice was soft. "What's going on, Carrie?"

I looked at her, feeling comforted by her concern. I dropped my eyes to the appetizers we always nibbled on. I wasn't hungry.

"I feel like Gavin and I are drifting apart," I confessed. Saying it out-loud made me wince.

"Hon, you're just getting over the honeymoon stage," Leslie said. She popped a piece of bread into her mouth. "Trust me. It's normal."

I raised an eyebrow. "No offense, Leslie, but when your longest relationship has been with Lexi the barista over on Third Avenue, I'm not so sure you're the one to be giving me relationship advice."

She shrugged and grinned, accepting my comment without denial. "Just saying."

"I'm sure it's just a phase," Dena said. "The two of you have been through so much, it's bound to make things feel weird when everything's becoming routine."

"When was the last time you two had sex?" Leslie asked.

I glared at her but her smile only got bigger. I might have lost many of my inhibitions when it came to talking about sex when I was with Gavin, but it didn't mean it was open season in public.

"Come on, Carrie," Leslie coaxed, giving me her 'loosen up' look. "I'm not asking what positions you did it in. I just want to know how long it's been."

"A couple days." I said. "Friday night after we went out to eat." I flushed. "And the day before that too. At my office."

"Damn." Leslie laughed. "You're getting more than I am."

I brushed my hair out of my face as I frowned. "It's not the lack of sex, even though it's less often than it had been before." I struggled to define what I was feeling. I wasn't sure I wanted to share, even with my friends, but I had to talk to someone and, for once, it couldn't be Gavin. "There's something missing." I glanced up at them. "Don't get me wrong. It's still amazing and he can do things…" My face heated up. "But the passion that had been there before, it's gone. There's no spark."

"Do you still love him?" Dena asked.

"Yes," I answered immediately. "More than anything."

"More than anything?" For once, Leslie was being serious. A few seconds ticked by while she chewed her lip. "More than your work?"

I flinched. How could she ask that? "Of course," I snapped.

She held up both hands in a gesture of surrender. "I'm just saying that if you'll ignore your oldest friend because you're working…"

"Love has nothing to do with it." I scowled at her. "The work I do is important. It saves lives."

"Carrie," Dena spoke before I could really get going. "We know that what you're doing is important, but you have to take care of yourself too. And, if you really do love him, Gavin is part of that. If you don't take the time to work on your relationship, you're going to lose him."

I slumped back in my chair. Dena never talked that much outside of the courtroom, so I knew when she made a little speech, it was something I needed to listen to, no matter how much I hated it.

"Taking some time for yourself and Gavin doesn't make you a bad person," Leslie said.

I closed my eyes for a moment. That's what it was, I knew. I didn't enjoy working more than I enjoyed being with Gavin, but I felt guilty if I wasn't doing whatever I could to save people. I ran myself ragged, barely able to excuse myself for needing time to sleep. And it was killing Gavin and me.

I thought back to the other night and how bad I'd felt asking Gavin to reschedule his important trip. I wanted to make it up to him but was just so tired, so overwhelmed, all I really wanted to do was go straight to sleep. So instead of being honest with him, or even honest with myself, I'd purposefully taken control and done everything I could to get us both off as quickly as possible. And it hadn't even been a warm-up for something longer. I'd just been so tired and knew I had a ton more work to do the next day. It had been more about finishing than it had been about being close.

"You're right," I finally admitted. I looked up and found my friends wearing nearly identical expressions of concern. "I have been feeling guilty any time I'm not working."

Leslie reached across the table and took my hand. "You can't fix the world, Carrie. And it doesn't mean you're a bad person if, every once in a while, you take a break from trying. Your own personal world is important too."

We drank a bit more in silence before I spoke again. "Gavin has a business trip to France coming up and he wanted me to come with him, but I had my meeting with Congressman White scheduled that day. Now that it's been canceled, should I tell Gavin I want to go? I don't want to seem like I'm doing it out of some sense of obligation or anything like th—"

"Go," Dena said before I could even finish the last word.

"She's right," Leslie agreed. "You need to spend some time with your sweetie and what better place to do it than France?" She gave me an impish grin. "But if you don't want to go, can I?"

I rolled my eyes and smiled as the mood lightened. As soon as I was done here, I'd call Gavin and ask him what I needed to pack. I wasn't sure what the dress code was for a business meeting about starting a sex club in the French Riviera.

EIGHT

GAVIN

When Carrie told me about the congressman canceling on her, I was frustrated and upset for her, but I'd have been lying if I said I also hadn't been excited that she could come with me now. The first class cabin, complete with excellent champagne, would've been dull and boring without her. With her at my side, cramped coach would've been more than tolerable.

Not that I was about to give up our seats.

I reached over and squeezed Carrie's hand. "Have I told you yet how beautiful you are?"

She blushed and I felt a surge of love go through me. I loved that I could still make her flush with a compliment. And I meant it. She was wearing a cute little dress with half-sleeves and a hemline that hit her thighs at the most frustrating place, short enough to tempt me with those gorgeous legs of hers, but long enough to be decent. I was thinking anything but decent thoughts when I looked at her.

"More champagne, Sir?" The flight attendant leaned closer than necessary as she refilled my half-empty glass. She smiled down at me and I automatically smiled back. I felt Carrie stiffen next to me and I squeezed her hand again. It might've been a bit mean, but I was actually glad she was jealous. I wasn't flirting with the attendant, but it was nice to know that seeing someone flirt with me still annoyed the woman I loved. If she hadn't cared, I'd have been worried.

As the blonde walked away, Carrie spoke in a half-serious, half-joking tone. "Look at the menu all you want, but you better not even think about eating anywhere but home."

I grinned and leaned close to her ear, keeping my voice low. "Babe, you're the only one I want to eat."

Her face went bright red and she glared at me. No matter how much I'd managed to loosen her up, I could still embarrass her, especially when it came to talking about sex in public.

Taking pity on her, I changed the subject for the moment. "I just realized there's something I don't know about you. Have you ever been to France?"

She rolled her eyes. "Sure, Gavin. I went all the time while I was juggling college and working as a lawyer."

Part of me wanted to threaten to spank her for her smart mouth, but I refrained. I'd promised myself that I'd never try to push what I wanted on her.

"I've been to Cannes twice and it's absolutely gorgeous," I said. "There's the Promenade de la Croisette, this spectacular avenue along the waterfront. There are beaches and restaurants, boutiques. Plenty of places to get good food and to shop." I put my arm around her shoulders. "Or we could check out the Musée d'Art et d'Historie de Provence." The French words rolled off my tongue and she raised an eyebrow, impressed. "It's an eighteenth-century mansion that has artifacts over thousands of years. Maybe more. I've never been there myself."

"You speak French, don't you?" she asked.

I shrugged. "Enough to get my point across."

She leaned up and spoke in my ear. "How do you say 'I'd rather just stay in our hotel and fuck your brains out' in French?"

My jaw dropped and I stared at her. Her face was flushed and I could tell she was embarrassed by what she'd said. That she'd done it on her own, without any prompting by me sent blood rushing south. It was all I could do not to take her in my arms and savage her mouth, run my hands all over her body, other passengers be damned.

She grinned at me, her eyes dancing. I could see she was pleased to have shocked me. "Now, about the club."

I blinked, surprised by the change of subject.

"Do you have any specific plans in mind?"

Here came a conversation I really didn't want to have, especially not after what had just happened, but I knew it was better to tell her now, rather than later. She'd be furious if I kept it from her.

"I don't know anything about the site yet," I said. "But I do know that Vincent wants it to be in the style of the original Club Privé." I hesitated, wondering if she was going to need me to be more specific.

"That makes sense," she said amicably. "I'm sure France has plenty of dance clubs, but one that caters to the desires of the rich and famous in Cannes would definitely be a gold mine."

My eyebrows shot up. Would it be possible for us to do this without any conflict? I approached the subject cautiously. "I'm surprised you're okay with it," I admitted. "I'd thought you'd object to there being..." I chose my words carefully. "On-site sexual liaisons occurring."

"I'm not a prude, Gavin." Carrie's voice seemed a bit tense, but she continued before I could tell her that I hadn't meant it like that. "My concern is only that the encounters be between consenting adults without the exchange of money. No one in the sex industry, forced or otherwise."

"Absolutely," I agreed automatically. "No prostitutes of any kind." Relief went through me. That had been much easier than I'd dreamed possible. Now, I just had to smooth over whatever it was that I'd said that had prompted the prude comment.

"Is everything all right here, Sir?" The flight attendant was back and, unless I was mistaken, she'd hiked up her skirt a bit. She crouched down next to me, one of her full breasts pressing against my arm. "Because if there's anything I can do for you, anything at all, please don't hesitate to ask."

"That's it," Carrie snapped.

Oh shit. I looked over to see her eyes flashing. For a moment, I thought she was going to hit the flight attendant, but instead, Carrie stood and grabbed my hand.

"Come with me."

I stood, confused about what was happening, but there was no way I was going to stop her. As we headed down the aisle, I put two and two together... and my cock did as well. It was hard in an instant, making it a bit interesting to walk. If I was right, Carrie was going to initiate something that even I had never done before.

She glanced behind us, but didn't even hesitate as she reached for the door to the bathroom stall. She backed inside, pulling me after her. I could barely get the door shut behind me, but as she picked herself up to sit on the sink, I forgot about the tiny space we were in.

She pulled her skirt up, giving me a glimpse of the creamy

skin of her inner thighs and a hint of a pair of dark gray panties that matched her dress perfectly. With my gaze fixed between her legs, she pulled aside the crotch of her panties and slid her finger into her pussy.

"Fuck," I breathed.

"That's the point," she said. "Come on. We don't have much time."

I actually fumbled with my pants in my rush to get them open and I had a moment of thanks that we didn't have to mess with condoms. Then I was pushing inside of her tight, wet heat. I pressed my face against her neck, muffling my moans, and then I felt the sting of her teeth against the base of my throat and my body jerked. She cried out as I went too hard, but when I stilled, she wrapped her legs around my waist and pulled me toward her.

"Je préfère juste rester dans notre hôtel et baise la cervelle," I whispered.

"What?" Her voice was barely audible.

"That's how you say it in French," I said as I drew back.

"Just fuck me." Her nails dug into my shoulders and I could feel them through the thin cotton of my shirt.

That was all the encouragement I needed. I thrust into her as hard and fast as I dared, each of us trying to contain our cries of pleasure. And then...

"Folks, we have begun our descent into Nice Côte d'Azur International Airport, we'll be at the gate in about twenty minutes. If you are up and about, please return to your seat now. Flight attendants, please prepare the cabin for landing. Thank you for flying with us today."

"Fuck," I growled.

I felt a hand between our bodies, fingers brushing at the

base of my cock as Carrie found her clit. A moment later, her body tensed around mine. I kept pumping, faster and harder into her pulsing pussy. I was so close; I needed to come to.

A loud knock at the door broke my rhythm.

"You need to vacate the bathroom." A stern woman's voice came through the door.

"Just a minute," I practically shouted. My balls were aching, my cock throbbing with my need for release.

"Now, Sir," she said. "Or I'll be getting the key to unlock this door."

Carrie pushed at my chest and I cursed, knowing we were done. As much as she'd initiated and wanted this, the idea of being caught with our pants down, literally, terrified her.

"Fine!" I snapped as I yanked up my pants. I was so hard it hurt and I winced as I tucked myself back into my boxer briefs, and then zipped up my pants.

"Sorry," Carrie mumbled, her cheeks flushed. She climbed down off of the sink and then glanced down. "I'm thinking I should walk in front of you."

I looked down to where I was sporting a very obvious and large erection. Yeah, that wasn't going away any time soon. "That's probably a good idea."

The flight attendant pounded on the door again, but before Carrie could open it, I leaned down and gave her a hard, fast kiss. "You owe me," I said. "And I'm going to enjoy collecting."

Judging from the way her eyes brightened before she turned back toward the door, I had a feeling she was going to enjoy it almost as much as I would. It was almost enough to make up for the serious case of blue balls I was getting.

Almost.

NINE
CARRIE

I wasn't entirely sure what had come over me on the plane. All I knew was that I didn't like the way the flight attendant had been flirting with Gavin and I wanted to prove that I wasn't a prude, not even outside the bedroom. I'd remembered how insanely turned on I'd been when we'd fucked in the conference room, nearly getting caught by a janitor, and something inside me had just snapped. I wanted that feeling back. What I hadn't counted on was us reaching our destination before Gavin got to... arrive.

I knew it wasn't really funny, but I couldn't stop smiling as we made our way back to our seats, my face burning as I passed by people who looked at us with knowing expressions. And, of course, Gavin's comments about me owing him had my already wet panties soaked clean through. I hoped he came through on his promise to collect. I missed the way he'd possessed me when we'd first started having sex. How he'd once told me that I was his, that he would be responsible for my pleasure.

How either of us managed to sit still through the plane landing at the Nice airport and then wait for everyone to exit, I didn't know. After that, it was customs and security checkpoints, all the while both of our bodies were screaming for us to finish what we'd started. At least I didn't have any physical evidence of the strain I was under. Poor Gavin wasn't just sporting a decent hickey at the base of his neck, but he was still at least half-hard too.

When we were finally through all of the checkpoints and had our bags, he took my hand and we hurried toward the exit. Vincent had sent a limo to pick us up and I breathed a sigh of relief when I saw a distinguished looking man holding a sign with Gavin's name on it. He introduced himself as Dave and then insisted on loading our bags while we got into the back of the limo.

I started to slide across the seat to the opposite door when Gavin's arm wrapped around my waist and he yanked me back against him. The door closed, leaving us with the dim sunlight coming through the tinted windows. Gavin put his mouth against my ear as he pulled me half onto his lap. His hard cock pressed against my ass.

"I hope you don't have any immediate plans for when we get to our room," Gavin said. "Because I plan on fucking you sense-less the moment the door closes behind us."

I shivered with anticipation and hoped the ride would be a short one. I wasn't sure I could handle a long wait.

"Mr. Paoli has arranged for you to stay in the InterConti-nental Carlton Cannes," Dave said as he got into the driver's seat.

"How far is it from here?" Gavin asked, his arm tightening around my waist.

"Depending on traffic, Sir," Dave said. "About ninety minutes."

I closed my eyes. I was going to explode, and if I felt that way, I could only imagine how Gavin felt. The string of oaths he uttered in my ear gave me a pretty good idea.

Dave glanced in the rearview mirror and then pulled out into traffic. "You know, Sir," he said in a politely conversational tone. "One of the best features about this car is that with the push of a button, I can put up a privacy screen that prevents you from seeing or hearing anything I'm doing. We can still communication through an intercom, but if I want to sing along with the radio, which I do often, it won't bother you."

Gavin's hand was already on my thigh, pushing my skirt up, as he spoke. "That would be quite appreciated, Dave. You go ahead and sing along with the radio all you like."

"Thank you, Sir."

A moment later, a panel slid into place and Gavin's fingers were pushing their way into my pussy.

"Fuck." My head fell forward as he roughly thrust the digits into me. I'd had enough time since my orgasm so I wasn't overly sensitive, but the nerves were still awake enough that it didn't take much for them to start humming again.

"Yes," Gavin said. "That is exactly what I'm going to do."

He pulled out his hand and half-lifted me. I heard the sound of his zipper and then he was lowering me onto his raging erection. I moaned as he slid inside. I was still stretched from before and he was able to bury himself completely without hurting me. That was a good thing because I didn't think I'd ever felt him so hard.

"I'm not going to last long," he warned me. "So if you want to come, you're going to have to help yourself along."

I nodded but didn't move. My eyes were squeezed tight, absorbing the sensation of fullness. Of all the things Gavin could make me feel when he touched me, this was one of my favorites. I loved the way we fit together.

He gripped my hips hard and lifted me up enough that we'd both have room to move. Except, I didn't need to move. Gavin held me in place as he slammed up into me. I cried out, putting a hand on the ceiling to brace myself. His second thrust was stronger than the first, sending jolts of electricity racing through me.

Neither one of us spoke as he drove into me over and over, each stroke bringing a wail to my lips at the bruising force. I hoped the limo was as sound proofed as Dave had said, otherwise, he was getting quite an earful. The hand not on the ceiling moved between my legs. The pressure inside me was building again and I could already feel Gavin starting to lose control. I began to rub my clit, the friction making my muscles tremble.

Just before I got there, Gavin pulled me down hard and his cock went deep. I would've screamed if I'd had the air. As it was, my body went rigid, riding that edge between pleasure and pain, waiting for the last push to decide where I would go. I felt him coming inside me and shuddered. Just a little more.

Gavin's fingers closed around my wrist and I whimpered. I was so close.

"I should make you stop," he said. His voice was rough and I could feel his heart thudding in his chest, but he was in control. "Make you go the rest of the way on the edge."

My pulse stuttered.

"What do you think about that? I had all that time with no release. Shouldn't I make you touch yourself the rest of the way to the hotel, but never let you come?"

He flipped up my skirt and spread my legs so that my pussy was completely exposed. He was still inside me and I could feel our combined juices slick on my thighs. If Dave chose to lower the divider, he'd see everything.

"Is that what I should do?"

I shook my head, desperate for release. "Please," I whispered.

"Please what?"

"Please let me come."

He paused, as if he was considering it, and then released my hand. "Alright," he said. "But you only have thirty seconds before I buzz Dave to open the divider."

A thrill of fear went through me.

"Better get started."

If he'd waited any longer to let me start, I might've come down too much to be able to make it, but as it was, I was so close that he'd barely made it to fifteen before an orgasm ripped through me. I cried out his name and heard him swear as my pussy squeezed his now-soft cock. He pressed his lips against the side of my neck as wave after wave of pleasure washed over me. And then he slid out of me and a mini-orgasm hit me.

As he pulled me onto his lap, cradling me against his chest, I realized something. "You didn't buzz Dave."

"No." He sounded amused and I looked up to see his deep blue eyes sparkling. "Just wanted to make things more interesting."

"Ass," I muttered as I buried my face against his chest.

He kissed the top of my head. "I don't know about you," he said. "But this was a great way to start our business vacation."

I nodded in agreement. Leslie and Dena had been right. Some "us" time was exactly what Gavin and I needed. We'd get through this and come out stronger than ever.

TEN

CARRIE

I'd never adjusted well to time changes and the five-hour difference between New York and France was playing havoc with my sleep cycle. Despite being exhausted from the flight and the sex on the car ride here, I hadn't been able to fall asleep right away, and I must've woken several times during the first part of the night. This time when I woke, however, I knew I'd been out for at least a few hours. I was still jet-lagged, but far from non-functioning. Especially if my nose was correctly identifying coffee.

I opened my eyes and stretched, my hand brushing the empty space next to me. I turned my head. Gavin wasn't there. I sat up and blinked the last of the sleep from my eyes. The light coming through the window seemed wrong until I glanced at the bedside clock and saw that it was past nine. And this was why I hated time differences.

A warm breeze blew across me, drawing my attention to the open French doors on the far end of the room. I climbed out of bed and picked up the thin silk robe lying across the back of a nearby chair. I slipped it on over my nightgown and then followed the smell of coffee and saltwater. As I stepped out onto the balcony, I was torn between the views. On one hand, I was looking out over the ocean and one of the most beautiful beaches I'd ever seen. On the other hand, Gavin was standing at the railing, dressed in a pair of khakis and an open white cotton shirt that showed off his gorgeous body.

Lust won out and I walked up behind him and slipped my arms around his waist. I rested my cheek against his broad back, letting myself breathe in the scent of him. My hands flattened out on his stomach and the muscles beneath my palms jumped.

"Good morning, sleepyhead," he teased. "There's coffee behind you."

I lingered for a moment, but my need for caffeine was too great and I reluctantly released him. As I moved toward the second greatest smell in the world, I spoke, "How long have you been awake?"

"A couple hours," he said. "I'm determined not to sleep away our vacation."

I glared at him as he turned to face me. "How are you not jet-lagged?"

He shrugged. "You know me; I can sleep whenever and wherever."

I rolled my eyes and took another long drink of the premium roast. He held out his hand to me and I took it, setting down my cup. I wanted coffee, but I wanted him more. I stepped into his embrace and wrapped my arms around his waist, purposefully staying under his shirt so I could feel his skin against mine. His hands rested on the small of my back and I could feel the heat of him through the thin silk of my robe and nightgown.

"This is nice," I said and pressed my lips against his chest. He made a sound that sent a spike of arousal through me.

"Definitely different than New York spring weather, isn't it?" Gavin said.

I nodded in agreement. I loved my home, but there was something to be said for the sunshine and near sixty-degree weather at the end of April. Back in New York, we were just finishing up with the cold and snow, and were heading toward the hot and humid days of summer.

"It'd be nice to get away from the city once in a while, wouldn't it?" he said. "Maybe spend the first couple months of the year over here. Come down after the holidays and not head back until the weather changes."

I imagined what it'd be like, waking up like this every morning, and I couldn't say that I disliked the idea.

"You know," he said carefully. "If this deal goes through, I might need to spend a couple months here to get things started. Now that your work with the congressman is on hold until after the elections, maybe you could work from here for the summer."

I looked up at him. "If you're offering me this every day, I might never want to go back to New York." I smiled and reached up to push some hair out of his face. He'd need a haircut soon. "This vacation was a brilliant idea," I said. He beamed and my stomach flipped. I loved that smile.

"You've been working too hard," he said. He wrapped a curl around his finger, then tucked it behind my ear. "We both have, and I've missed you."

I swallowed hard. "I've missed you, too."

He bent his head and brushed his lips across mine. When he pulled away, his expression was troubled. "I feel like we're drifting, Carrie."

I felt my breath catch in my throat. He'd been feeling the distance too... "Then let's not." I put my hand on his cheek.

"We're here for a week. Let's focus on each other, not get all wrapped up in other things. Let's work on us."

He nodded. "That sounds perfect." His eyes darted away and he sighed. "Except I have a brunch meeting with Vincent."

"We are here for that," I said, trying not to be disappointed. I'd known coming into this that Gavin had to spend some time working on the club. "But the rest of the time is just us."

"Agreed," he said. "Get yourself from room service brunch and I'll be back by noon." He cupped my chin and tilted my head up. "We'll go shopping and you can model sexy dresses for me." A smile played across his lips for a moment before he bent and kissed me.

My mouth opened under his and I moaned as he slid his tongue into my mouth. It curled around mine and I dropped my hands to his ass, squeezing the firm muscles until Gavin took a step back. His eyes were dark, his breathing heavy.

"I have to go." His expression plainly told me that he'd prefer to stay and finish what we'd barely started.

I definitely wanted him to stay too, but I knew this was important. For Gavin, what had happened at Club Privé hadn't just been business. It was personal. He needed to do this for himself as much as for the business.

"Hurry back." I smiled at him as he headed into the room. I took a moment to appreciate the view from behind before following. I was hungry. By the time Gavin had finished buttoning up his shirt and was on his way out, I'd ordered a few things from room service and then gone into the bedroom to change.

After I was done, I still had some time to kill before the food arrived, so I headed back out to the balcony. I'd been all caught up looking at Gavin before, but now I could appreciate the rest of the view.

The private beach had the white sand and deep blue water that dreams were made of. It looked like paradise. Only the hotel guests were allowed on this part of the beach, so it wasn't as crowded as I guessed the public beaches were. There'd be room to walk or sit privately and not have to worry about being disturbed.

Other guests were down there already and I watched them as I waited. It didn't take long for me to notice a few things. First, the bathing suits the women wore often covered less than some of my lingerie; many were even topless. Second, basically every woman I saw was gorgeous. There were tall ones and short ones. Some that were model-thin, others had curves, but every one of them was beautiful. And most looked like they were younger than me. Considering I was only twenty-five, that was saying something.

Another pattern quickly presented itself and I frowned as I realized it. Other than the occasional man holding another man's hand, every guy down there was either with one of these gorgeous women or being pursued by one. Most of the men were in their fifties and had these twenty-something's hanging off their arms.

Back home, I'd been used to women flirting with Gavin and shooting me dirty looks when they realized we were together, but this was different. Even in this short amount of time, I could tell that the women here were going to be more direct in their approach. They wouldn't have any problem telling him what they wanted. And a man like Gavin, rich and gorgeous, would be what every woman wanted.

I nervously smoothed down the skirt of my sundress. I'd

brought it because it was cute, and it had been one Krissy had helped me pick out for Gavin before. He'd always said he'd liked it, but now I felt underdressed. These women were sexy, unashamed of their bodies and willing to flaunt them. Gavin had helped break down some of my inhibitions, but it wasn't until now that I realized how far I had to go. When given the choice, I still dressed like a kid. Not in a "trying to recapture my youth" kind of way, but more in a naïve kind of way.

Someone knocked at the door and I went back inside to answer it, thoughts still spinning through my head. I'd been taking Gavin for granted, I realized. I knew he loved me and I hadn't even considered that maybe I should be trying to make sure I was worth it. We had sex and we both got off, but had it really been soul deep satisfying? In the car yesterday, that had been the first time in a long time that I'd heard Gavin use that authoritative voice for real. Sure, he'd kind of used it when we'd been role-playing, but he'd never needed to pretend to be someone else before. When had he stopped dominating me, pushing my boundaries? A better question was, why had he stopped?

I opened the door and greeted the handsome young waiter with a polite smile.

"Where would you like me to set up?" he asked.

"On the balcony." I gestured even though I knew he knew where it was. I didn't miss his appreciative look as he passed me and that made me feel a bit better about my appearance, but I didn't want some waiter flirting with me. I wanted Gavin.

I needed a plan. A better one than just coming to France and spending time together, hoping that would magically fix whatever was wrong with us. The first step, I decided, would be to take advantage of our shopping excursion this afternoon to get myself a sexy new wardrobe. It wasn't that I didn't like wearing those kinds of clothes. A part of me really enjoyed it. It was just that I still felt awkward, like I was a child playing dress-up. I wasn't going to let that stop me anymore. If I wanted to keep Gavin, I was going to have to grow up.

And we were probably going to need to talk about why things had changed. That, however, wasn't something that could be done now, so I could turn my attention to the amazing food being set out in front of me.

"Is this your first time in Cannes?" The young man's English was good, but heavily accented.

"It is," I answered as I plucked a strawberry from a plate. "It's beautiful."

"Yes," he agreed. "And beautiful places attract beautiful women."

I blushed. "Thank you."

He gave a little bow. "Is there anything else you need?"

I shook my head and reached into the bag Gavin had thoughtfully set aside for tips. I handed the young man a bill.

"Thank you," he said. "And if there is anything you need at all – a tour guide, companionship – please do not hesitate to ask. My shift ends at five."

I stared at him as he left and wondered if he'd seriously just propositioned me. Wow. Apparently, it wasn't just the women who knew what they wanted. Even though I had no intention of being with anyone but Gavin, I had to admit, it was nice to have been thought of in that way.

I leaned against the railing as I picked my way through my meal. I could definitely get used to this.

It took me more time than I'd thought to get to Gaston-Gastounette from the hotel and I silently cursed myself for not having left before Carrie woke up. As much as I'd enjoyed being able to talk to her, especially since we'd been able to touch on how this part of this trip needed to be about us, I was frustrated that I was now running late. Again. This wasn't the kind of impression I wanted to give Vincent.

I'd never been at Gaston before but I knew that this was one of the hottest places to go for lunch, so it wasn't a surprise that it was packed. I strained to look over the heads of the people waiting to get in and quickly spotted Vincent. He was at the back with a woman sitting on either side of him.

As soon as I reached him, I apologized for being late and Vincent waved a dismissive hand. I took a seat in the only chair left and offered polite smiles to both of the women.

"Gavin, this is Felice, one of France's most popular pop singers." Vincent caressed the arm of the petite brunette next to him. "Only twenty and already the hottest thing out there. And very talented in many ways."

I smiled at her, wondering if I was just imagining the innuendo in Vincent's words. "Pleased to meet you, Felice."

Her dark eyes looked over me as she smiled and I had the distinct feeling that I was being mentally undressed. Something told me I was going to have to watch out for this one. She looked like the kind of woman who was used to getting what she wanted, and if she wanted me, I'd have my hands full.

"Pleasure," she said. "I look forward to know you."

"Likewise," I said.

"She doesn't speak much English," Vincent said. "But she knows all of the important words, don't you?"

"Yes," she said, not protesting when Vincent's hand rested on the back of her neck for a moment.

"And this," he turned to the other woman, "is Marguerite. She's Felice's best friend slash entourage slash assistant. They go everywhere together." He brushed back some auburn hair from Marguerite's face. "And they do everything together. Isn't that right, girls?"

And there was that innuendo again.

"Yes, we do," Marguerite said. Her eyes flicked to me and she gave a polite smile, but I didn't see any of the admiration in them that I saw with Felice. Until her gaze turned to the other woman. Unless I was mistaken, Marguerite had a crush on her friend. Maybe more.

"I'm Felice's manager," Vincent explained. "And once the club opens, Felice and performers like her will be the entertainment."

"In more ways than one," Felice added in her thickly accented English.

I caught a flash of annoyance on Marguerite's eyes and then it disappeared.

"She's quite the entertainer," Vincent said before he called over a waiter.

I wasn't sure which was worse, listening to Vincent imply that he'd had sex with both women or that neither woman protested his comments. I hoped we'd get down to business soon as I had no desire to hear anything about Vincent's sex life, but as the brunch progressed, it became obvious that Vincent was the kind of guy who preferred to lead with pleasure and business came last.

I focused on eating my bouillabaisse and hoped he didn't notice I was being rather quiet. Neither of the women talked very much either, but I felt Felice's eyes on me the entire time and whenever I'd look up, she'd be staring. Before Carrie and I had gotten together, I would've enjoyed the attention. Hell, Felice was the kind of woman I might have taken for a ride around the block a couple times. But things were different now and I found myself wishing that she'd turn her attention back to Vincent.

It was a relief when she and Marguerite excused themselves to the restroom. At least I'd have a few minutes of being left alone with Vincent.

"What do you think?" Vincent asked as soon as the women were out of earshot. "Aren't they a hot pair of asses?"

I gave him a tight smile.

"Everyone knows Marguerite has a thing for Felice," he said, confirming my suspicions. He winked at me. "Makes it that much easier to get them both in bed. Marguerite will do anything for the chance to eat that pussy."

I stared at him.

"What do you say?" Vincent asked. "When we're done eating, let's head back to my hotel. You and I can watch the girls go at it and then take turns with them. I don't mind sharing."

Making sure my voice didn't sound judgmental, I said, "No thanks. I'm just here for business."

Vincent scowled. "Business is boring. Why do you think I want to start a sex club? That's exciting. Today should be about fun."

"It is fun, I'm enjoying getting to know you better." I tried for an easy smile and a change of subject. "I want to hear more about your vision for the club. When can we see the building so I can get started on some ideas."

Vincent leaned back in his seat, his expression clearly stating that he didn't like that I wasn't going to join him in a foursome. I wondered if he even remembered Carrie had come with me or if he thought a pretty face and hot body would be all I needed to cheat. Maybe he thought because we ran a sex club, we were in an open relationship. I made a mental note to be careful with Carrie around Vincent. I wasn't sure I'd be able to control my temper if he propositioned her.

"We're scheduled to see the site tomorrow," he said, then looked around. "Now, I hope this isn't too much mixing business with pleasure for you, but there's a big music conference in town this week. That's why it's so crowded."

I felt Felice's hand trail along my shoulder as she passed by on the way to her seat. I stiffened, but didn't shrug her off. I didn't want to offend her, not if she was going to be performing at the club.

"Tonight's the biggest party of the week," Vincent continued. "I want you to come. It's a huge hip-hop artist throwing it and it'll be a great time to mingle with the celebrities. Make connections."

He was right, I knew. Making connections was important in this business. "Sounds great," I said. "I'll be there." Besides, Carrie liked music. She would enjoy it.

"You come?" Felice asked.

"Sure," I said. "And I hope to see you there." I smiled at Marguerite to include her as well. "It'll be nice to get to know you better."

Vincent looked pleased at that and I breathed a sigh of relief that I'd salvaged the brunch. The last thing I needed right now was for things to go south on this deal.

TWELVE
GAVIN

By the time I got back to the hotel, I was more than ready for an afternoon of just me and Carrie. It had been too long since we'd had any real alone time. We'd need to be back at the hotel before six to make sure we were ready for the party at seven, but when most of our time together had been measured by just an hour or two, nearly six hours seemed like a luxury.

"How'd the meeting go?" Carrie asked as soon as I entered our room.

"Let's not talk business," I said as I crossed the room and wrapped my arms around her. The meeting had left me with a bad taste in my mouth and all I wanted to do was be with her. I'd work with Vincent, but it didn't mean I had to like him. Maybe it was better that way. Howard had pretended to be my friend and I'd let that blind me for longer than I cared to remember.

"Okay," she said. "So what do you want to talk about?" She put her arms around my neck and looked up at me.

"How about how amazing you look in that dress?" I

captured her mouth before she could say anything. Her fingers twisted in the hair at the base of my neck as I nibbled at her lips, forcing myself to be gentle when what I really wanted to do was make her cry out. Bite down, then soothe the bruised flesh with my tongue, suck it into my mouth... I pulled back and smiled down at her. "Now, what do you say we go shopping?"

She returned the smile. "You're probably one of the few straight men in the world to ever utter that line."

I laughed and released her. She went to get her purse and I watched her go. I really did love that dress. The color was perfect on her and it was just right for walking around Cannes, but I wanted to get her into something sexy. The memory of her in various outfits she'd worn at the beginning of our relationship flipped through my mind. I never wanted her to feel like I didn't love who she was, but I sometimes thought she didn't give herself enough credit, especially when it came to how amazing she looked in designer clothes.

"Lead the way," she said as she hooked her arm through mine.

If I had to describe a perfect afternoon, this would've been it. The sun was shining and the temperature hovered around sixty degrees. A light breeze came in off the ocean, just enough to keep the sun from being too hot. People were out and about, but the sidewalks weren't even close to as crowded as they normally were back home.

"Where are we going?" she asked after a few minutes.

"La Croisette," I answered. "It'll take us right along the waterfront and we can see the yachts while we shop. There's also places where celebrities have put their handprints in the cement."

She wrapped her other arm around mine and leaned her

head on my shoulder. My heart gave a skip. I loved this woman so much that it hurt sometimes, especially when I thought about how far apart we'd drifted. It was foolish to think that a day of shopping could fix everything, but maybe it could at least make things better.

I lost track of time as we walked, letting myself enjoy the weather and the company. Palm trees, clear blue sky...all the things I needed to forget about the busy lives we'd left behind.

"Hey, babe, is that...?" Carrie's voice was low. I followed where she was looking and saw a familiar face. Even if she hadn't been sporting blue hair once more, the entourage would've clued anyone in that this was a celebrity out and about.

"She must be in town for the music festival."

"There's a music festival?" Carried glanced up at me.

I nodded. "Vincent told me earlier. He thinks it'd be a good idea for us to go to a party tonight. I forgot about it." I kissed the top of her head. "You distracted me."

She titled her head up for a quick kiss. "That sounds great, but I'm definitely going to need a new dress then. If I'm representing the club in front of all those celebrities, I can't go dressed like this."

"You'd be gorgeous in a potato sack," I insisted. "But I'd definitely love to see you in something with some slink."

"Then let's head up there." She gestured toward a plaza with a large metal sculpture in the center. "I'll bet those are some pricey shops." She winked at me and then grinned.

I decided right then that I didn't care how much whatever dress she wanted cost. Price wasn't going to be an object this week. If the business deal flopped and we had to discuss a change to finances at some point, fine, but for right now, there would be no limit.

A rush of cool air hit us as we walked in and a pair of finely dressed sales women immediately greeted us. Carrie glanced at me and I smiled.

"Surprise me," I said.

As the sales women began their pitches, I headed toward the couch in the center of the store. Another husband or boyfriend was already sitting there. We exchanged the nods of men who had resigned themselves to spending as much time as necessary waiting for the women in our lives to find the perfect dress.

I checked my phone while I waited, but there weren't any messages from Vincent. I wasn't sure if that was a good thing or a bad thing. I'd gotten the impression that he'd been a little annoyed at me for not wanting to play this morning, and that made me a bit nervous about our deal since we hadn't officially signed anything. I just hoped, in his case, no news was good news.

I wasn't sure how much time had passed, but the other man's wife had come out in two different dresses before Carrie emerged. Taking her time had paid off. It was perfect. A deep crimson – my favorite color on her – it complemented her skin tone perfectly. The neckline was plunging, far more daring than anything I would've imagined her choosing for herself. My mouth went dry as my eyes followed it down between her firm breasts until it ended at the base of her ribcage. The simple tie top kept her shoulders bare and, as she turned, her back as well. That part of the dress exposed everything down to the base of her spine, confirming that she wasn't wearing a bra. I shifted in my seat and tried to will away the beginnings of an erection.

Unfortunately, the hemline barely covering her ass and the fabric clinging to her body didn't help. Then there were the six-inch matching heels.

Fuck me.

"I believe he approves." One of the sales women smiled at Carrie.

I nodded. "He most definitely does." My voice was hoarse. I stood and hoped I wasn't as hard as I felt. I reached into my pocket and withdrew my credit card.

As we left the shop, Carrie was beaming.

"Did you really like it?" she asked.

I gave her an incredulous look. "Are you kidding me? It was all I could do not to take you on the couch right there."

She reached over and took my hand. Her arm bumped against mine as she moved closer. "I know we have this party to go to, but do you think we have some time?"

I raised an eyebrow, hoping she meant what I thought.

Color rose in her cheeks. "Do we have time for a quickie?"

I squeezed her hand as blood rushed south. "Hell yes," I answered immediately. As I realized what time it was, however, I had to add, "But I think it'll have to be in the shower. We're cutting it close."

"Then we better hurry," Carrie said as she quickened her pace. "We don't want a repeat of the airplane."

No, I silently agreed with her. I most certainly didn't want that.

THIRTEEN

From the moment I'd seen the look in Gavin's eyes when he saw me in that dress, I knew there was no way I was going to go to some party without fucking him first. The insatiable appetite I'd once had for him had come back with a vengeance, and I was going to feed it.

As soon as we got back to our room, I put my purchases – including some new panties he hadn't seen yet – in the bedroom while Gavin went to warm up the shower. I then immediately stripped and headed into the bathroom. My stomach was twisting into knots as I went. One of the things I'd had turning over in my head all afternoon was how to approach this whole change in our sex lives. It had been when I'd suggested the quickie that I'd decided the best way to do it. And I wasn't going to wait.

Gavin pushed open the sliding glass door and held out his hand. As he backed into the shower, taking me with him, I let my gaze wander. No matter how many times I saw him naked, he still took my breath away. His body was like a work of art, a sculpture of male perfection. His chest and abs were defined, not from being too thin or because he was bulky. His waist and hips were proportioned to the rest of him and those deep v-grooves pointed to the most exquisite piece of flesh I'd ever known.

He was only half-hard and already bigger than average. I swallowed hard and knew exactly how to begin. The warm spray beat down on me, soaking my hair and caressing my body. Gavin's eyes darkened as they traveled over me, then widened as I went down on my knees. The tile was hard and still cool against my skin. I looked up at him as I put my hands behind my back. The position pushed my breasts out, but I knew that wasn't the only reason he'd caught his breath.

"Carrie?" He breathed my name as a question.

I reached out and took his hand, guiding it to the back of my head. Once it was there, I clasped my hands behind my back again. I watched his Adam's apple bob as he swallowed and then my eyes flicked down to his cock. It was fully erect now, meaning he didn't really need my mouth on him to get us where we needed to go, but I wanted him to do it anyway.

He moved forward, pulling my head toward him at the same time. The tip of his cock brushed against my lips and I opened my mouth. My tongue darted out, swirling around the tip. We didn't have time to make this last, but I wanted a taste. Then he was pushing his cock forward, sending the thick shaft sliding across my tongue until he almost reached the back of my throat.

I looked up at him from under my lashes and found that he was staring at me. The intensity in his gaze made me shiver despite the heat of the shower. His fingers tightened in my hair, sending little pinpricks of pain through my scalp. I moaned and my pussy throbbed. I'd forgotten how good that felt.

Too soon, he was pulling back. When I didn't stand, he pulled me to my feet. His eyes met mine and I could see there was a question he wasn't sure how to ask. I kept our gazes locked and backed up until I was against the wall. Then, without a word, I held out my hands, my wrists crossed over each other. When he wrapped his hand around them, I nodded.

He groaned as he pinned my hands above my head and pressed his body against mine. His free hand moved under my thigh, lifting my leg around his hip. My heel rested against his ass, allowing me to feel the flex of muscle as he drove into me.

I keened, my entire body shaking with the sudden force of the intrusion. The second stroke was just as intense and I cried out again, this time, forcing it into a single word so he would know not to stop.

"Yes!"

Again and again he thrust into me, making me feel every inch of him. My fingers curled and flexed, wanting to touch him, needing to find some sort of outlet for the sensations coursing through me. But he held me tight, refusing to give me that respite. He swiveled his hips, grinding the base of his cock against my clit.

"Gavin!" I writhed against him, desperate for something I couldn't put into words. All I knew was that I was going to explode, that this pressure inside me was going to be too much very soon.

"Come for me," he panted. "Come for me, baby."

I whimpered. I wanted to do as he said. I needed it. But I couldn't quite get there. And then his mouth was on my breast, his teeth and lips worrying at the soft flesh until I knew I'd have a mark. A mark that would be visible in my new dress. A mark that would show everyone that I belonged to him.

He gently pulled on my nipple with his teeth and I came. His arms moved to wrap around my waist, holding me tight as he thrust up into me twice more, then stilled, buried deep inside me. He pressed his face against the side of my neck and I felt the heat of every shuddering breath as he came. His muscles trembled under my hands as I ran them down his back.

After a minute, he pulled back, a reluctant expression on his face. "We need to clean up and get dressed. Besides, I have another surprise for later."

"A surprise, huh?"

He looked down at me, a flicker of uncertainty in his eyes. "Yes, and I hope you'll like it." He swatter my ass. "But for now, we better hurry."

As much as I wanted to explore what had just happened, I knew we didn't have the time. We washed in silence, each of us lost in our own thoughts. I didn't know what had Gavin so preoccupied, but I was thinking about how much I'd enjoyed what we'd done. I'd liked giving him that control. The feel of his fingers circling my wrists, restraining me, had twisted something inside me that hadn't made itself known since the beginning of our relationship. And judging by his reaction, he'd liked what we'd done too. We may not have had the time now, but I was more resolved than ever to have a discussion with him about why he didn't do those things anymore.

We were in the middle of dressing when our phones rang at the same time. When I saw who was calling, I was glad Gavin was distracted by whoever had called him. Mine was from the front desk. I pulled on my shoes and quickly left the room, hoping I could get down and back before Gavin noticed I was gone.

As I rode the elevator, I glanced down to make sure my

dress was staying in place. The hickey Gavin had put on the side of my breast was indeed visible and I knew it should've embarrassed me. Instead, the heat that spread through me was one of arousal. I had no reason to be ashamed that the man I loved had marked my body.

When I reached the lobby, I kept my head up as I walked from the elevators to the front desk. I could feel eyes on me as I went, but refused to look. I knew some of those gazes would be ones of admiration, but there could be some condemnation too. I didn't care about any of that.

"Here you are, Miss Summers." The young woman behind the desk handed me my package after I scribbled my signature on the delivery form.

I thanked her and headed back to the elevator. While Gavin had been at his meeting earlier today, I'd decided I wanted to give him something. Forty-five minutes online and a big chunk of money later, I had my gift being delivered to the hotel. I peeked in the little box. The cufflinks were perfect. One had my initials, the other had his daughter's. I'd even had the script matched to the tattoo of his daughter's initials on his back. I couldn't wait to see him open them.

When I entered our suite, Gavin was still on the phone. I could hear him in the bedroom, his voice hushed and hurried, as if he wanted to get off the call right away. I glanced at the clock. We were running late.

"I'll have to figure out how to get away, but I'll be there."

A moment later, he appeared in the doorway, fully dressed, but looking rushed. "Babe, where'd you go?"

I smiled at him, enjoying the way his eyes were drawn to my body as I walked toward him. "I had to run down to the front desk and pick something up." I held out the box and it took him a moment to refocus his gaze on it. "I wanted to get you a little something."

"You didn't have to do that," he said as he took the box from me.

"I know," I said. "But you got me this gorgeous dress and I wanted to get you a present too."

"Trust me," he said, his voice low. "That dress is as much for me as it is for you."

A moment of heated silence passed between us.

"Open it." I was afraid if I didn't break the moment, we'd never make it to the party.

He opened the box and his face lit up. "Wow, where did you get these? They're amazing!" His mouth came down hard on mine, his tongue pushing its way between my lips. Desire went straight to my core, heating my entire body. And then he was stepping back, the expression on his face saying he'd rather stay in the rest of the night.

"Here, let me." I fastened on each one and then admired how they looked. "Perfect."

"Thank you." He ran his fingers over the one with his daughter's initials and then reached for me. His hand cupped my chin, tilting my head so that he could brush his lips against mine. As he straightened, his eyes dropped to the mark he'd made on my breast. He lowered his hand from my chin and gently touched the darkened flesh.

I made a sound in the back of my throat and his hand covered my breast, squeezing it. My eyelids fluttered and the pressure spiraled into pleasure. I moved closer, ready to say to hell with the party, then jumped.

Someone knocked on the door.

I swore silently as Gavin dropped his hand and moved to

answer it. I looked down and made sure my dress was in place, then turned just in time to see a gorgeous, petite brunette walk into the room. My eyes widened when I saw what she was wearing and suddenly my daring dress didn't seem so daring. Even Krissy wouldn't have worn something like that.

The top half of the young woman's body was wrapped in a scarf. Literally. She had a filmy scarf tied over her breasts, the material so thin that I was pretty sure I could see the outline of her nipples. If she'd been any bigger, the material wouldn't have covered everything. And then there was her skirt. If it could be called that. The waist of it rested so low on her hips that if it dipped the tiniest bit, I'd be able to confirm that her pussy was bare. The skirt was so short that she almost risked flashing everyone just by walking, and I was positive she wasn't wearing panties.

"Carrie, this is Felice."

"I escort."

I glanced at Gavin, hoping there was a language barrier issue here.

"She's a singer so she knows her way around the Cannes music scene," he jumped in quickly to explain. "Vincent's her manager. He must've asked her to escort us to the party."

I forced a smile and held out my hand. "It's a pleasure to meet you."

She smiled back but it didn't reach her eyes. As soon as she turned back to Gavin, it was obvious her reaction was limited to me. "We go now?"

Gavin gave her a warm smile and looked over at me, he eyebrow raised in question. "Ready?"

I nodded and followed them out of the room. It was on the tip of my tongue to ask her if she was going to get cold, but I didn't want to sound catty. Gavin always had women hitting on him. That was one of the things that came with dating a man like him. Not all of the girls looked like they were barely legal and would drop to their knees in a second if he asked though.

Felice rattled something off in French and Gavin laughed. I suddenly wished I'd taken French in high school. Maybe I could look up how to say, "keep your damn hands off my boyfriend" in case I needed it.

When we walked outside, I hooked my arm through Gavin's and he smiled down at me. I started to return the smile when I saw Felice link her arm through his on the other side. She shot me a glare that disappeared as soon as he looked at her. I waited for him to tell her to let him go, or at least politely remove her arm from his. Instead, he began to walk and we fell in step beside him.

He was just being polite, I told myself. He didn't want to make Felice feel like a third wheel. It was the gentlemanly thing to do. She could have her hand on his arm all she wanted, but I knew whose bed he'd been in when the night was done. And I wasn't planning on us getting much sleep.

I kept my peace as they chatted in French, distracting myself by taking in the sights of Cannes in the evening. It wasn't difficult to see where we were heading once we rounded the corner. What looked like a few thousand people were making their way toward the Grand Hotel. We didn't need Felice to show us the way after all.

"The guests here are from all over Europe and North America." Gavin's voice drew my attention away from the beautiful sunset. "These are the people we want spreading the word about the club. And some of them might even want to perform there." He glanced at Felice. "Vincent's already said he wants Felice as an entertainer."

I had a pretty good idea that her brand of entertainment wouldn't always involve singing, but I decided I'd better keep that to myself. I'd promised Gavin that if things at the club happened between consenting adults, I was fine with it. Instead, I changed the subject by pointing toward a large, dark-skinned man with several tattoos. "Mimi handled his divorce case."

"That's great!" Gavin exclaimed. "You should talk to him."

Shit. That hadn't been what I wanted. I didn't want to remind one of the East Coast's most thug-like rappers about his divorce from some reality star. Fortunately, by the time I looked back, he'd been swallowed up by the crowd. Maybe I'd be lucky and I wouldn't see him again tonight.

We were walking through a press of bodies now, down to almost a shuffle as we made our way to the front of the line. Felice flashed a smile at the massive man at the door and he stepped aside, motioning the three of us through. We walked into the lobby, following the people in front of us, and then found ourselves outside again. The hotel had a massive garden that had been turned into a dance party.

The music pulsed around us, a rhythm that was familiar even though the lyrics weren't. I glanced toward the place where guests were dancing and was half-tempted to ask Gavin if he wanted to go.

"We dance," Felice said, pulling at Gavin's arm.

He shot me an apologetic look as he allowed her to drag him away. I watched them dance, though what Felice was doing looked a lot more like writhing than dancing. I thought back to how Gavin and I had danced the first night we'd met and a pang of jealousy went through me. I told myself that he wasn't interested in Felice, that he was just humoring her, but it was hard to keep thinking that way when she was rubbing her body on him like a cat in heat.

I grabbed a glass of champagne from a passing waiter and drank half of it in one gulp. I tore my gaze away from Felice and Gavin and started looking around. I recognized a few other big name stars, but most of the people around me were indie artists or local ones. I liked music, but I wasn't exactly up on the latest hits. Still, there had to be someone here I could talk to about the club. If I wasn't going to enjoy this as a date, I'd at least prove my worth to my boyfriend's business. Besides, I told myself, if I found a hot guy who wanted to dance with me while we talked, it would be a nice bonus. After all, why should it only be Gavin having fun on the dance floor tonight?

No hot guys were asking though and three more songs played before Gavin returned, a laughing Felice clinging to his arm. Oh yeah, this was going to be a fun night, alright.

I tried not to let Gavin see how annoyed I was as the night progressed, but it wasn't easy. Felice demanded all of his atten- tion and every time he wasn't looking, she'd shoot me a smug grin that clearly said she knew exactly what she was doing. She dragged him around like he was some prize for her to show off, leaving me to follow if I wanted. Sometimes I did, sometimes I didn't. I nursed a second glass of champagne and reminded myself that I didn't want to make things awkward for Gavin by bitch-slapping the singer who'd be working in the club.

I was gratified to see him checking his watch every so often, but I would've felt a lot better if he'd made a point of making sure I was with him, of letting people know that we were together.

"There are a lot of great possibilities for talent here," Gavin said as he and Felice found me at the edge of the party.

I was working on formulating an appropriately supportive response when a beautiful auburn-haired woman approached. A glance at Gavin told me he knew her too.

"Carrie, this is Marguerite, Felice's best friend and assistant."

"Pleased to meet you," I said. She got a warmer smile than Felice since she didn't start clinging to my boyfriend.

"Likewise." Her handshake was firm and her face gave away nothing.

"Where's Vincent? I haven't seen him here yet?" Gavin said looking around.

Marguerite nodded. "He had some business to attend to. He hopes he can make it later tonight. Knowing Vincent I doubt he will show." She turned to Felice and said something in French. Judging by the confused expression on Gavin's face, he hadn't gotten most of it. "We must be going," she said in accented, but flawless English.

"It was good seeing you both again," Gavin said as Felice released his arm. "We should get together before I leave and do something. Drinks maybe."

"I would like that." Felice gave him a predatory smile before her friend took her arm and the pair walked off.

Gavin picked up a glass of champagne and drank in all in one long draught. I smiled. Maybe he hadn't been having as much fun as it had appeared.

"Excuse me." A woman's voice came from my right and I turned, my eyes widening.

A pretty blonde was standing less than two feet away,

flanked by a pair of men with arms the size of my thighs. "Kelsey Larson."

"I know who you are, Miss Larson." I shook her outstretched hand. "I'm a huge fan. You do great work drawing attention to human trafficking."

"As do you, I hear. And, please, call me Kelsey."

I didn't try to hide my surprise. "You've heard of me?"

Kelsey's smile widened. "I have, Miss Summers."

"Carrie, please." I couldn't believe it.

One of the foremost entertainers working to promote awareness of the sex trade and human trafficking, Kelsey Larson was the poster child for the movement. Born to a Russian prostitute, Kelsey had been abused since birth. Sold to an American businessman when she was eight, she endured four more years of horrific abuse before escaping and taking three more sex slaves with her, all under the ages of ten. Now in her late twenties, she was a best-selling author, a chart-topping country star, producer and director of the documentary My Rapist's American Dream, a re-telling of her life. Rumor had it, she'd be nominated for an Academy Award for her work.

"I've heard that you're working on a proposal for Congressman Joshua White. I'd love to hear about it."

Out of the corner of my eye, I saw Gavin check his watch again. Maybe it hadn't been Felice boring him. Whatever it was, it could wait. I began to explain how the proposal was designed to fill in loopholes in sex trafficking laws, as well as address the statute of limitations. Kelsey was amazing. She asked all the right questions, giving advice on some points I hadn't thought of, as well as how certain things should be worded. We were right in the middle of a discussion on international policy when Gavin put his hand on my shoulder.

"Babe, I need to go do something." He sounded distracted. "I know you're busy here, so I'll see you later?"

I nodded, slightly annoyed that he hadn't lasted more than twenty minutes without being the center of attention. I'd stayed in the background while he and Felice had gone all over the place together arm in arm. Everyone probably thought she was his girlfriend, and I hadn't complained to him once. Now, he was going to bail just because I was talking to someone about something important? I suppressed a scowl because I didn't want Kelsey to know something was wrong, but all of the excitement of talking to her was muted by Gavin's exit.

A quarter of an hour later, Kelsey and I exchanged contact information and promised to connect once we both returned to the States. With her support of my proposal, I could really gain some traction while I was waiting for Congressman White. Maybe even give him a bit of push to move ahead before the elections.

As Kelsey walked away, I looked at my watch and then around at the crowd. It was only eleven o'clock and I knew that meant the party was just starting. I just wasn't interested in mingling, not by myself.

I sent a text to Gavin saying I was heading back to the hotel and then started to walk back the way I'd come. I wasn't sure what he'd planned when he told me he'd see me later, but at the moment, I didn't care. He'd left and I was going to do the same. If he wanted to be off doing whatever, that was his business.

I tried not to feel abandoned as I walked back to the hotel alone, but it wasn't easy. I'd gotten this beautiful dress because I knew Gavin would like me in it. We'd had what I thought had been great sex, and he'd loved the gift I'd given him. I really thought we had been on our way to getting things back on track.

Instead, I spent most of the night watching my boyfriend with another woman and now he was off somewhere, leaving me in a strange place where I didn't speak the language. I looked at my phone and nearly growled... he couldn't even bother to text me back. What could he be doing that was so important he couldn't just acknowledge my message?

I was good and annoyed by the time I reached our room, so distracted that I was halfway through the main area before I heard noises coming from the bedroom. My stomach twisted and my heart told me to turn around and leave, but I didn't listen. I forced my feet to go toward the unmistakable noises of passion.

When I pushed open the door, it took my brain a moment to register what I was seeing, and then the picture became clear.

Felice and her friend, Marguerite, were lying in our bed, naked, and in a position that left absolutely no doubt as to what they'd been doing just moments before.

"What the hell?" The question came out flat.

Felice smirked at me from where she was laying on her back, legs spread wide. Despite her thick accent, her words were perfectly clear. "Gavin invite us to join him."

Carrie was going to be pissed. She'd texted to say she was heading to the hotel and my damn phone died before I could text her back. I knew she'd been annoyed at the party, watching Felice drag me around, but it wasn't like I had much choice in the matter. I couldn't afford to piss off someone who so obviously had the ear of my potential partner. And then I'd needed to leave so I could get to Monique in time. I'm sure that hadn't gone over very well either, and only Kelsey Larson's presence had stopped Carrie from saying anything right then.

My hand tightened around the package, hoping the ends would justify the means and Carrie would be so overjoyed with her present, the rest of the night would be forgotten. I hadn't realized at the time that my subterfuge would backfire in my face. What I'd meant to be a build up to the romantic surprise would, in fact, probably just make her mad.

I could only hope she'd had a good enough conversation with Kelsey to be only mildly annoyed at my behavior. Once I explained and gave her the custom-made necklace I'd commissioned, I knew she'd understand. I hated knowing I'd upset her, though, even if it was only for a bit and for a good reason.

Based on when I'd gotten her text and how long it would take for her to get from the party back to the hotel, I knew I was probably only a few minutes behind her, and that was good. The less time she had to stew in our hotel room, the better. I was also really hoping she hadn't changed out of that magnificent dress yet. I'd been looking forward to peeling it off of her from the moment she'd tried it on in the store.

Just the thought of her in that dress sent blood rushing south and I could feel my cock twitch in my pants. I tapped my foot impatiently as the elevator seemed to crawl along. I crossed the distance to the room in record time, my key card already in hand when I got there. The light flashed green and I stepped inside, fully expecting Carrie to be waiting for me, wanting an explanation.

Instead, the main area was empty and I frowned. Had she gotten into the shower already? I hadn't thought I was that far behind her. I was a bit disappointed that I wouldn't get to see her in that dress again, but considering how well the shower before the party had gone, I wasn't exactly going to say no to another wet encounter.

I slipped the package into my pocket and headed for the bedroom. I was partway there when I heard Carrie's voice screaming, "Get the hell out of my room!"

All my plans were forgotten as adrenaline lit a fire under my feet. I burst into the room, then skidded to a stop. My brain processed things in snapshots. Carrie standing at the foot of the bed, an expression of horrified anger on her face. In the bed were two women—naked, limbs entwined. Fuck. Felice and Marguerite.

Shit.

I looked down at Carrie and her eyes were flashing. "Babe," I said, trying to lighten the mood, "if you wanted to spice up our sex life, all you had to do was ask."

As soon as the half-ass attempt of a joke left my mouth, I knew it was the wrong thing to say. By a lot.

"Fuck off!" She snapped at me, her face a mask of pure rage.

I heard Felice giggle as Carrie stormed out of the room, but I didn't even bother to look down at either woman. I followed Carrie, calling out her name. She was already at the elevator when I reached the hallway.

"Carrie, wait! It was a joke! A stupid joke!"

The door opened and she stepped inside. I didn't even need to see her face to know my shitty joke had landed wrong. Everything about her said she was furious. I didn't blame her. If the situation had been reversed I'd been pissed as hell to find two naked men in my bed. Pissed didn't cover it; someone would have gotten hurt.

I managed to squeeze inside just as the doors began to close, but before I could say anything, Carrie grabbed the front of my shirt and shoved me against the wall. I was so startled, I couldn't believe she was able to move me without any resistance. It went a long way in proving just how angry she was.

"You bring me to fucking France, leave me alone at a party for the whole night while you go off dancing with that... that slut!" She jabbed a finger back toward the room. "Then, when she finally leaves, you take off, saying you have to 'do something.' Like being with me for more than twenty minutes is so awful."

My jaw dropped. I could hardly believe this was Carrie. I'd seen her angry before, but I never imagined I'd see that fury directed at me... not like this.

"When I finally leave, I text you, hoping like some insecure little schoolgirl that you'll say you're on your way, but I get shit." She let go of my shirt, but didn't step away. "Then, I get to the room and find two naked whores fucking in our bed." She took a deep breath, and let it out with a growl. "You still think this is about some fucking lame joke you made?!"

Pieces were starting to fall into place, though I still had no idea why the women were in our room or how they'd gotten there. "Carrie, I-"

"And don't say you're sorry!" She cut me off. "I don't care if you're fucking sorry! How dare you leave me alone all night. You dragged me here so I could support you and the business we're supposed to be partners in, and then blow me off like I'm excess baggage—"

"Whoa, whoa." I finally found my voice. "Let me explain."

"You think you can explain away all of this?" She took a step back and crossed her arms in what I'd come to recognize as her 'not taking any shit' stance. "Try me. Give it your best bullshit."

Fuck. I took a minute to figure out the best place to start. An apology was probably a good idea and I had a shitload to apologize for.

"Babe."

Her eyes narrowed at the endearment.

"I'm so sorry for how all this has played out. It's not what I wanted." I smoothed down the front of my shirt. Seeing Carrie so riled up had thrown me. "And that." I gestured toward a general space outside. "I don't know what the hell that was. I had no idea either of those women would do something like that."

"Felice said you invited her."

Shit. Now I got it.

"I sure the hell did not. Neither of those woman had an invitation from me," I said firmly. I locked eyes with her. I didn't want there to be any doubt about this. "I did not state or imply that I was interested in any kind of sexual relationship with either of those women." I sighed. I had to be completely honest with her. She deserved that. "But part of this is my fault."

Carrie shifted her weight from one foot to the other. I reached out and hit the stop on the elevator. I wasn't going to fuck this up by trying to rush it.

"I should've made it crystal clear that I wasn't interested the first time she indicated she was," I confessed. "I never encouraged her, but I let it go. I did it because I didn't want to risk her ruining my deal with Vincent. And I need this deal."

I could see her face morph into disgust, but I continued anyway. She deserved to know the whole truth. "I haven't been entirely forthcoming about how things were going back home. With all the renovations and changing the club from what it was..." I ran my hand through my hair. "It' cost a lot more than I'd planned, and with that and... other expenses..."

"My business," Carrie said, spitting out the words.

I nodded. "I love what you do," I assured her quickly. "And I love that I can help you do it, but it does cost money. Money that I've had no problem spending, but with the club not being open, and not taking in as much when it is, it's not being replaced as fast as it's going out. And we're not even a quarter of the way done with the changes yet."

A concerned expression overtook the anger on her face. However she thought this conversation was going to go, this wasn't it.

"A club here is what I need to get things going again. I didn't want to risk the deal, but I never imagined anything like this would happen either."

"Stop right there," Carrie said. "I just need to know one thing right now. The rest of it can wait. There are two naked women in our bed right now. Did you invite them there and then backpedal because I didn't like your little surprise?"

"Carrie," I said the only thing I knew she wouldn't question. "I swear on my daughter's life that I didn't ask either one of those women to come here."

A look of relief washed over her, but her eyes still looked troubled. "Why were you so distant all night? Taking calls? Acting secretive? Why did you have to leave me alone so much?"

I smiled. This one I could answer and provide proof that she'd like. "I was trying to surprise you with this." I reached into my pocket and pulled out the package. I held it out to her.

Her entire body stilled for a moment and then she took it, glancing at my face and then down to the rectangular box in her hands. I kept my eyes on her face while she opened it. I'd been waiting all day to see her expression and I'd be damned if I'd let some stupid misunderstanding ruin this moment.

She lifted the lid and her eyes widened. Her face softened and a soft exhale came from between her lips. "Gavin, it's beautiful."

I smiled, relieved. I'd gotten the idea when we'd passed by a shop and Carrie had expressed a liking for the intricate workings of a gold and ruby necklace. The delicate gold filigree had been shaped like a rose. The one I'd commissioned was a heart, and not just some simple heart with gold and jewels. It was two entwined hearts and I knew she understood what I was trying to say. Our hearts were just as linked as those two pieces of metal.

"I had to get it from the jeweler before she took off for some sort of convention thing in Munich," I explained.

"I love it," she said, her voice barely over a whisper. She closed the box and took a step toward me. She raised herself up on her tiptoes and brushed her lips against mine. "Thank you."

"You're very welcome." I wrapped my arms around her waist and she leaned her head on my shoulder. "I'm sorry tonight ended like this. It's not what I had in mind."

She sighed. "Me either."

"Think we can salvage it?" I asked, trying not to sound as doubtful as I felt.

"I'm just tired, Gavin," she said. "I want to go bed." Then she groaned and banged her head against his chest. "Except our bed is occupied. And I'll be damned if I'd sleep in it now anyway."

I chuckled, in complete agreement. "Tell you what," I said. "I'll go in and check. If the women are still there, we'll get another room. If they're gone, I'll get housekeeping to come up and change the linens."

She nodded and when we reached our floor, I took her hand. I'd fucked up at the party, choosing to hang with Felice instead of the woman I love. It wasn't even close to making up for it by taking her hand in an empty hallway, but I wanted her to know I felt it.

I paused at the door and looked down at her.

"I'd rather not go back in there," she said and leaned against the wall. "I already saw more than I wanted to."

I gave her a quick kiss and then headed inside. I walked straight to the bedroom, fully prepared to give Felice and Marguerite a piece of my mind. But, as I looked into the bedroom, I found the women still in bed and asleep, arms around each other. It'd take more energy to rouse them, get them dressed and out than it would just to go downstairs and tell the front desk we needed another room. Money would be a problem soon if things didn't pick up, but it wasn't now and I believed the cost was worth the reward of getting my ass out of here. It'd be worth every penny, if just for the peace of mind that came with knowing those two women wouldn't know where we were.

I grabbed a few of our things and walked back into the hallway where Carrie was waiting. I grinned at her. "Guess we need another room."

I was still trying to figure out how to tactfully tell Vincent what had happened when I walked into the café for our breakfast meeting. Carrie and I had gone to our original room first thing this morning and the women were gone, so we'd gotten our things and moved them to our new room. I hadn't even asked Carrie if she wanted to stay in the first one. I knew I didn't. Our new room had just as nice a view and no images of naked people that weren't us.

Vincent grinned at me as I walked toward him. "Good morning, Gavin. And how are you this fine day?"

Someone'd had a good night. At least a better one than I'd had. The only thing that had made it salvageable had been seeing how much Carrie loved that necklace.

"I'm not doing too badly," I said as I slid into the seat across from him. "But I have to admit, I didn't sleep very well last night."

Vincent's smile widened. "Really?"

"I had a couple of visitors last night," I said. "Quite the surprise."

He waggled his eyebrows, the gesture somehow looking appropriate with his eighties attire. "Did you enjoy that? It was Felice's idea, but I didn't discourage it."

My smile was tight. "Let's just say my girlfriend didn't appreciate finding two naked women in our bed."

Vincent sighed and leaned back. "Well, I'm sorry to hear that. Let me know if you want a private repeat performance. Felice would be game any time and Marguerite's up for anything that gets her in bed with Felice."

"No, that won't be necessary." I shook my head. I paused as I ordered scrambled eggs and coffee. Once the waiter left, I told Vincent what he needed to know. "Here's the thing. I'm not sure exactly what you think Carrie and I have together, but it's not..."

"It's not what?" He sounded mildly amused.

"It's not an open relationship," I said. I figured that was the most tactful way I could say it. "It's only for us. Carrie and me. No one else."

Vincent threw up his hands in a gesture of mock surrender. "I see. I'm sorry. It's my fault. I should've been at the party and felt you out about what Felice wanted to do. I got caught up at a business dinner I couldn't get out of. I assumed, because of the kind of club you ran, that your tastes were a bit less... conventional."

While I'd always hated that assumption, I understood it. And it at least explained why Vincent thought what he did. It made me feel better that I wasn't giving out that kind of vibe, the kind that said I wanted to be with anyone but Carrie.

Vincent continued, "Anyway, my friend. I promise you won't see Felice again, at least not until she performs at the club.

I can't say she won't try to hit on you. She likes you." He waved a hand. "Then again, this is France, and in France, men like us, we have a new girlfriend every week... or every hour." He winked at me.

I smiled because it was what Vincent expected, but I was glad when the waiter brought our food. I could keep busy eating and not have to fake enjoying some parts of the conversation. I still appreciated his business sense and he wasn't actually a bad guy. A couple years ago, I might've even taken him up on his offer. Now, I was more about the business than the schmoozing.

"But enough talk about women," Vincent said. "Do you want in this deal or not, because if you don't, I'll have to find a new partner ASAP. I want this club to open sooner rather than later."

"Yes," I said. "I'm in." I held out my hand.

Vincent took my hand and we shook on it. The tension I'd been feeling about the deal eased some.

"Where do I sign?" I asked.

"You just did." Vincent leaned back in his seat. "Between us, a handshake is golden. We'll let the lawyers handle the paperwork tomorrow."

I knew I wouldn't completely relax until I had physical signatures, but I felt better that Vincent was on board.

"But before that. Allow me to make up for the disaster of last night. I'm meeting with a couple of old friends tonight. You come along and let me meet your beautiful girlfriend. I've heard so much about her, I feel like I already know her. I would enjoy meeting her."

That didn't sound too bad, and I could use the chance to make up for what had happened with Felice. "That sounds great. Thank you. We'll be there."

Before Gavin had left for his meeting with Vincent, he'd spoken with the front desk and filed a formal complaint regarding our two unexpected visitors. But based on the look I'd seen on the desk clerk's face, it was obvious he didn't believe what had happened had been a mistake. He clearly thought Gavin had just gotten caught fooling around and was trying to make things look better for himself. Everyone else could think that all they wanted, but I knew the truth. Gavin had sworn on his daughter's life. He'd never do that lightly. Skylar was the most important person in his life and being number two to her made me love him even more.

The fact that I knew he wasn't lying didn't make me any less annoyed at his recent behavior. The necklace was a start, but I fully intended to get everything I could out of him, and I wasn't thinking money.

While Gavin was at his meeting, I enjoyed our new room, including the tub where I soaked in lilac-scented bubbles for almost an hour. I didn't bother dressing when I got out, sticking with the complementary hotel robe. I sighed as I wrapped myself up in it. A year hadn't been long enough for me to get used to these kinds of luxuries.

I frowned as I thought it. Why hadn't Gavin told me about the financial situation? I loved that he wanted to support the work I did, but most people who ran pro bono businesses like mine spent time getting donors. Having to do that instead of relying entirely on him wouldn't be a hardship. It's what I would've done if he hadn't offered to pay for everything.

And then there was the whole thing about how the club wasn't making as much as it used to. I hadn't been there since we'd changed it into a regular club, so I hadn't known that attendance was down. I'd assumed that just taking the sex element out wouldn't be detrimental. There were plenty of regular clubs in New York that did just fine. But, I was forced to admit, there were more than a few that declared bankruptcy and closed after only a few months.

When we got home, Gavin and I were going to sit down with the books and I was going to have him show me everything. I needed to know how badly this was hurting us. If he wanted me to think of the money as ours and we were supposed to be partners in the business, he couldn't keep me in the dark anymore. Not that I'd been particularly curious, I acknowledged. All that was going to change, I promised myself. I was going to be more involved and we'd find a way to get things back to the way they had been, even if it meant I had to consider the possibility of bringing sex back into the club. There'd be a lot of negotiation on how that would work, but it was something I knew might need to be discussed.

I heard the door open and pushed aside all thoughts of

money and business. This was all personal. I walked into the main area.

"I talked to Vincent and fixed it. He's going to make sure nothing like that happens again." Gavin took a step toward me.

"Great," I said, my voice dripping with sarcasm. "I'm so glad Vincent is going to make sure it doesn't happen again." I crossed my arms. I knew Gavin trusted the man, but I didn't. "And what about you? What are you going to do?" My voice was flat. "Can you fix what I saw? How am I supposed to get that image out of my head?"

He looked wounded. "Carrie, I-I don't know what..." He held out his hands.

"I want you to fix it," I said. I reached for the belt of my robe and waited until I was sure he was watching before I untied it. "I want you to fix me."

The expression on his face tightened as I slipped the robe off my shoulders. All I wore was the necklace he'd given me last night.

"Right now, I need you to make me forget everything I saw. I want you to inject me with your mind altering drug... over and over."

He took two long strides and was right there in front of me. He cupped my face in his hands and kissed me. It started off slow, his lips moving gently, parting mine. Then, as one hand slid to the back of my head, the kiss deepened. His tongue slid into my mouth, thoroughly exploring as if for the first time. Searching and seeking what I was willing to give.

I'd expected something harsh and needy that would get me wet and aroused, ready for sex, but this... this made my knees weak. I remembered our first kiss, how it had made my head spin and my heart beat faster. I'd wanted him then and I wanted him now. Maybe even more.

He wrapped his arms around my waist and lifted me, carrying me to the love-seat. He put me down on the seat and then knelt in front of me. He rested his hands on my knees for a moment and then pushed them apart. His palms slid up my thighs until he was able to curl his hands around my hips. He pulled me toward him, until he was able to lean forward and press his lips just below my belly button.

I shivered in anticipation but didn't rush him. He placed feather-light kisses across my abdomen, then down my hipbones before stopping just above my pussy. His eyes flicked up to me and my stomach tightened at the heat I saw there. Then he lowered his head and licked one long, broad stripe across the sensitive flesh. I moaned as his tongue slipped between my folds and teased at my entrance.

"Fuck," I breathed as his mouth did all the wonderful things I was familiar with. He knew exactly how to alternate attention between my pussy and my clit, never paying too much attention to either one as he worked me toward climax. His tongue and lips applied just the right amount of pressure to my clit to send ripples of pleasure through me.

When he slid a finger inside, I pushed my hips toward him, wanting more. A second finger joined the first, giving me deep, even strokes as his mouth moved and circled my clit. I cried out when he began to suck on the little bundle of nerves, alternating suction with his thrusting fingers. Then he curled his fingers and made a 'come here' gesture that rocked my world. It was appropriate... it was going to make me come right here.

"Yes!" I practically screamed the word as he repeated the movement, over and over until I came. My muscles tightened, trapping his fingers inside me as an orgasm rushed over me. And still, his tongue kept working over my clit until I was pushing at his head, needing relief from the overstimulation.

He raised his head, but didn't remove his hand from between my legs. He leaned higher and wrapped his lips around one of my nipples. I moaned at the sensation and then gasped as he pushed a third finger inside me. He twisted his fingers, stretching me as his teeth scraped over my breast. I put my hand on his head, running my fingers through his soft hair. His thumb brushed against my clit and my fingers fisted in the silky strands. He groaned against my breast. My free hand rolled my other nipple, trying to match the pull of his mouth, the dual sensations mingling with the pleasure his hand was giving me until I was coming again.

This time, Gavin kept his fingers working until I was begging him to stop. It was too much. I let out a half-sob of relief when his hand withdrew. My pussy and clit throbbed, each pulse sending another wave of pleasure through me. I'd closed my eyes when the climax had started and now, as it began to fade, I opened them again. Gavin had undressed, but was back to kneeling between my legs. His cock was hard, curving up toward his flat, sculpted abs, and at the sight of it, the ache between my legs returned, as if no number of orgasms could satisfy without having him inside me.

He pulled me off the couch and turned me around so I was kneeling, my arms resting where I'd just been sitting. He gripped my hip with one hand and I could feel the other between us, positioning him.

"You want to forget?" he asked quietly.

I nodded. "I want to forget everything that isn't us, right here and now."

Gavin's hips snapped forward and I wailed. Even as stretched as I was, the sudden penetration sent a shockwave through me. He was so long and wide that he reached every inch of me, stretching me, filling me, until there was no room for anything else. And he didn't stop or wait for me to adjust. His second thrust was as hard as his first and I cried out.

"Yes!"

This was it, this was what I wanted. When he was pounding into me, reaching those places only he could reach, there was nothing else in my mind. Only the way our bodies moved together, how perfectly we fit together. His pace rode that line between pain and pleasure, keeping my brain from having the capability of focusing on anything else.

My nipples rubbed against the fabric of the couch until they almost hurt, but I couldn't hold myself up against the force of Gavin's thrusts. When his hand slid around my stomach, so the tip of his finger could tease my clit, I swore. My head fell forward. I shook as I came again, but it didn't fade away. As Gavin continued to rub my clit, his rhythm increased. Wave after wave of pleasure washed over me until I could barely breathe. Every muscle in my body was quivering and I could feel my brain struggling to process everything.

With a drawn-out groan, Gavin buried himself deep inside me and came, his arms wrapping around my waist. He slumped over me and pressed his lips against my shoulder blade.

"Did it work?" he asked, his breath harsh against my back.

I frowned, my overwhelmed brain trying to make sense of the words.

"Did I make you forget?"

I chuckled and he hissed as the laughter made all of my

muscles contract, including those in my pussy. He was soft inside me, overly sensitive. "Yes, Gavin. It worked."

"Good." He straightened and pulled out, hissing as his withdrew. As he helped me to my feet, he lightly touched the necklace I was wearing. "What do you say we put that back in the box and take a nice, long bath while I tell you about the party we're invited to tonight and how I want to show you off."

I smiled as he slid his arm around my waist and we walked to the bedroom. I never liked fighting, but make-up sex almost made it worth it. Almost.

I watched Carrie as she teased her golden curls into submission, frowning at her reflection. It was her serious face, not her upset one, and it made me smile. I stepped behind her and slid my arms around her waist.

"You're gorgeous," I said and kissed her temple, breathing in the scent of her conditioner and that extra that was just her. My cock gave an interested twitch despite the amazing sex just a few hours ago. I knew we needed to go to this party, but all I really wanted to do was bend her over the dresser and take her again.

"You're not so bad yourself." She smiled at me in the mirror. "Help me put on the necklace?"

I took a step back so she could pull her hair up. I reached around her and picked up the necklace. As I fastened it around her neck, I let my fingers brush across the base of her neck. She shivered, and when I leaned down to kiss the place where her shoulder and neck met, a moan escaped.

"Keep that up and we'll never make it to the party." She turned to face me and wrapped her arms around my neck.

"Maybe that wouldn't be such a bad thing." I pulled her close so she could feel how much I liked that idea.

She raised to her toes and softly kissed my mouth. "Tempting as that is, you know we have to go. As you said earlier, we need this." She took a step back, then reached down between us and cupped my now very-interested cock. "Save this for after."

I let out a breath and ran a hand through my hair as she moved away to find a pair of shoes. I wondered how long we'd have to stay before we could make our excuses and leave without insulting anyone. Then again, I thought with a touch of humor, Vincent might be understanding if I told him I wanted to leave so I could fuck my girlfriend into next week.

"So, where's this party?" Carrie asked as she straightened.

"The Hotel Majestic Barriére," I said. "And have I mentioned how amazing you look in that dress?"

"Once or twice," she said with a smile. "Though it never hurts to hear it again."

"Well, you do," I said. The women at the boutique where we'd gotten the dress Carrie had worn last night had been thrilled when I'd called and asked them to send over their second choice. It was just as perfect as the other one and matched her necklace as if they'd been made together.

"Let's go," she said. "The sooner we get there, the sooner we can leave and you can get me out of this amazing dress."

I smiled, knowing we were thinking along the same lines meant more to me than the promise of sex. Carrie and I had seemed so out of sync recently, it was a relief to know we still had it.

The Hotel Majestic Barriére was impressive, but I could only think about how much I wanted to be back in the room with Carrie. As we entered the event room, however, I forced myself to focus. Vincent had said the deal was set, but I still wanted to make a positive impression on the people here. I knew that in any business, no matter how iron-clad the contract, the right word from the wrong person could end it all.

"Gavin!" Vincent came toward me with a huge smile on his face.

Neither Felice nor Marguerite were with him so I breathed a sigh of relief. "Vincent." I smiled and held out my hand. He shook it heartily and then turned to Carrie. "This is Carrie Summers, my girlfriend and partner at Club Privé."

"It's a pleasure to finally have a face to go with the name." Vincent took Carrie's hand and gave a little bow before kissing it. "And what a lovely face it is."

"Thank you." Carrie sounded a bit stiff, but I doubted anyone other than me would notice. "It's nice to finally meet you as well."

"I'd like you both to meet a friend of mine." Vincent straightened and extended his hand behind him.

The woman who stepped forward wasn't what I expected at all. I'd assumed most of the women who spent time with Vincent were like Felice and Marguerite. Early twenties and looking like some sort of college sorority girl. This woman, however, wasn't like that at all. Sure, she was drop-dead gorgeous, the kind of woman who would've looked at home on a runway, but that was the only similarity. The woman currently giving me and Carrie an appraising look was in her thirties, maybe a bit older if she was one of those perpetually youthful kinds of people. She was dressed in a long, elegant gown that flattered her slender figure and managed to be tastefully simple while still being apparently expensive. She had sleek, dark hair pulled back from her face and eyes a shade of brown so dark that they almost looked black.

"Alizee Padovani," she said in heavily accented English. She shook my hand with a firm handshake many women in business tend to get after a while. No matter how much progress was made, business was still a predominantly male-dominated field. Unfortunately, women had to often work harder to prove themselves. A firm handshake went a long way in not appearing weak.

"Gavin Manning and Carrie Summers." I put my arm around Carrie's waist to make our relationship clear.

"Pleased to meet you," Alizee said.

She turned to Vincent and rattled something off in what sounded almost Italian. It wasn't strange for Europeans to be multi-lingual, but I wasn't quite sure what language she was speaking. Vincent replied in the same language and then chuckled. It was odd, I thought, how respectful Vincent was being with Alizee. She seemed exactly like the kind of woman he normally enjoyed ogling.

"So sorry," Alizee apologized as she looked at me, a quick glance toward Carrie included her as well. "That was rude of me. I was simply telling Vincent that I must be going." She gave both Carrie and me a nod. "I'm sure I will be seeing you over the course of the next few days. Good night."

Vincent waited until Alizee was out of earshot before speaking again. "Alizee is a very wealthy business woman from Corsica."

That explained the language thing. While the official language was French, there was a Corsican language and if she was mingling with some of the old money families on the island, being able to speak it would definitely be a plus. I hadn't realized Vincent knew the language as well.

"She owns a dozen or so of the most successful bars and clubs along the Rivera, which means she can either be our worst competition or an ally."

"An ally?" Carrie asked. "It seems to me that anyone who is trying to reach your same target customers would be competition, no matter how friendly."

"Smart woman." Vincent gave Carrie the kind of charming smile that would've bothered me if he'd been more her type. "In most businesses, this would be true, but one of the reasons I wished to open a branch of Club Privé here is that none of Alizee's clubs cater to exactly that particular clientele."

I snagged two glasses of champagne from a nearby waiter's tray and handed one to Carrie. She took it but barely glanced at me as she continued to question Vincent.

"A lot of sex clubs have issues with underage girls and prostitutes. What measures are you going to take to make sure everything at the club is legal and consensual?"

I tried not to wince at her words. At least she hadn't mentioned Howard's involvement back home.

"That is indeed a problem many clubs face, no matter who they serve." Howard's expression was the perfect combination of serious, enough for Carrie to know he wasn't blowing her off, but not severe or forbidding enough to completely bring down the mood. "I have actually budgeted for extra security, whose main purpose will be to ensure that all activity is legal, safe and consensual."

Carrie looked reluctantly impressed. I had to admit, I was too. I hadn't expected Vincent to have anything in place already.

I'd fully planned on needing to have a discussion with him regarding prohibiting prostitutes from working the club.

"In fact," Vincent continued. "If you would like, I could introduce you to the man who will be the head of security."

"I'd like that," Carrie said, glancing up at me.

I nodded and put my hand at the small of her back as we followed Vincent through the crowd. Her skin was soft against the palm of my hand and my blood heated with the touch.

As we walked, Vincent would pause every so often to speak with someone, offering them a handshake and a hearty smile. He always introduced us both as the partners in his newest business venture and never made it seem like one of us was more involved than the other. To my surprise, he didn't make a single sexual comment to any of the people he talked to, not even when one of the women overtly flirted with him. He was every bit the gentleman and I wondered which part of him was the real Vincent Paoli. Who did he put on an act for, the group or the individual? And if the leering wasn't who he really was, why did he think that was the type of person I wanted to deal with?

I mulled over the question as we mingled, meeting others who would be involved in the club. There were politicians who would be in charge of permits. Members of boards who approved zoning requirements. The owner of the construction company Vincent had on stand-by. The head of security and a manager Vincent was bringing over from another club. Each one was charming and pleasant. They were all enthused about working on the project and had a thorough knowledge of what their part would be.

Before I knew it, Carrie and I were dancing to a slow song and a couple of hours had passed. The words were in French, so I knew Carrie didn't understand them, but they were perfect for us, talking about lovers finding each other through insurmountable odds.

"All right," Carrie said suddenly. "I'm convinced."

"Convinced about what?" I asked, wondering if I'd missed something while I'd been listening to the song lyrics.

"Vincent," she answered. "He seems like a genuinely talented businessman with a lot of important connections. He knows what he's doing and the obstacles he's going to have to face."

"So you trust him?" I asked, trying to hide my surprise.

She made a thoughtful face. "I trust that you trust him," she said. "I admit that my vision isn't exactly unbiased here, so I'm trusting what you say."

I smiled and pulled her closer. She rested her head on my shoulder and slipped her arms underneath my jacket. Her fingers traced patterns on my back as we danced.

As the song faded into another, she spoke, "How many dances do you think we'll have to do before we can make an escape? Because I have a totally hot boyfriend I can't wait to get back to my room so I can tear off his clothes."

I immediately stopped dancing and started scanning the crowd for Vincent to tell him goodnight.

The ride back to the hotel and then up to the room was excruciating. Part of it was because I wanted to do exactly what I'd said to Gavin. Tear his clothes off, ride him like a pony...

But I knew that would have to wait. I'd told him I would trust him about Vincent and I meant it. Part of what had been missing in our relationship was that element of trust. I hadn't even realized it until those women showed up in our room. If I'd truly trusted him, I never would've needed to ask if he'd invited them. In that moment, however, I'd wondered if he'd planned it; if he decided to spice things up because he wasn't satisfied with what we had. I'd worried our sex life wasn't enough for him. That I hadn't known had told me our communication was in trouble, and I needed to fix it.

When we stepped into our room, I kicked off my shoes and walked toward the love-seat. I grew warm at the memory of what had happened here this morning, but reminded myself that there would be time for that later. This was more important.

I sat down in the chair instead and looked up to see Gavin approaching, a puzzled expression on his face. He draped his jacket over the arm of the love-seat and sat down, loosening his tie as he went.

"Is something wrong?" he asked. "I thought you said you had a hot boyfriend whose clothes you wanted to tear off."

I smiled, but my heart wasn't in it. I had no clue how to broach this subject. Gavin had taught me a lot about things I never thought I'd want sexually, but we'd never covered this. So much had happened between us those first couple months that I sometimes forgot we hadn't gotten to do the normal "new couple" stuff where we slowly revealed things about ourselves. Instead, right away, it had been intense, personal stuff that most people waited at least a few weeks, maybe even months, to get into.

"I wanted to talk to you," I said. I folded my hands on my lap. "But I'm not really sure where to start."

He looked concerned and he reached out to cover my hands with his. "Just say it, babe. You're scaring me."

If only it was that simple, something I could blurt out in a single sentence. "It's about... sex."

Now he looked confused as well as concerned. "Sex?"

I took a breath and reminded myself that I wasn't talking to some stranger. This was Gavin. The man I'd loved almost from the first time I'd seen him. The man who'd saved me, in more ways than one. He knew my body better than I knew it myself. We'd been through so much and had never turned away from each other. I'd trusted him with my heart and soul, with my body and mind. How could I say I loved him, trusted him, if I let this go?

"When we first started sleeping together, you said there

were things you wanted to teach me, things you wanted to do to me." It was the memory of what he'd said rather than embarrassment that made my face flush.

"Yes?" Gavin said the word slowly, more a question than a statement.

"Why'd you stop?" The question was more blunt than I'd intended it to be, but at least I got it out there.

"Why did I stop what?" He shook his head. "I don't understand what you're trying to say."

"Why don't you want to do those things to me anymore?" I looked down at our hands. "You once said you wanted to spank me. You tied me up. Teased me."

Gavin's hands tightened around mine.

"You don't talk about any of that anymore. Didn't you like it? Was..." I forced myself to ask the question I'd hidden inside the darkest parts of me. "Was I not good at doing... that?"

Gavin swore under his breath. He hooked his finger under my chin and raised my head so that our eyes met. "Why would you think that?"

"Because you stopped. Stopped doing it. Stopped talking about it, telling me what you wanted to do." I blinked at the sudden burn of tears. I hadn't realized until now that part of the reason I hadn't wanted to talk about this was because I was scared that I was the reason things had changed. Not because of work or things like that. Those were my fault. But rather I hadn't been what he wanted.

Gavin's fingers tightened almost painfully on my chin. "Babe, that isn't it at all."

He kissed me, his lips hard against mine. The kiss was brief but fierce, sending electricity straight through me, right down to my toes. He released my chin but kept his gaze on me. His eyes were blazing.

"After what happened with Howard." A flash of anger crossed his features at the name. "I didn't think you'd want anything to do with that lifestyle. I assumed you'd always associate what he did with what I wanted to do."

I started to shake my head, wanting to protest, but he continued on without letting me say anything.

"Every time I asked you to do something, I felt like I was forcing it on you, like you only agreed because you thought that's what I wanted." He reached out and twisted a curl around his finger. "How could I claim to love you when I made you do things that bothered you? I could live without the bondage or any of the other stuff I used to be into. I couldn't – I can't – live without you."

A rush of relief went through me, so strong that it made my knees shaky.

"Gavin, everything you did, I loved." I pushed back his hair, letting my fingers linger. "I didn't ask you to teach me about your lifestyle, about the things you enjoyed because I felt like I had to."

I leaned forward to kiss him, my tongue tracing along his bottom lip before I bit down on the soft flesh. Gavin made a sound that made me instantly wet. His hands gripped my shoulders and I knew he wanted to pull me to him. Instead of letting him, however, I pulled back and he let me go. Before I gave over control, I needed to make sure he understood I was telling the truth.

"I wanted you to teach me because I wanted to try new and different things," I continued. "I still want that."

"Carrie," he began.

I held up a hand and he stopped. "You introduced me to this world I'd never known existed, and then, suddenly, I was back to my plain vanilla life." I started to look away, but forced myself to meet his eyes. "Every time you touch me, I feel like I'm on fire, but lately, when we've had sex, it seems like there's this part missing. It was still great and I never faked coming, but it wasn't quite..."

"Satisfying," he finished quietly. "I felt it too. There'd be glimpses of it, of what we used to have, but it wasn't the same."

"I think it was because we haven't been honest about what we want in the bedroom." I allowed a half-smile. "Or the living room or the shower."

He smiled back, but I could see he was being cautious. "So what do we do? How do we fix this?"

"We have to be honest with each other," I said. "About everything." I took his hand between both of mine. "I need you to tell me about the things you want, what you enjoy. Your fantasies."

I could see emotions warring on his face and I understood it now. He was fighting against his nature, against things he thought might scare me. One of the reasons I truly fell in love with him was his protective nature. That's who he was and I loved him for it, but he needed to accept that I meant every word.

"The other day," I said. "When I put my hands behind my back and you had to guide my mouth, did you like that?"

Gavin's Adam apple bobbed and I felt his hand twitch between mine.

"Did you hold back?" I asked. "Did you want to fuck my mouth harder? Deeper? See how far I could take you?"

I saw him hesitate, but then he nodded.

"But you didn't because you thought it would be going too far."

"I never want you to be uncomfortable or feel like I'm using you." Gavin's voice was rough.

"What if I want you to use me?" The question came out before I knew I was going to ask it.

"Fuck," Gavin muttered. "You can't say stuff like that, Carrie."

"Why not?" I pushed. "You once told me that the BDSM lifestyle isn't about pain or control. It's about trust." I picked up his hand and placed it over my heart, my skin burning where it touched his. "I've trusted you with everything."

"And I trust you," he replied.

I shook my head. "Not with everything. You pulled this part of you away from me and hid it. I know you did it for a noble reason, but the why doesn't matter." I slid his hand sideways and down until he was cupping my breast. "Trust me. Talk to me. Be that man again who teased me with all of the toys in Club Privé, promising to show me his world."

"It's not you I don't trust," he said quietly. "It's me."

That stopped me for a moment. "What are you talking about?" Now it was my turn to be confused.

"I don't want to hurt you or scare you," he admitted. "What if something I want is going too far?"

"Then I'll say stop, and you'll stop," I said simply. "We have safe words for a reason. You told me that. Do you ever doubt you'd stop if I asked?"

"No," he answered immediately. "I'd never do anything like that."

"Then let me tell you a secret." I gave him a moment to think about what my secret could be. "I liked it when you pulled my hair. When you were in control. I liked when you told me that I wasn't allowed to touch myself because my pleasure was yours." His hand tightened around my breast. "And when you said you wanted to spank me, it made me wet."

"Carrie, babe, please." There was an almost desperate note in his voice.

"Just one thing," I said. "Tell me one thing you like, one thing you want to do to me."

He took a breath. "I liked tying you up. Restraining you." He looked down as if he didn't want to see my expression.

I slid off the chair and down onto his knees. I caught a glimpse of surprise on his face as I reached for his belt and I knew what he was thinking. He was wrong though. I wasn't going to give him a blow-job. Well, not unless that's what he wanted me to do. I pulled his belt from its loops and then looked up at him. He looked puzzled now.

I looped the belt and then held it out to him. He took it, but still wasn't understanding. Apparently, I needed to spell it out for him.

I said three simple words and watched his expression change.

"Tie me up."

When I told him to tie me up, I really thought he was going to argue, but I supposed denying himself for nearly a full year had whittled away at least some of that restraint.

Then, he changed right before me. His expression. His eyes. Everything.

"Hands," he commanded.

I held them out. I recognized that tone. I liked that tone.

He slipped the circle of leather around my wrists and watched my face as he pulled it closed. I knew, at least for a little while, he'd need my reassurance that whatever he did was okay, so I nodded.

"Stand."

It was more awkward than I'd realized to go from kneeling to standing with bound hands, but I managed to do it. He stood as well and took the end of the belt. He led me across the room and into the bedroom. He paused there for a moment, scanning the room as trying to decide his next more. When I saw his eyes light up, I knew he'd gotten an idea.

The bed had four tall posts at each corner, almost like you'd see on a canopy bed, only this didn't have a canopy. I supposed they were some sort of decorative thing, but right now, it seemed that Gavin had another purpose in mind. He led me to a post at the base of the bed, stretched my arms above my head and then fiddled with the belt and the post. I couldn't see what he did, but when he stepped back, my hands were fastened high above my head.

He walked from one side to the other, apparently checking to make sure whatever he'd done would hold. Out of the corner of my eye, I saw him give a satisfied nod and begin to strip off his clothes. I tried to turn to watch, but he'd picked a place that was just out of my sightline, even if I craned my neck.

His voice was low, caressing my skin. "A total denial of sight forces focus onto the other senses."

I heard him walking toward me but couldn't see where he was. No matter how much I trusted him, it was unnerving.

"But, sometimes, allowing sight that is limited provides for an experience that is just as exciting." He was right behind me now.

I inhaled sharply as his hands skimmed over my bare back and then down over my hips. His touch was light, but that didn't change the charge that flowed across my skin. Then his hands slid beneath the sides of my dress, moving across my stomach and then up to my breasts.

"Knowing that I'm here, just out of sight." He cupped my breasts, the fabric of the dress straining against the intrusion. "That if I wasn't speaking, it could be any man behind you."

His thumbs flicked across the tips of my nipples before he pinched the sensitive flesh between thumb and finger. I moaned and he chuckled, that deep, sensual sound that always made my pussy throb. I hadn't realized how much I'd missed that laugh until I thought about how little I'd heard it recently.

"Lucky for you," he said. "I don't share." He pulled his hands from under my dress and went back to my hips.

I stared at the bed post, my breath coming faster, my pulse racing. Not being able to see him but knowing he was there, naked, hard and ready for me... it was a new form of torture. I wanted to touch him, taste him, but I couldn't do anything except feel. When his hands slipped beneath the hem of my dress, I instinctively parted my legs. I was wet and aching.

"I know what you want," he said. His fingers teased at the edge of my panties. "You want me to touch you." He ran a finger along the crotch of my underwear. Hard enough to make me feel it, but too light to give me anything.

"Yes, please," I said.

"Not yet."

He removed his hands and I felt his mouth press against my spine. I shivered as his lips traveled down my back, stopping at the place where my dress began before they moved up again. He ran his hands over my dress, teasing at my nipples through the thin fabric. His mouth pressed against my ear and I could feel the heat radiating through his body, his cock hard against my ass.

"You asked me what I liked, what I wanted to do with you. Do you still want to know?"

There was an edge to his words, but I could still hear an undercurrent of tension that didn't have anything to do with sex. He was testing the waters, trying to see if I was going to back out.

"Tell me." I pulled at my restraints, wanting to turn and look at him, meet his eyes and let him know that he could tell me anything.

That was why he was talking now, I realized. He didn't want me looking at him when he said certain things. He was still afraid I'd react badly because of what had happened with Howard.

"Tell me, Gavin," I said.

"With you like this," he began. "I'd love to teach you what it feels like to have a flogger used on your back."

I remembered our conversation back when this had first begun, when he'd said something similar.

"Not just on my back, right?" I asked. When I felt his body tense, I knew he'd remembered too. "You once said you could make me come with one. Is that what you'd like to do to me now?"

"Very much." Gavin's hands slid down the front of me and under my dress. His fingers slipped beneath the waistband of my panties and then down between my legs. "Right here." He pressed a finger against my clit and I moaned. "I'd love to have this all swollen and throbbing, then take it into my mouth, soothe it."

"Fuck." I swallowed hard.

"I want to claim every inch of you, Carrie. Fuck your mouth. Your ass. Leave no part of you untouched." He nipped at my earlobe. "Push you further than you'd ever thought you'd want to go. Right now, I want to take you, hard and fast. Make it so you'll feel me for days."

"Do it," I said. My voice was shaking, but not with fear. The desire inside me was hot and sharp, almost painful in its intensity. I didn't know if it was what Gavin was saying or that he sounded like his old self again. Whatever it was, I didn't want to lose it again.

I felt a tug against my dress, then a tearing sound. I realized what he'd done even as the pieces of my dress fell forward, hanging loose from my shoulders. My jaw dropped. Had he seriously just ripped the seam of my dress? Before I could ask, he was yanking my panties down to my ankles and nudging my legs apart.

"Oh fuck!" I yelled as he buried his cock deep inside me with one thrust. "Fuck!"

He wrapped one arm around my waist, keeping me still as he pounded into me. The other hand was busy at my breasts, fingers pinching and twisting my nipples until they were burning.

"Yes!" I cried out. I pulled at the belt, unable to stop myself even though I knew I couldn't get free. "Fuck, Gavin, please, baby. Please," I begged.

"Please what?" Gavin asked. He swiveled his hips and I keened.

"Make me come," I begged and squeezed my eyes closed. I was at that edge between pain and pleasure, so close to coming that my body was starting to tremble. All I needed was him to touch my clit and I'd come, I knew it.

"What if I don't want to?" he asked.

I couldn't figure out how he was able to talk when I could barely breathe.

"What if I want to deny your release? Keep you on that edge for hours?"

I whimpered at the thought of that sweet torture, the way the pressure would build and build but not dissipate.

"I want to do that," he said. He lightly bit at the back of my neck. "Does it frighten you?"

I shook my head.

"Why not?" he asked without missing a single deep, penetrating stroke.

"Because," I gasped. "I trust you." My arms were starting to ache. My wrists hurt. My nipples were throbbing, sending pinpricks of pain through me. I knew that my pussy was going to be sore tomorrow. And I was so close to climax that it almost hurt. But still, I trusted him to take care of me. "I trust you," I repeated.

"Fuck," Gavin groaned. The arm around my waist tightened and he pressed his face against the side of my neck. He was mid-stroke as I felt him start to come.

I waited for his fingers to finish me off, to do what I couldn't, but he stilled, holding me against him as his cock emptied into me. My head fell forward, my body tense with pent-up energy. I pulled at the belt, making frustrated noise when nothing happened.

"I've got you," Gavin whispered in my ear.

He brushed his thumb over one of my swollen nipples and I flinched. When he pulled out, my knees almost gave out. Every cell in my body was screaming for relief. As soon as he untied me, I'd have it. It wouldn't take much.

Something brushed against my calves and I opened my eyes, looking down. Gavin was moving between me and the bedpost. He slid his hands around the backs of my thighs, pulling me closer until he was able to maneuver my legs over his shoulders, placing his mouth right where I needed it.

He kept his hands on my ass, holding me still as his tongue darted out and flicked against my clit. A shudder ran through me. His tongue began to circle and dance around that little bundle of nerves until I was shaking. The moment his mouth covered it, I was gone.

My body went rigid as a burst of white light flooded over me. My hips bucked against his face and he only sucked harder, making me scream. Even after his lips released me, he wasn't through. His tongue dropped lower, lapping up every drop of our mingled juices. He thrust his tongue into me, sending another climax rolling over me as the first started to abate.

Again and again his mouth brought me until I was gasping, my nerves misfiring with every pass of his tongue. Only when I was sobbing, begging him to stop did he finally lower my legs to the floor where they immediately buckled. I cried out in pain as my shoulders wrenched and the leather cut into my wrists, but I didn't have the energy for anything else.

Gavin stood, one arm around my waist to hold me up as his other hand released the belt. As soon as my arms dropped, Gavin scooped me up and carried me to the side of the bed. He pulled off the pieces of my dress and my panties before sliding me between the sheets. He knelt next to the bed and I watched as he freed my hands. He frowned as he saw my wrists, red and most likely bruised from how hard I'd been struggling. I mustered up enough energy to reach out and put my hand on his cheek.

"That was perfect," I whispered.

Relief and pride mingled on his face. He gently pushed me back as he climbed into the bed, maneuvering until he had me half-laying on his body, his arms around my shoulders, one of mine around his waist.

"I missed this," he said softly. "I hadn't realized how much keeping this from you was pushing us apart. I've missed being close to you. And I've missed this part of our sex life. I knew I could live without it, but I hadn't thought it would mean this much."

I pressed my lips against his chest. "Don't hold back on me again."

"I won't," he promised. He kissed the top of my head. "And thank you for making me deal with it."

I nodded, suddenly exhausted. I closed my eyes and listened to the steady thrum of his heart. As I sank toward the darkness, I thought that maybe this trip hadn't been such a bad idea after all.

I was starting to regret having told Gavin to fuck me so hard I'd feel it the next day. Oh, I'd enjoyed every second of it the night before and I even liked the smug smile on Gavin's face the next morning when I grimaced as I sat down. What I wasn't enjoying was how difficult it was for me to walk normally and act like every movement wasn't causing my nipples to chafe against my bra and my pussy to throb in protest. If we'd been back home, it wouldn't have been too bad, since most of my work was done from my office where I could suffer in private. Here, however, we had an appointment to see the location for the club today. And since it had apparently been rescheduled once, there was no way I could ask for it to be postponed. Especially since I had no desire for Gavin to try to explain why.

As we climbed into the car Vincent had sent for us, Gavin's eyes flicked down to my wrists and he frowned. I reached over and took his hand, lacing my fingers between his. The belt had left faint black and blue marks around my wrists and I knew he was thinking back to my bruised wrists after Howard had tied me up. I raised our hands and kissed the back of his. I'd considered putting concealer on them and if they'd been any darker, I probably would've, but they were light enough that no one would notice unless they were really looking. Besides, I wanted him to know I wasn't ashamed of what we'd done. Granted, I wasn't exactly trying to advertise it, but I wasn't going to hide it either.

"Are you having second thoughts?" I asked. I needed to know if he was going to close down again.

"Are you?" he countered. He traced his finger across one of the bruises, careful not to actually touch the skin.

"Not a chance." I squeezed his hand. "I'm looking forward to what we do next."

He visibly relaxed and I breathed a sigh of relief. Hopefully, that'd be the end of it. I loved that he was worried about me, and I appreciated everything he'd been willing to sacrifice, but I wanted us to move past what Howard had done, and we couldn't do that if he was tiptoeing around what he wanted, afraid I'd freak out.

I leaned against Gavin and he put his arm around me as we watched the scenery go by. The weather was just as gorgeous as it had been the day before, sunny and the perfect temperature. If we could get through with the inspection of the location in good time, maybe we could check out more of the sights Cannes had to offer.

We were on Rue des Féres Pradignac soon, driving past various bars and nightclubs. I didn't catch any of the names, but they all looked high-end. About three-quarters of the way down the street, the car slowed down and pulled up to the curb. Vincent was already waiting outside.

"Gavin! Carrie!" He beamed at us both and gave me an enthusiastic, but not exactly inappropriate, hug. "It is good to see you again."

I smiled and nodded but didn't speak. A figure was stepping out of the shadows and my smile tightened.

"Good morning." Alizee gave Gavin and me warm and professional smiles. "Vincent asked for me to come take a look at your location. He wished for my opinion as I am, if you do not know, well-versed in the business of pleasure in this part of the world."

"He mentioned that you own quite a few bars and clubs," Gavin said. He gestured up the street. "Any of these yours?"

Alizee nodded, but didn't elaborate on her own businesses. "Vincent chose wisely." She folded her arms and looked at the front of the club. "This building is perfectly located. There are bars and clubs there, there and there." She pointed to the businesses across the street and next door. "They are for dancing and drinking, but no girls. No sex. Putting a club here that caters to sex will draw customers from those clubs, but not take enough of their business to cause problems."

I wondered if Vincent had really thought of all that or if it had just been a great deal on a building in the right section of the city. I didn't see any other places that looked like they would be up for sale.

"Shall we take a look inside?" Vincent opened the door and made a gesture for Alizee to enter first.

She did, and then I followed. Gavin came after and Vincent last. The interior of the building was dark so I stepped to the side while I waited for my eyes to adjust. They didn't have to do much since the overhead lights came on a moment later.

Gavin stepped to my side as we looked around. The place

was dusty and had an air of disuse, but it was obvious that someone had been caring for it enough that there didn't seem to be any of the pest problems that empty places back home would've had after just a couple days.

A bar ran along one side, the shelves behind it looking like they could hold a fair amount of liquor. Other than the bar, the rest of the building was empty. The ceiling was high, with simple lighting. The floor was wood, typical for a dance club. The space itself was impressive, but it was down to nearly the bare bones.

"Vincent has explained to me that you are quite the visionary when it comes to the design of these clubs." Alizee stepped between Vincent and Gavin, though it was clear she was only talking to Gavin. "Tell me, what do you see here?"

I looked up at Gavin. I hadn't been there when he'd created the club back home, but I'd seen how impressive it had been. Despite all of the negative things I associated with it, the design had been amazing.

"We don't want something identical to the club in New York," Gavin began. He walked into the center of the room and looked up. "But we want the feel to be the same. Something sensual. Seductive."

"This is good," Alizee said. She took a few steps toward him, her eyes narrowing as she watched him.

I frowned. I wasn't sure I liked how she was looking at my boyfriend. It wasn't anything overt and she hadn't said or done anything that was even the slightest bit inappropriate. Just a feeling I had, something in my gut that said maybe I shouldn't trust her.

"I'm thinking we work with the wood that's here," Gavin continued with his vision, oblivious to what was going on in my head. "Strings of lights instead of pulsing ones. Something to differentiate it from the other dance clubs. Long, filmy curtains." He turned back to Vincent and shrugged. "Just my first impression. And I'll put together a couple different ideas so we can decide together on what we want." He looked at me to make sure I knew he was including me in the decision.

I smiled, hoping he couldn't read the thoughts on my face. As Alizee began discussing the practicalities of some of Gavin's ideas, I tried to look like I was paying attention, but I was more concerned with keeping my eyes on the other woman. I watched her movements, where her hands went, how she tilted her head, the way she smiled. I'd watched Leslie and Krissy flirt enough to know all the signs. After just a few minutes, I was forced to admit that either Alizee was very subtle or I wasn't reading her right.

Or, I thought, it wasn't that she was interested in Gavin sexually. Maybe there was another agenda here. If she had other clubs and bars in the area, it was possible Vincent was wrong and she saw our club as a threat. Maybe she was looking for weaknesses, or trying to steer us in the wrong direction.

That might've been a possibility, I conceded, if Vincent hadn't acted like the woman walked on water. He knew what he was doing, and I seriously doubted he'd invite someone who'd hurt his business venture.

It was just that I still couldn't shake the feeling that something was off about her. I wanted to pull Gavin aside and ask him about it, but I knew this wasn't a good time. Especially since I'd just spent a good portion of yesterday talking about how I trusted him. I'd feel him out about Alizee later and see if he'd gotten the same vibe from her. If he hadn't, I wouldn't push the matter. I'd chalk it up to some lingering issues on my part and let it go.

With that decided, I turned my attention back to the conversation.

"It will be a good idea for you to meet with the owners of the other establishments around here," Alizee was saying. "You will want to establish a mutual agreement where you refer customers in accordance with their desires. For example, should a customer ask for a dance club, you could point them across the street. In turn, any customers who inquire about things of a sexual nature, that club would recommend this place."

That was really smart, I thought.

"Well, Vincent will be taking care of that," Gavin said. "Carrie and I live in New York, so most of the personal connections will be his responsibility."

"No." Alizee shook her head. "You are to be the face of the club." She glanced at me. "You and your beautiful lover."

Gavin protested, "Vincent–"

"We will work out those details later," Vincent hurriedly said.

I got the impression that Vincent didn't want to take sides.

"Right now, we must discuss the changes we need to make to the space," he continued. "Alizee knows the best contractors in the city. She will be able to direct us to the best pricing."

"Right," Gavin agreed. "Well, the first thing we need to look at is the foundation. Make sure it's solid. Once that's done, we'll want to take a look at the basic structure. We'll want inspectors who know the required standards we'll have to meet."

I'd been distracted before by my own thoughts, but this time, the conversation itself wasn't one I followed very well. I knew, in theory, what all went into the design of Club Privé, but

I hadn't been a part of the day-to-day practicalities of it. There was a reason I was a lawyer and not a businesswoman.

I could see, however, what a savvy businesswoman Alizee was. She didn't just follow what Gavin was saying. She made suggestions, provided information. She was actually more involved in the conversation than Vincent was. And way more than me. When they'd started to walk through the building, Gavin had taken my hand so we walked side-by-side, and he wasn't shutting me out, but it was obvious I wasn't serving any real function here.

When there was a pause in the conversation as Alizee and Vincent started talking rapidly in whatever language they spoke, I tapped on Gavin's shoulder. He looked down.

"I'm going to step outside and call the office. I want to see how things are going. Find out if Zoe's heard how Robyn's doing."

Gavin glanced at his watch. "It's close to five back home. Did you really make Zoe work full days when you're gone?"

I rolled my eyes. "No, Gavin. I'm not a slave driver. She's supposed to stop in for a few hours every day to get the mail, sort through email, that kind of stuff. I asked her to come in later in the day so if I did call, I didn't have to bother her on her time off."

"Good idea." He smiled at me and kissed my forehead. "If we're done before you are, I'll meet you outside."

I nodded and headed back toward the exit. I blinked a few times as I stepped out into the bright afternoon sunlight. I pulled a pair of sunglasses out of my bag and slipped them on before fishing out my phone. I walked down the sidewalk as I waited for the call to go through.

"Carrie?" Zoe's voice crackled, then cleared. "Is everything okay?"

"It's fine, Zoe." I smiled at her concern. "I just wanted to check in. Anything new going on?"

While Zoe filled me in on motions and files received, I turned and started heading back toward the building. As I did, I noticed a man across the street leaning against a beat-up car. His eyes were on me and, as I passed, he nodded. I gave a half-smile, grateful I had the phone as an excuse not to respond. I wasn't sure if he was flirting or just being polite, but I didn't feel like meeting any strangers at the moment.

"And what about Robyn?" I asked. "Have you heard from her?"

"No." Zoe sounded frustrated. "And the D.A. called yesterday. Said if Robyn doesn't show up to testify in front of the grand jury, chances are, Little Tino's going to walk. Again."

I sighed. "Well, keep me posted and let me know as soon as something happens." I refused to say 'if.' I was still holding out hope that Robyn would come to her senses and testify. She just had to admit what a part of her already knew, that Little Tino was using her. I didn't understand how she could let him do that to her. Did she really think so little of herself, or was she actually so in love with him that she was willing to ignore everything that told her what a dick he was?

"Are you and Gavin having fun?" Zoe asked.

I smiled, even though she couldn't see me. "Yes, we are."

"That's great," she said sincerely. "You two deserve it. Now don't worry about anything back here. You guys just enjoy your vacation. Everything will be waiting for you when you get back. I promise."

"Thanks, Zoe."

"Anytime."

As I ended the call, I heard a man's voice call my name.

I turned, expecting to see Gavin. Instead, the stranger from across the street was coming toward me, taking long, quick strides that were closing the distance between us at a rapid rate. There was no way I could outrun him.

TWENTY-ONE
CARRIE

"You are Carrie Summers?"

The man was just a few feet away now and I was frozen to the spot.

"My name is Pierre Bastillo." He stopped before he was within reaching distance, as if he'd figured out that his approach was freaking me out. "I am a journalist."

A journalist? The fear I'd been feeling at being accosted by a stranger was replaced with confusion. Why was a reporter in France trying to talk to me? Better yet, how did a reporter know who I was? Even back home, once the insanity surrounding Howard had died down, no one really paid that much attention to me. It was actually one of the most frustrating things about what I did. I tried to get the media to do stories about human trafficking, but they were always overshadowed by the more "important" stories. Like whichever celebrity had posed nude this week.

"I was at the party the other night and saw you speaking with Kelsey Larson."

I relaxed slightly, but still kept my guard up. No respectable New Yorker would accept only that for an explanation. I clutched the strap on my bag, remembering the instructions from my self-defense class that explained how to use a purse as a weapon.

"All right, Mr. Bastillo," I said. "But that still doesn't explain how you know who I am."

"Pierre, please." He gave me an easy smile, flashing white teeth against tanned skin and showing off a single deep dimple. His eyes were a bright, sparkling green. "I am sorry if I frightened you." He held up his hands, palms out. "I assure you, it was not my intention."

"Well, intention or not, it does cause worry when a stranger knows her name but doesn't say how," I said wryly. I'd stopped thinking I was in trouble, but I didn't relax my stance. Again, growing up in the city had taught me to be cautious, especially when talking to a strange man. No matter how good-looking or seemingly polite.

"I apologize," Pierre said. "When I saw you speaking with Ms. Larson, I wondered who you were as Ms. Larson appeared to know you. I researched and discovered your firm in New York."

That made sense at least. It wouldn't have been hard to get a picture of me at the party. Show it around a bit and get a name. My name plus a photo would easily lead him to my firm. I had to make myself easy to find. What good was an attorney who specialized in helping victims if the victims couldn't find them? Gavin had been nervous about me putting myself out there, asking what would happen if a sex trafficker decided to come after me. I'd told him that I couldn't ask the victims to be brave and stand up to their abusers if I wasn't willing to risk myself. He hadn't been happy about it, but he hadn't mentioned it since.

"Yes, I'm a lawyer," I said, giving Pierre a small smile. "I'm still not sure why that merits being approached by a French reporter."

"Fair enough," he said. "That is the saying, is it not?"

I nodded. He actually spoke English better than a lot of Americans, and with only a hint of an accent.

"I have been asking my editor to allow me to write a piece on sex trafficking in the French Rivera, but he has not been very... supportive of the idea," he said. "I wanted to speak with Ms. Larson, but was unable to set up an official interview until next month."

"You want to interview me?" I tried not to sound too suspicious. Back in New York, when reporters had wanted to talk to me, it hadn't been to shed a light on the horrors of the modern-day slave trade but rather to pry into my sex life with Gavin or to sensationalize what Howard had tried to do... or both.

"That would be one option," he said. "But I would prefer to use your expertise in the field.

"In the field?" I echoed.

He nodded and reached into his pocket. "I have decided to pursue the matter without my editor's approval in the hopes of writing a story that he will insist on publishing." He held out a business card. "Or one that I can perhaps sell to another publication."

I took the card. Pierre Bastillo, journalist. There was a number and an address on the front. I flipped it over and saw another number hand-written on the back.

"The number on the front is for my work phone. The one

on the back is to my personal mobile." He gave me another of his charming smiles.

I was willing to bet he was used to that smile getting him a whole lot of things. To be honest, if I hadn't been with Gavin, it might've worked on me too. Now, however, I was only interested in the work offer.

"What are you thinking?" I asked. "You want to know about the kinds of cases I've worked? The sorts of patterns I've noticed?"

"That would be the first step," he said. "And I would share the things that I have found here in Cannes. I would want your opinion about them, if my instincts are correct or if you believe I am wrong."

I glanced behind me to see if Gavin or the others were coming, but there wasn't anyone. I turned my attention back to Pierre. "I'm waiting for my boyfriend. We could talk a bit now."

Pierre glanced at his watch. "As much as I would love to chat with you now, I'm afraid I have an appointment I cannot miss."

"I'm only here for two weeks," I said. "But my boyfriend will be taking care of some business periodically. I could contact you then."

"That would be perfect." Pierre hesitated, and then added, "I was also wondering if perhaps you would not be adverse to also participating in some field work. Interviews and the like."

I knew what Gavin would say to that. Absolutely not. There was no way he'd want me to go wandering around Cannes alone, much less with a stranger. And definitely not a stranger who was a reporter digging into a dangerous crime. Gavin had already told me back home that he didn't like me getting person-ally involved with the cases I worked. At least there, I had to be careful I didn't overstep my bounds because I didn't want to risk having a case thrown out for misconduct or anything like that. Here, I didn't have to think about any of that. I was a tourist tagging along with a journalist. This was about exposure and awareness, not prosecution. It wasn't my job to build a case.

"I'm in," I said with a smile. I dug into my bag until I found one of my business cards. I scrawled my cell number on the back. "I'd prefer to call you from the hotel to avoid roaming charges on my phone, but if something big comes up, please let me know."

"I will," he said. "I really must be going now, but I am grateful that you are agreeing to do this. I believe it will make a real difference." He held out a hand.

I shook it. "Thank you for coming to me, Mr. Bas – I mean, Pierre."

"It was my pleasure," he said as he held my hand just a moment longer than necessary. "I look forward to seeing you again."

"And I do you." I quickly added, "I can't wait to see what we'll be able to accomplish." I didn't want him getting the wrong idea. I wasn't certain he was flirting with me, but better safe than sorry. I might've been able to spot a woman flirting with a man from a mile away, but I was more clueless when it came to men flirting with me.

He gave me another of those smiles and then headed back the way he'd come. I watched him go. I was definitely feeling better about having time to myself while Gavin was off with Vincent planning things. He'd said that the only thing he had to do was check out the location and close the deal, but I knew my boyfriend. He was a perfectionist and he wasn't going to leave the details to people he didn't know, no matter how much he said he trusted them. As soon as I'd heard the excitement in his voice when he was describing what he thought the club should look like, I knew he'd want to be involved in the design. I also knew he'd feel guilty and not do it unless I convinced him that I had things I could do while he was busy. I just had to figure out how to sell it right.

I also needed to figure out how to get this story back home. The international exposure would definitely help put pressure on Congressman White to throw his support behind my proposal. It always made politicians look bad when other countries were dealing with problems and they weren't. Americans never cared about a problem as much as they did when they were being ridiculed for not caring.

Between how well things were doing with Gavin and me, and the possibility of being able to do some good while I was here, this trip was definitely turning out to be better than I'd ever hoped.

TWENTY-TWO
GAVIN

I could tell Carrie was getting bored before saying she was going to step outside. She was the kind of person who had ideas to improve once the main things were set. Once the space was designed and she could visualize how everything looked, I was sure she'd have suggestions about how to make things flow more smoothly, or she'd spot potential problems. And while I knew she liked hearing my ideas, when we started getting into the real business-type stuff, that was beyond her usual involvement and I knew she wasn't enjoying herself.

When she left to call Zoe, I was able to focus solely on the club. Vincent had been right. Alizee really knew what she was talking about. She had suggestions to make the process go faster, names of companies who'd do the best work for the best price. I was starting to wish I had someone like her back home to help me with the renovations when she put her hand on my arm.

There wasn't anything overtly sexual about the move and she didn't keep it there longer than was appropriate, but it seemed like it was much more personal than our relationship called for. If one of Carrie's friends had done it, I wouldn't have thought anything of it, but I'd known them for a year. Alizee was a wonderful businesswoman and she apparently had a history with Vincent, but I barely knew her.

"Should you wish to go with your curtain idea, you will want to contact Fleur Roux," she continued what she'd been saying, seemingly oblivious to how I'd tensed at her touch. Either that or she was just too polite to say anything. I was betting on the latter. She was far too intelligent to have not noticed.

"Is she in Cannes?" Vincent asked.

"No, Corsica," Alizee said. "But her prices and quality more than make up for the short distance you would have to travel." She handed Vincent a card to keep with all of the others she'd given him. "Mention you know me and she will give you a discount."

"I'd like a copy of the city's building code," I said. "I want to read it before solidifying designs for approval. I don't want to do something that will have to be undone because it's against some obscure subsection."

"You will find," Alizee said. "Anything, and anyone, can be bought for a price." She brushed her hand against mine, the gesture so casual that I wasn't sure if it had been intentional. "Design as you will. Let Vincent handle how to make sure it is allowed."

I wasn't about to turn a blind eye to another partner's illegal dealings, even if it meant I'd have to tweak certain aspects of my plans. For all I knew, I wouldn't even have to change anything. Yet another reason I wasn't going to say anything now. I'd talk to Vincent later if the issue came up.

"Will you be hiring local women as the entertainment?" Alizee asked.

That was as good a lead in as I'd get to make sure my partner knew where I drew the line for sex in the club. "I suppose we'll hold auditions for any dancers or singers," I spoke before Vincent could. "But I've found it's a good idea to have both male and female waiters and bartenders. I'd also recommend both genders for dancers and singers. You'll want to draw both men and women as customers to allow for proper pairing ratios."

I saw a brief frown crease Alizee's face and then it was gone. Vincent's smile looked a bit forced, but neither of them said anything. I moved on.

"Of course, I'm sure once the club's popularity takes off, we'll have plenty of managers contacting us to have their singers perform. Anyone who wants to put a little sexuality into their reputation will line up to get in here." I motioned toward the far end of the room. "That's the perfect place for the stage."

The temperature in the room had chilled slightly when I'd made my little speech, but things warmed up again as we started going over the technicalities of wiring and sound systems. A few minutes later, I found myself between Alizee and Vincent as we walked the length of the bar. Vincent was in the middle of a story about how he'd found this place when I felt a hand on my upper arm. I looked over at Alizee.

"Are you going to be designing places for customers to indulge their fantasies? Their desires?" Alizee squeezed my arm, then slid her hand down, staying in contact until she reached my wrist. "Vincent said you have a room in your club in New York."

My thoughts flashed across the ocean. Club Privé did indeed have a private room for members. I'd used it with Carrie the night she'd shown up at my club. It had also been where I'd found her naked and tied to a bed while Howard suggested we rape her together.

"There is one," I said vaguely. "But there isn't a second floor here. I'm not sure how that would work."

"I have a thought," she said.

She took a step closer to me, invading my personal space. I thought about taking a step back, but I didn't want to offend her.

"Couches," she said in a low voice. "Surround couches with curtains. They are sensual, allowing for some privacy while providing the excitement that comes with exhibitionism." She looked up at me. "You do find that exciting, no? Knowing others are hearing you? That they could interrupt?"

I did take a step back now, but I combined it with a turn so that I was starting to walk again. "Not really my thing."

That was at least mostly true. The suggestion of being caught was exciting. Fucking in the middle of a large room where only curtains kept others from seeing me... that wasn't really my thing. Especially if it meant others would see Carrie. That wasn't even negotiable.

"A shame," Alizee said from behind me. "It can be very arousing."

I was suddenly very glad Carrie was outside. Since we were discussing a sex club, it wasn't weird that we were talking about sexual preferences, but I had a feeling Carrie wouldn't see it that way. And that's all it was. Alizee knew I had a girlfriend and we were working together on a business. Anything else was just me worrying about how Carrie would take things.

"So, Gavin, what do you think?" Vincent asked as he made a sweeping gesture to include the entire building. "Should I make an offer or look elsewhere?"

"If you do not take advantage of this opportunity," Alizee said. "I will. This is prime real estate. With your joined vision, I believe it will go far."

I looked at Vincent and shrugged. "I think she just said it for me."

"Excellent!" He beamed. He rubbed his hands together. "This calls for a celebration. Drinks?"

I didn't point out that it was barely afternoon. "I'd love to, Vincent, but I think Carrie and I would like to spend some time together. See the sights." I smiled at him and then at Alizee, taking care not to stay longer on one than the other. No need to give her the wrong idea. "Besides, if we're going to be coming to Cannes on a regular basis, we need to learn the lay of the land, right?"

"Enjoy this beautiful city with your beautiful lover." Vincent winked at me. "May I suggest the beach? I am sure Carrie would look quite stunning in a bikini."

"Shall we three meet tomorrow for lunch?" Alizee said. "I will bring my contact information and advise the best scheduling to complete your project in the most timely manner."

Yeah, I really did wish I had someone like her back in New York. I hadn't even wanted to call the foreman to see how things were progressing.

"That sounds wonderful," Vincent said. "Will you be able to complete concept art by then?"

I thought for a moment. Carrie and I could spend the day together and then I could spend tonight and tomorrow morning putting things together. I nodded. "I'll have some options together."

"Very good," Vincent said. He looked at Alizee. "Thank you again for all of your assistance."

"My pleasure," Alizee said. "Shall we get that drink now, Vincent, my dear?"

She took his arm and the two of them headed toward the exit. I followed. When I stepped outside, I looked around for Carrie. She was standing a few feet away, watching a good-looking man walking across the street. Puzzled, I started toward her.

"Hey, Babe," I called.

"Hi!" she said brightly as she turned. "You're never going to guess what just happened to me!"

I kissed her cheek as she told me about the reporter who'd just asked her for input into a story on sex trafficking in Cannes. I smiled down at her, enjoying the way her entire face was lighting up. I loved seeing her that way, even if the situation was something that I found a little concerning. If we were back home, I'd do some checking up, making sure no one was taking advantage of her, but I didn't really see some random person in France tracking her down for a story that was all over. As long as she stayed in public, I wasn't going to tell her I didn't think this was a good idea. Actually, I thought it was a great idea. Just the thing to keep me from feeling guilty while I was working on the club with Alizee and Vincent.

This trip really was turning out to be great in many ways.

Pierre was thrilled to hear from me so soon, probably more so than was a good idea, but I wasn't going to read too much into it. Gavin and I were here for a week and a half. I fully intended to spend the time we had together having fun. When Gavin was busy, however, I wanted to do some good.

We'd had a great time yesterday, checking out the sights. We'd watched the boats, walked along the public beaches. The weather had been perfect and the people great. I loved my hometown, but Cannes was definitely ahead in those two columns. One of the ways the two cities were alike, unfortunately, seemed to be the same thing going on in every big city in the world. Today, I intended to do something to at least shed some light on that problem.

Pierre was already sitting at a table in the café where we'd agreed to meet. He smiled and stood as I approached.

"Ms. Summers," he said and gave a little bow.

"Carrie, please," I said, sitting down across from him.

"I am thankful you called," he said. "I was hoping to begin some investigations today."

"So where do we begin?" I asked.

"With coffee." He winked at me.

"Coffee?"

Pierre signaled the waiter. "Yes, coffee. And we talk. You share with me the things I should be looking for. I tell you what I have been working on. I ask questions. You ask questions."

"So this is an interview?"

"No," he said. He shook his head. "I will not be including anything we discuss in my story."

I took a sip of my coffee. Wow. That was amazing. I was impressed that Pierre managed to get it right. "This is great."

"I am so glad that you like it." He flashed that brilliant smile at me. "Now, let us talk."

Pierre and I began to chat. The flow of information came quickly, moving from one area to the next. I told him how young people were targeted, the common characteristics of the ones who were caught up in the sex trade. I expected questions about what had happened with Howard, but Pierre never mentioned it. He had to have heard about it. No one in the media in any major country could've missed that story.

"Is any of this information helping?" I asked halfway through, wondering if I was providing anything Pierre didn't already know. I was glad he'd asked for my help, but pretty much everything I'd said so far could've been found in an internet search.

Pierre nodded. "I would like to know more about the methods by which people are trafficked. How they are moved from one place to another."

"Okay," I said. I fell silent for a moment, gathering my

thoughts. "Well, there are lots of different ways the trafficking works. Some underground, some more blatant. It can be anything from internet sites where buys are set up, to back rooms."

"Are those not the smaller operations? A few people here or there?" Pierre asked.

"Most of the time," I agreed. "The larger operations are the ones most difficult to uncover because they have so many moving parts. Usually they've been able to grow so large because they have people in the government, people who look the other way and cover up the messes."

Pierre nodded. "I understand."

"The vast amount of money that changes hands in this business can be used to grease a lot of wheels," I said, not bothering to keep the bitterness from my voice.

One of the things that had always sickened me the most about the people involved in the human trafficking industry was how easily a person's life was traded for money. Normal people pictured traffickers as the flashily dressed pimps who stood on the street corner, cat-calling obscenities to the decent folk who walked by. In reality, the majority of traffickers were average-looking, middle-aged men who had wives and kids.

"How are those operations run?"

I gave Pierre a puzzled look. I didn't spend much time in the courtroom, but I knew a leading question when I heard one. He was trying to get me somewhere. I just didn't know where.

"It depends on if it's local or overseas," I said. "Most of the local girls are runaways who end up getting into it because they need money." I thought of Robyn. "But there are those who end up getting picked up by someone in the industry, a pimp or a guy who's hired to break in the new girls. They pretend to be a boyfriend and eventually get the girl to have sex with other men." I paused, then amended, "It happens to boys too, but it's more prevalent with girls."

"It is much the same here," Pierre said. "Though that's usually the story of those on the streets."

"Most of those girls are on the streets," I agreed. "But these are tricks sometimes used by men who want to sell their victims. Foreign girls are usually brought in with the promise of a good life, a job as a nanny or in a factory. Some are sold by their families, others kidnapped."

"And it's your job to find who these people are and stop them?"

I shook my head. "What I do is work within the legal system to help the victims in any way I can."

"I heard how you helped the young woman who had been kidnapped by a wealthy man from your city."

I stiffened. Here it came, the questions about Howard.

"This man, he used a club to find buyers and hide what he was doing, did he not?"

"He did," I replied. I wasn't going to offer anything else until I knew what he wanted.

"Is that a common practice?" he asked. "Using a club to cover for a trafficking operation?"

Okay, so he wasn't trying to get personal. At least not yet. "It's not exactly uncommon."

Pierre nodded and leaned forward, the expression on his face suddenly serious. "This is what I think is happening in Cannes."

I relaxed. He really was after a story here, not me.

"There is a woman who owns many clubs and bars," he began.

My stomach sank.

"I believe she is using them as a means to traffic." He glanced around, as if making sure no one was listening. "She lives in Corsica, which I believe is her base of operations, but she uses the clubs here to distribute her... product."

"Do you have any proof?" I wanted to ask for a name but I was afraid of what he'd say. I needed to know how much of this was speculation.

"Not yet," he admitted. "But that is what I intend to do with you. I wish for you to help me build a case against Alizee Padovani."

I MUST'VE SPENT a good twenty minutes silently cursing as Pierre had filled me in on his suspicions. Everything he said sounded pretty circumstantial, which made matters worse. Alizee could be a trafficker, but coincidences do occasionally exist. Technically, Gavin could've had a good circumstantial case against him for what Howard had done. I didn't want to jump to any conclusions.

The problem was, if Alizee was getting involved in the club here and was what Pierre claimed, that meant she could damage the business. Not to mention, Gavin would be stabbed in the back again. I just didn't know if I should warn him now of the possibility or wait until I had solid proof. What would happen, though, if we left before Pierre and I found evidence? Could I let Gavin keep working with her without knowing? For how long?

I was pretty sure Pierre sensed that something was off because after he laid everything out for me, he said he had some things to do and I should take the rest of the day to think over what he'd said. He promised to call tomorrow to see if we'd be able to meet again, and we said our good-byes.

The whole way back to the hotel, I mused over what to do. I wanted to be honest with Gavin, especially since we'd talked about working on our communication, specifically not hiding things from each other. But, I also didn't want to start a fight and I knew if I accused Alizee of being like Howard without any proof, he'd be angry. He'd already been annoyed at my distrust of Vincent. An accusation like this would be worse, especially since I knew it would probably look like I was jealous. I wasn't, of course, but I knew it could come across that way.

By the time I arrived at the room, I'd made my decision. If it came up in conversation, I'd tell the truth. If Gavin asked me what I thought of Alizee, I'd drop a couple hints about how I didn't trust her. If I had solid proof, I'd tell him. Other than that, I was going to keep my mouth shut and hope that Pierre was wrong. I didn't quite trust Alizee, even without the speculation, but for Gavin's sake, I didn't want Pierre to be right.

Gavin was already in the room, but was on the phone, so I waved as I headed to the bathroom to freshen up. When I came out, he was off the phone and smiling.

"We checked out the public beaches yesterday, but didn't swim. I was wondering if you wanted to go down to the private beach this afternoon." He came over to me and put his hands on my waist. "I happen to know there's a dark red bikini in your bag that I'm dying to see you in."

"Oh really?" I asked. "And how do you know that?"

"I might've seen it when I was looking for one of my t-shirts in your bag." He grinned. "You do have a bad habit of stealing my shirts to wear to bed."

"I wasn't planning on wearing anything to bed most of the time we're here," I teased.

His eyes darkened. "Keep talking like that and I don't think I'll want to leave the room."

I took a step back. "In that case, I better go change for the beach." I started toward the bedroom and then stopped as a thought hit me. I turned back to face Gavin. "You know," I said. "That is a topless beach."

He scowled. "I don't think so."

I raised an eyebrow. Was he honestly telling me what to do? I'd been joking when I'd first said it, but now I was seriously considering it, just to remind him that he didn't own me.

"And what if I want to go topless?" I asked. I folded my arms and lifted my chin. "Are you going to forbid me to do it, Gavin?"

I saw the war on his face. He wanted to say it, to tell me no, but he also didn't want to be that guy, the one who controlled the woman he was with. I waited to see which man would win. Would we end up in a fight or would he let me make my own choice?

Less than fifteen minutes later, we stepped onto the hotel's private beach and Gavin looked down, waiting to see what I would do.

TWENTY-FOUR
GAVIN

I gritted my teeth to hold back a comment when Carrie reached behind her to untie her top. I knew this was a private beach and that anyone behaving inappropriately would be dealt with by the hulking security guards who stood around the perimeter, but that didn't mean men weren't going to be looking. And I didn't like the idea of men looking at Carrie. Actually that was an understatement. I hated it. I'd forgotten just how much it bothered me.

When she wore sexy dresses and men watched her walk by, or the times when they stared at her cleavage, I enjoyed putting my arm around her waist, letting them know she was taken. But even when she wore her most revealing dress, it wasn't a bathing suit. When we'd been on the beaches yesterday, I'd thought about what it would be like to have men seeing her in a bikini. I'd never dreamed she'd consider going topless.

I loved how far she'd come from the quiet, fairly self-conscious woman I'd met a year ago, to someone comfortable enough with her own body that she'd go half-naked in public. It was like the thing with Alizee, when she'd talked about exhibitionism. It was one thing to taunt and tease the idea, but something else entirely to actually do it.

No matter how much it bothered me, though, I didn't tell Carrie not to do it. It wasn't my decision to make. I refused to be one of those possessive jerks who acted like their girlfriends or wives were their property. Still, it didn't stop my hands from clenching into fists as she untied her top and let it slide off.

Fuck.

Her breasts were perfect. I knew some guys liked them smaller and others preferred them large, but hers were exactly what I wanted. A little more than a handful, firm but not fake-feeling firm. There was no doubt they were all natural. Her nipples were a slightly darker rose color and perfectly proportioned to the rest of her. I'd once spent hours on her breasts alone, teasing and sucking, playing with her nipples until they were hard and sensitive.

Dammit. I shifted, wondering how in the world I was supposed to keep an erection away when she was right there. I had a difficult enough time not getting hard when she was in regular clothes. Hell, I thought she was sexy in sweats.

Carrie reached over and took my hand, reminding me that we weren't in the privacy of our home or hotel room. I gave her a tight smile and looked around. Other women were walking around without tops, but my gaze slid right over them, searching for the men who were staring at my girlfriend.

"Come on," she said. I could hear a note of amusement in her voice as she pulled me toward the ocean.

I followed, barely feeling the water flowing over my feet and lapping against my ankles. She laughed as a wave hit her knees and the sound made me smile for real. I loved hearing her so happy. And if this made her happy, I'd be damned if I ruined it. It wasn't like there weren't hundreds of other beautiful women showing their breasts. It was a cultural thing. No need to freak out about it. Yeah, I needed to keep telling myself that.

I grabbed Carrie around the waist and lifted her out of the water. She squealed as I spun her around, sending both of us into a wave that splashed over us. She gasped as the water soaked us both and squirmed in my arms, turning around so we were facing each other. Her nipples were hard as they brushed against my chest. The response was immediate as I felt my cock stiffen in my trunks.

I brushed my lips across hers, not trusting myself with anything more serious. Her, half-naked and wet, in my arms, would be a test of even the most iron self-control. I wanted to ravage her mouth, slide my hands beneath her bottoms, feel how tight she was, how ready for me. I wanted to walk us deeper into the ocean, pull out my cock and fuck her right there.

"If I go home without a tan, Leslie and Dena might kill me," Carrie said. She took my hand again and led us out of the water.

A quick glance down told me she looked almost as amazing from the back as she did from the front. Of course I already knew that, but wow... that bikini was something else. I used my free hand to tug the wet material of my trunks away from my body, hoping to draw attention away from my pretty impressive erection. I was seriously regretting suggesting coming to the beach.

We headed for a pair of chairs sitting out in the sun and Carrie immediately settled on one, leaning back and closing her eyes. I sat in the other one, drinking in the sight of her, that body I knew so well. I knew how every inch of her felt, how soft her skin was between her breasts. The dip over her ribs and the slight swell of her firm stomach. I knew how tight and hot her pussy would be if I slipped my fingers inside her.

"Dammit, Carrie," I muttered under my breath. How was I supposed to relax when she was so fucking distracting?

I closed my eyes and tried to focus on the heat of the sun and the sound of the waves. Anything but my girlfriend. Slowly, the tension began to seep out of me. It didn't last long though. As soon as I heard male voices coming closer, I opened my eyes. I needed to know if they were looking at her. One glanced her way and I scowled, but as soon as he put his arm around the other man's waist, I started to relax. Then I heard part of their conversation as they passed.

"...think they'd be interested in joining us?"

"I doubt he swings both ways."

"Pity. Maybe they'll let us watch."

I didn't have any proof that they were talking about us, but it managed to ruin any chance I had at being able to sit back and enjoy the sunshine and scenery. I managed to make it through another thirty minutes without losing my mind or my temper, but my body was so tightly coiled that I knew I was going to need to blow off some steam or I was going to go crazy. Carrie had said that she wanted to know the kinds of things I enjoyed. I fully intended to show her a side of me that was a bit darker than what she'd seen before.

"We're going back to the room," I said suddenly. I sat up and looked over at Carrie.

She raised an eyebrow, but didn't move.

I turned so that I was facing her, close enough to touch even though I didn't.

"I told you once that you were mine," I said. I pitched my voice low and watched her shiver as I spoke. Damn, I loved how she responded to me. "Now we're going back to our room and I'm going to show you what that means."

Her eyes darkened with desire and she sat up. She reached the small bag where she'd stashed her top and pulled it out.

"No," I said firmly. She gave me a puzzled look. "You wanted to go without it. Wanted men to look at you. Now you don't get to put it back on as long as we're on the beach."

I stood and held out my hand. She took it, smiling as I threaded my fingers between hers. I fully intended to make sure she understood that I hated knowing other men had seen her breasts, but I also wanted her to know that I wasn't actually angry with her. Worked up, hell yes. Wanting to vent some frustration in a positive manner, definitely. Acting out of anger, no. Anyone who truly understood the BDSM lifestyle knew where the line was and respected it.

By the time we reached our room, I knew I was going to be getting pretty close to it, but I'd never cross over. The moment the door closed behind us, I spoke, "Stop."

When she immediately did as I said, I knew this was going to go well. I reached out and yanked the tie for her bikini top. It fell to the floor, exposing her now-lightly tanned breasts.

"Did you enjoy men staring at you?" I asked as I stepped closer. I kept enough space between our bodies that we weren't actually touching, but close enough that she could feel me there. "Did you like knowing that they were imagining what it would be like to touch you?"

I reached around her and covered her breasts. I squeezed until she made a soft noise. Judging by how quickly her nipples hardened against my palms, she wasn't going to protest at least a bit of rough treatment. That was good. I wasn't particularly feeling gentle at the moment.

"Well, you may have enjoyed having men ogle you, but I didn't." I put my lips next to her ear. "But I think you knew that. In fact, I think that's why you did it." I pinched her nipples, hard, and she whimpered. "I think you decided to take off your top because you wanted me to punish you." I dropped my hands and slid them down over her stomach and back around to her ass. "Is that right, babe? Do you want me to punish you?"

She didn't answer, but that was okay. The game worked whether she admitted it or not. The only thing that really matter was if she said her safe words. Anything other than that was just part of the experience.

I took a step back and pulled off my shorts. I was already hard from her show and the anticipation of what was coming. "Walk over to the window."

I saw her shoulders tense, but she didn't protest and walked over to the floor-to-ceiling window. They were closed so the air conditioning could run while we were gone, but I didn't want them open at the moment anyway. It was the illusion of the thing that mattered. We had an ocean view and were too far up for anyone to see us unless they happened to have binoculars on the beach or in a boat. It was a risk, I supposed, but that's what made it so exciting. The curtains were already drawn back so Carrie stopped a couple feet away, obviously not trusting that no one would be spying.

"All the way to the glass," I said.

She hesitated, but then crossed the remaining space until she was directly in front of the window.

"Put your hands on the window."

I saw her breasts heave as she took a deep breath, then followed my directions. I closed the distance between us and placed my hands on her waist. I rubbed my thumbs up and down her spine before hooking my fingers in the waistband of her bottoms and pulling them off. She stepped out of them without having to be told and I straightened. I moved off to the side and then looked at her reflection in the window.

"Take a step back, but don't move your hands." I reached up and unpinned her hair, letting it fall over her shoulders and down her back. "I want your ass out."

She shifted her stance until she was standing the way I wanted her. I took a moment to savor how she looked. I wanted Carrie to enjoy this as much as I did. The thought of her begging me to spank her was heady, but there would never be another first time, and there was nothing like watching someone experience it for the first time.

"Do you remember what I told you?" I asked as I ran my hand down the length of her spine. "That, if done right, spanking could be as much of a turn on as oral sex?"

She nodded. "I remember."

"I once threatened to spank you for disobeying." I reached under her and gave a light tug to her nipple. "I didn't do it then, but I'm going to now." I buried my hand in her hair and turned her head until she was looking at me. "I'm not going to be gentle."

Her eyes darkened to nearly black and I swore silently at the desire I saw there. My guess had been right. She'd done all this on purpose, wanting to see what I'd do. She didn't want me to be gentle. My hand tightened in her hair and she made a sound that made my stomach tighten. What had I been missing with her all this time?

I kept my hold on her as I raised my other hand. I wanted to see the expression on her face the first time I made contact. I might not have planned on being gentle, but I wasn't going to start off as hard as I really wanted to. Not for someone who'd never done this before.

She gasped as my hand came down, a loud crack sounding in my ears. A slight sting went through my palm and my cock grew impossibly harder. It had been too long since I'd been able to indulge this part of me. I landed another smack on her other cheek. Her face was flushed, her lips parted, and as I spanked her harder the next time, she made a sound that was half-pain, half-pleasure.

I let go of her hair and she turned her head forward. My hand came down again and elicited another of those wonderful noises. My other hand moved underneath her, fingers roughly pushing between her legs until I found her clit.

"Oh!" Her head jerked up, her eyes wide as I rubbed against the little bundle of nerves, quick circular motions that her body wasn't quite ready for.

My fingers were still working over her clit when I spanked her again, twice in rapid succession, hitting the same spot. I could feel her skin heating up and my palm was getting hot. Her hands squeaked against the glass as they slid an inch downwards, but she didn't pull away. Even as she yelped when I struck her ass again, she stayed where she was.

I ran my hand down further, ignoring the whimper as I lost contact with her clit. By the time my fingers reached her pussy, my hand was soaked. I pushed two inside, making her gasp.

"So wet," I murmured. "Are you enjoying your punishment?"

I didn't expect an answer, not when I had two fingers inside her and was still spanking her with my other hand, but she had other ideas.

"Yes," she breathed. "Oh, yes."

Fuck.

I was tempted to put her down on her knees and fuck her mouth until I came, but that could wait. Maybe later tonight, after I was ready for a second round. For right now, I wanted to bury my cock inside her and make her scream my name.

First, there was one other thing I wanted to do. A taste of things to come. I pulled my fingers out of her and she made a sound of frustration. As I stepped around to stand behind her, I groaned. Her cheeks were red. Not the kind of red that bruised or caused any harm, but the kind that would make it tender for the rest of the day.

I leaned over her body, hearing her hiss as I rubbed against her ass. I cupped her breasts as my chest rested flush against her back. My fingers immediately began to twist and pull at her nipples, fast, hard tugs that made her cry out.

"These," I spoke low in her ear. "Are mine to see, to touch. Mine to pleasure." I scraped my teeth against the side of her throat. "I'm the only one who gets to bring you pleasure. The only one who gets to see you come."

Our eyes locked in the window's hazy reflection.

"How would you feel if another woman saw me naked?"

A sound very much like a growl came from Carrie. Her eyes flashed and I chuckled.

"Exactly." I tweaked her nipples again. "The next time you decide to do something like that, these are going to pay."

She shuddered, but the expression on her face made it clear it wasn't in protest. She might've just been learning the game, but she'd been made for it.

"It'll be a flogger to these pretty little tits you're so proud of." I kissed her shoulder. "And if you're really bad, maybe even to your clit."

"Fuck," she whispered.

"You said you wanted to know what I liked," I said as I straightened. I ran my finger down her crack and circled her asshole. "And soon, we'll work on the pleasures that come from here."

I watched her eyelids flutter. Damn. If just a light touch could do that, what would she do when it was my tongue? A finger? My cock? So many different ways I wanted to take her, and I couldn't wait any more. I was so hard that it hurt.

I nudged her legs with my knee and she walked forward until she was standing straight, her hands still on the window, her swollen nipples touching the cool glass. If she still had any qualms about being naked in front of the window, she didn't voice them.

I bent my knees slightly and positioned myself at her entrance. I pushed forward slowly, knowing if I went too fast, it'd be over too quickly. I needed the tight pressure of her, the resistance that came from her pussy stretching around me. Listening to her moan as I entered her though was almost my undoing. Worse was when she began to beg.

"Gavin, please." Her fingers flexed against the glass. "Please, baby."

I closed my eyes as I reached the end of her. She fit me perfectly, as if we'd been made for each other. People laughed at things like that, said it was just biology, but I knew that wasn't the case, especially for someone built like me. Our bodies were like two halves of a whole, and I saw now that we were even more sexually compatible than I'd dreamed. I could feel her pussy quivering around my cock, feel her muscles trembling beneath my hands. This wasn't someone who was tolerating something her lover wanted. She was hovering on the edge of an orgasm, ready to explode at any moment.

"Think you can come from my cock alone?" I asked. I could hear the strain in my voice as I pulled back until I was almost out and then pushed back inside. "I think that should be part of your punishment. If you can't get off like this, you don't get to come."

"Please!" She looked at me, her expression desperate. She was closer than I'd thought.

I gave her a wicked smile and repeated those slow, even strokes until I was sure I could last long enough to make her scream. The entire time, she continued to plead with me, her entire body shaking as I kept her hanging right on that edge. Finally, I shifted my hips as I thrust again, pressing my cock against that spot inside her I knew would take her over.

She gave a strangled yell as she came and I swore. Her pussy contracted around my cock, squeezing it almost painfully. I could feel my own body reaching for its release, wanting to join her. I fought it back, determined that this wouldn't be it. Before she could come down from her high, I drew back and then slammed into her again. She keened, her body going rigid. I gripped her hips and began to pound into her, each thrust pushing her up onto her toes.

"Gavin, yes. Gavin. Fuck, baby. Yes."

My name fell from her lips and drove me harder and faster. She'd once told me she'd never been vocal in bed before, and knowing that I could make her say things, do things, that she'd never imagined, was a heady aphrodisiac.

I could feel my balls tightening, the heat in my stomach ready to come apart. I was close. And so was she. I didn't think she'd technically stopped coming after that first orgasm, but her body was building toward something bigger, I was sure of it.

I pressed myself against her, changing the angle of my thrusts and giving my mouth access to her neck. I sucked on the side of her throat, pulling the skin into my mouth until I knew she'd have a mark. My mark.

"Mine," I growled against her neck as I buried myself deep.

She cried out and I felt her come again. The sound of her pleasure and the spasming heat of her was too much and I came, feeling my wet heat surge from my body. I wrapped my arms around her, holding her tight as I emptied myself into her. I pressed my face against her shoulder, breathing in the scent of her as pleasure washed over me. I sank down to my knees, taking her with me, our bodies still joined as I cradled her on my lap.

We sat there as our breathing slowed and the sweat on our skin dried. Only when my knees began to protest the awkward position did I move her, feeling a pang of loss as I slid out of her. I stood, pulling her with me, and slid my arm around her waist.

I looked down at her, concerned. "Are you okay?"

She smiled at me and stretched onto her tiptoes to brush her lips across mine. "I'm great. Thank you."

"No," I said. "Trust me. Thank you."

She rolled her eyes and leaned her head against my shoulder. "What do you say we go get cleaned up and then order room service?"

"That sounds perfect," I said.

We were half-way to the bedroom when I heard my phone ringing. I fully intended to ignore it, but Carrie pulled away.

"I'll get the shower warmed up," she said. "You answer the phone."

"I don't have to."

"Go." She gave me a gentle push and then headed into the bedroom.

I kept my eyes on her still-red ass even as I walked over to the table and picked up my cell phone. I didn't recognize the number, but it looked like it was local.

"Hello?"

"Bonjour, Gavin." A woman's throaty voice came over the phone. "This is Alizee."

"Hello." I frowned. Why was Alizee calling me instead of Vincent?

"I would like to discuss a few things with you and Vincent."

At least she got right to business. I would've felt a bit awkward having to make small talk while standing naked in my hotel room. Business was weird enough.

"Tomorrow morning, you and Vincent will have brunch on my yacht."

Did she just tell me what to do? I really hoped it was just a language barrier thing making what should be a request into a demand. She was already far more involved than a non-partner technically should've been, but I agreed with Vincent... it wouldn't be a good idea to piss off someone who could be considered a business rival or who had so many connections in Cannes.

"We will discuss things then," Alizee continued.

"Okay," I agreed. I listened as she told me where to go and then said a polite good-bye. I stood there for a moment after the call ended. I'd have to tell Carrie about the meeting but didn't think it'd be a good idea to let her know all the details. I didn't want her to have any reason to think there'd be a repeat of what had happened with Felice and Marguerite. Especially not after that little display of possessiveness I'd just put on. Any argument about a double standard wouldn't go over well.

With that in mind, I started toward the bedroom. There was no way I was going to ruin what was shaping up to be an amazing night.

TWENTY-FIVE
GAVIN

I felt guilty for not giving Carrie the details about my meeting today, but I convinced myself I wasn't actually lying to her or denying anything. If she'd asked specific questions, I would've answered them. I knew it was a cop out, but I allowed myself to be deluded into thinking I was doing the right thing.

Then, I showed up at the slip where Alizee had told me come. Warning signs flew up when I didn't see Vincent anywhere.

Alizee stood on her yacht, looking stunning in a gold bikini that showed off a figure most women would kill for. She smiled and motioned for me to come aboard. Hoping that Vincent was just below deck, I headed up. Alizee held out a glass of champagne.

"I'd better not," I declined with a polite smile. "It always takes me a couple minutes to get my sea legs back. I don't want to spill anything."

"Nonsense," Alizee said. She held the glass closer to me. "Please."

I had a feeling it'd be pointless to argue. Alizee struck me as the kind of woman who always got what she wanted, no matter how strongly someone protested. I took the glass but didn't drink anything. I was all for having a glass of wine with lunch, but wasn't so sure a liquid brunch on a boat was a good idea.

"We'll be casting off shortly," Alizee said. "My crew is made up of only the best. I am sure that sea legs will be quite adequate for smooth sailing."

I looked around. "Where's Vincent?"

"Oh, he will not be joining us." Alizee smiled at me, her eyes floating down to my lips. "He called a while ago. Apparently, something he ate last night did not agree with him. He fears he has food poisoning."

I wasn't entirely sure how to respond to that. I felt bad that Vincent was sick, but I was also annoyed that the brunch hadn't been canceled. While I appreciated Alizee's help, she was going to be working much more closely with Vincent. I wouldn't be involved in most of the day-to-day stuff getting the club going. Although I was willing to spend some time working, I didn't want to spend it with a strange woman when I had a beautiful girlfriend I could be with. A beautiful girlfriend who was going to spend the rest of the morning and early afternoon with a good-looking French reporter because I'd told her I had to work.

I forced a smile and opened my mouth to offer some sort of excuse as to why I should leave, but the boat lurched and we pulled away from the dock. Dammit.

"Come," Alizee said. "We shall eat first, then talk business."

I considered asking her to tell her crew to back up and let me off, but I knew that would come off as rude. Even if Vincent was the main one dealing with Alizee, I didn't want to do anything to offend her. Besides, she hadn't really done anything that would merit that kind of behavior. Even her flirting wasn't something I couldn't logically explain away with culture or personality.

I took a drink of my champagne as I followed her. Alcohol seemed like a good idea after all. I was really glad I hadn't said anything to Carrie about the kind of meeting I was having. When she asked later, I'd keep it vague and simple, tell her that the meeting was fine. Boring stuff talked about. She didn't need to know about how it was just me and a scantily-dressed Alizee on an expensive yacht. Well, us and the crew, but crews on boats like this were in the background, trained not to be seen, not to see.

"I had the chef keep the meal light," Alizee said as she led me around to the back of the boat where a table and chairs had been set up. "I wasn't sure how you or Vincent would be on the water."

I looked down at the array of food spread across the table. Light, yes. Cheap, not even close. There was the rich people staple of caviar and crackers. Cheeses that I knew easily ran hundreds of dollars. Fruit that had to be imported.

"Help yourself." Alizee waved her hand over the table and then picked up a strawberry. "These are delicious with champagne."

As we ate, Alizee and I made small talk. She never tried to pry into anything personal, keeping the conversation mostly on my life in New York City, though she seemed to avoid mentioning Carrie. I wasn't sure if that was intentional, because she didn't want to say anything to acknowledge I had a girl-friend, or simply because the questions she asked didn't lead there. Either way, I let her direct the non-business part of the conversation. I didn't want her to get the wrong idea that I was interested in her that way. Everything I asked was associated with work.

"Have you been to Cannes before?" Alizee asked as the boat slowly turned, giving us a beautiful view of the coast.

"Yes," I said. "But only for a few days, and I rarely had time to enjoy the sights before." I gave my most charming smile. "And never with my girlfriend."

"Ah, yes, Ms. Summers." Alizee turned toward the coast and walked over to the side of the boat. "She is quite lovely."

"Yes, she is," I agreed as I followed Alizee.

"How involved is she in the club?" Alizee asked. "She did not seem too interested in our conversations before."

"She's more of a silent partner," I said. "She's very busy with her work."

"And what does she do?"

"She's a lawyer. Works on sex trafficking cases," I said.

"And how does that work with your sex club?" Alizee asked, lifting her glass to her lips and staring out onto the water.

"Better than you'd think." I kept my answer vague. Vincent still didn't know that Club Privé had changed its focus. I wasn't about to tip my hand to Alizee.

We were circling around toward the dock and I was surprised we weren't staying out longer. I'd fully expected her to keep me out here for hours, especially once I'd discovered Vincent wasn't coming. Even if her flirting was just who she was and nothing personal, I'd gotten the impression she was the kind of woman who liked undivided attention from those she chose. And, at the moment, she'd chosen me.

"I've been to your America," Alizee said. "To New York, though I did not visit your club. I like America." She glanced at me and drained her glass. "But there are many things about my home country I like better."

I frowned. I wasn't sure where she was going with this.

"America likes to pretend that it is sexually free, but there are still many who do not see that where women are concerned. We are to be demure, sexually innocent, even if in pretend. We are to be the responders, never the initiators."

She turned towards me and gave me a look that said everything I'd been trying to pretend wasn't true actually was.

Shit.

"I work in a man's world, and I learned a long time ago that I must take what I want."

I really wasn't liking where this was heading. I was still trying to figure out the best way to politely decline her interest, but before I could, she took a step toward me.

"I know what I want, and I always get what I want."

I held out a hand to try to stop her but she ignored it and kept coming.

"I can make all your problems go away," she purred. "For a small price, of course."

What the fuck was she talking about? "Problems?"

She wrapped fingers around my wrist and shifted her weight until my palm was pressed firmly against her breast. She gave a throaty laugh as I quickly pulled my hand away.

"Don't underestimate me," she warned. "Just because I have breasts doesn't mean I'm soft. Or weak. I know you. I know about your, ah, financial issues. You need this deal very badly."

I turned from her, but she slithered closer, pressing against my back. Her hands snaked around, grabbing hold of the rail in front of me, trapping me between her and the warm metal. I could break free, of course, but I knew she had me trapped in a different way. Like I'd told Carrie, we weren't broke, but if this deal fell through, we were going to be in trouble very soon.

I didn't try to hide the anger in my voice. "What do you want?"

"Your surrender," she murmured and I could hear her breathe in my smell. "You give me what I want. I give you what you want."

Heat rose within me, but it wasn't anything remotely close to desire. I'd never hit a woman out of anger, but Alizee was seriously testing my self-control.

"What exactly do you think I want?"

She laughed. "You want it all, just as I do. You want your little girlfriend to be happy. You want your new dance club to thrive. You want to pay your bills and never let anyone know how close you are to desperation." Her hands moved from the rail to my stomach, one hand slipping beneath my shirt and touching skin.

She had stressed the word 'dance' when she referred to the club and I heard the underlying threat in her voice. I wrapped my hands around her wrists and pulled them away from me. Then I turned to face her.

"I'm not for sale."

She laughed again, her eyes glittering. "Of course you are. You would be foolish not to be. An hour of your time and attention removes all of your troubles."

It was my turn to laugh. I repeated, "I'm not for sale."

"Vincent will be very disappointed to hear this," she said, moving so that her body was nearly flush against mine.

Fuck. My mind screamed at me to push her way and then I realized that I was fucked either way.

Sitting wasn't exactly comfortable after last night, but I definitely wasn't going to complain. What had happened between me and Gavin had been one of the most intense experiences of my life. When he'd first mentioned spanking me, back when our relationship was beginning, I'd been turned on, but also nervous. I hadn't been at all sure I'd like it.

But, oh, I had. I'd more than liked it. I'd been wet from the first strike.

There were, however, consequences. One of which was how tender my ass was at the moment.

"These are the things I found about Alizee's businesses." Pierre handed me a folder of papers. "As you're in the club business, I hoped you would take a look at them, see if you can find anything suspicious."

I spread the papers out on the café table, but immediately realized the problem. "It's in French."

"So sorry," Pierre flashed that grin. "I'll translate."

For the next half hour, Pierre and I went over the papers.

He'd tell me what they said and I'd tell him if it was important. Most of it wasn't. A couple of the papers contained financial information, so I set those aside to go over more carefully and look for any sort of discrepancies that could indicate how money was being siphoned off into areas it wasn't supposed to be.

"There are some things that could indicate trafficking," I said as I turned over another paper. "Trips to places that are known for their poor human rights laws, places where people disappear and the authorities turn blind eyes."

"But these things can be explained for other reasons, no?"

"That's the problem," I said. "I'm not seeing direct proof."

"I am seeing one thing repeated," Pierre pointed at a line in one of the papers. "It seems that Alizee likes to use her yacht on some of her journeys. Because of her connections, I believe she receives only cursory checks at borders."

"You think she's using her yacht to traffic people," I said.

Pierre shrugged. "It's possible."

"Maybe we should go check it out," I suggested. "Maybe if no one is on board, we can get close enough to see if there are any hidden compartments, places where people could be smuggled."

"You're suggesting we sneak inside?" Pierre gave me a sly smile. "You would make an excellent reporter."

"I have to admit," I said. "I'm enjoying not having to think about how things will play out in court."

"Let us go then." Pierre stood and gestured toward his car.

As we rode to the docks, Pierre chatted about the mundane things, nothing too personal, but the kinds of questions that could be personal if either of us wanted them to be. He never crossed the line, but I got the feeling he was sussing me out, trying to determine if I was interested. I ignored the subtle signals and kept things polite and professional. Friendly was fine, but I wouldn't let it go any further than that. I also wasn't going to say anything preemptively. If he made a pass, then I'd handle it.

We parked in the main lot and walked down the dock toward the slip where one of the papers had said Alizee kept her boat. We were a few feet away when I realized it wasn't there.

"Well, that was a wasted trip." I sighed. I supposed we could start going over papers again, but I'd been looking forward to some sort of action. The idea of sneaking onto a boat gave me a thrill.

"Maybe not," Pierre said.

I turned to look at him and found him with binoculars, peering out toward the ocean.

"The yacht is out there." Pierre pointed. "I believe she's there with someone. Perhaps a contact." He held out the binoculars.

I took them and focused on the spot where he was pointing. I adjusted the sight, and then adjusted it again, desperate to sharpen the blurry image of the two people I instantly recognized.

It wasn't possible. Was it? No, it couldn't be.

There, in an intimate embrace, was Alizee...passionately kissing my boyfriend.

TWENTY-SEVEN

CARRIE

I was going to throw up.

My stomach lurched and I turned to run. If I was going to be any more humiliated than I already was, I wanted to be as far away from the public as I could get before it happened.

Gavin had kissed Alizee.

Part of me said it had to be a mistake, like what had happened with Felice and Marguerite. I'd jumped to conclusions then and had been wrong. I shouldn't do the same thing here.

There was only one problem with that line of thinking. Gavin hadn't lied to me before. Not a direct lie. Sure, he'd hidden where he was going during the party, but that had been because he'd been trying to surprise me with a gift. This morning, he'd said he had a meeting with Vincent. And then I'd caught him on a yacht with Alizee. Kissing her. It was possible, I supposed, that Vincent was there too and hadn't told Gavin that Alizee would be there. I shook my head; it felt too much like I was trying to convince myself. I'd never understood people who couldn't see what was going on right under their noses, but now I got it. Sometimes, it was too painful to face the truth.

I'd known Gavin had been out of my league from the moment I'd first seen him in that bar. I'd known what people said about relationships based on intense emotional experiences, but I'd always hoped he and I would be the exception to the rule.

All of this flashed through my head in a matter of seconds, processing even as I turned to run. I made it half a dozen steps when I felt a hand close around my arm.

"Carrie, what's wrong?"

Pierre. I'd completely forgotten about the handsome reporter who'd been the one to bring me here. The one who'd convinced me that Alizee was up to no good. Not that I hadn't already been suspicious. I turned toward him, struggling to regain my composure.

"The man on the yacht," I forced myself to say the words. "That's my boyfriend."

Pierre's eyes widened and he glanced back toward the boat. It was too far away for us to see what was happening now and I was grateful for that. If Gavin had lied about who he was going to see, it meant everything else came into question. And having seen the way Alizee had been with him before they'd kissed, it didn't take much imagination to figure out what he was most likely doing right now.

"I am truly sorry about that, Carrie," Pierre said sincerely. "But you cannot let him know that you saw this."

"Excuse me?" Now that the initial shock was wearing off, anger was overcoming the nausea. That was a good thing. It meant I didn't want to throw up anymore. I wanted to hit something. Or someone. Preferably two.

"Your boyfriend cannot know we were here."

"Oh, I fully intend to let him know I was here," I snapped. I pushed back a few curls that had escaped my ponytail. "And I'm going to tell him what a bitch Alizee is and how I hope the two of them are very happy together."

I was aware that I was probably overreacting, but I didn't care. I was getting sick of this shit. I was tired of constantly having women throwing themselves at Gavin, at watching him flirt and joke. I hated that he brushed it off as work stuff, saying he had to charm people, but that I should know he didn't want anyone but me. I wondered how I was supposed to know that. I wasn't a fucking psychic. I couldn't read his mind. And right now, that sounded like a line of shit a man fed to a naïve girlfriend or wife while he was out fucking anything that moved.

"You cannot tell him," Pierre repeated firmly. "If Alizee discovers we are investigating her, she will leave and all will be lost. She will change her operations and we will never be able to help those she is hurting."

I took a step back so that he wasn't touching me anymore. I was too pissed for any sort of physical contact, no matter how platonic.

"Gavin won't tell her. Not if he thinks she's involved in trafficking," I said. No matter how angry I was with him, I couldn't believe he'd risk people's lives.

The look Pierre gave me said he didn't agree. "Even if he does not say anything, she will be able to tell something is wrong. Whatever you say to him will change things between them."

"Fine," I snapped. "I'll just make up another excuse as to why I was there."

"And he will accuse you of following him. Spying."

"But I wasn't!" I immediately countered.

"And that is exactly the problem," he said. "Your boyfriend will say these things and you will defend yourself. The only way to do that will be to tell him the truth. And we cannot allow that to happen."

"I can't pretend like I didn't see that," I said. The sick feeling was back and I hugged my arms across my middle. Despite the warmth of the sun, I was cold.

"You must," Pierre insisted.

"How am I supposed to go back to our hotel room and pretend I didn't just see him kissing another woman when he told me he was at a business meeting?" I asked. "I can't just smile and pretend that everything's okay. If he touches me, all I'll be thinking about is her, wondering if he touched her the same way..."

Pierre grabbed my upper arms and I gasped in surprise. His fingers dug into my flesh and his eyes were flashing. "You must not speak of this to anyone! You cannot ruin what I have worked for!"

I pulled out of his grasp and put my hands on his chest, giving him a hard enough shove that he knew I meant business. I watched him regain control, but there was no apology on his face.

"Carrie, you must consider the big picture." Pierre's voice was tense. "We cannot allow emotions to sway our judgment."

I scowled at him. That was easy for him to say. It wasn't his boyfriend making out with some former model. "I'll take that into consideration."

"You must–"

"Back off, Pierre!" I snapped. "Don't tell me what I 'must' do. I'm not a cop or a reporter. I don't live or work here and I sure as hell don't work for you." I was so done with this. "I'm going to catch a cab and go back to my hotel. Give me a call if you have anything else on Alizee and still want my help, but I'm not making any promises."

I walked away before he could respond. I had a feeling I'd just gotten a glimpse of the real Pierre rather than the one with the charming smile. I could handle myself, so I wasn't worried, but I was definitely going to be more careful if I was out with him in the future.

I pushed that thought aside as I gave the cabbie the hotel name. I would deal with Pierre later. Right now, I had to figure out what I was going to do about Gavin and Alizee. I closed my eyes and fought back the tears that wanted to escape. I wasn't going to cry, and definitely not here in the cab.

What I wanted, more than anything else, was to open my eyes and be in bed, basking in the afterglow of an amazing night. I wanted Gavin to be honest with me, even if it meant telling me he was meeting with Alizee. I wanted him to tell me he was only meeting with her because Vincent wanted it, but that he hadn't wanted to be anywhere but in bed with me. I wanted to know for sure that what I'd seen had been Alizee making a play for Gavin seconds before he pushed her away.

But I knew I couldn't have any of that, and I probably couldn't even get an explanation either. As much as I hated to admit it, I believed Pierre had a point. I was just torn between doing what my heart wanted and what my head knew was right.

TWENTY-EIGHT

GAVIN

I put my hands on Alizee's shoulders and held her in place as I took a step back, breaking the kiss that never should've happened. I was stupid for not expecting her to act despite my evident disinterested. She'd said it herself. She was the kind of woman who knew what she wanted and went for it. I just happened to be in her line of fire.

It had been an aggressive kiss, the kind that would've had me hard in seconds if it had been Carrie pressed against me. With Alizee, my only thought was how to make this as polite but clear as possible.

Dammit. I was tired of the misunderstandings with the women in this country. A little bit of flirting was one thing. I mean, I made a living off sexual chemistry, but these women were taking things way too far. It was exhausting to constantly be on guard, wondering who was going to come on to me next. I nearly smiled, realizing how egotistical that sounded, but this wasn't the time for self-reflection. I had one of those women to deal with right now.

"Alizee, I can't do this." I paused, then amended my statement. "I won't do this." I didn't want her thinking it was only a matter of ethics. She had to know I was making a choice here... and the choice wasn't her.

Her dark eyes flashed with anger, but not before I saw the surprise cross them. She'd honestly thought I'd go through with it even though I was with Carrie. I wondered if it was arrogance on her part or if she thought all men cared about was sex, no matter where they stuck their dick. I really hoped it wasn't because she thought I, personally, was like that. I was starting to wonder if I gave off some sort of vibe that told women it was okay to seduce me even though it was clear I was taken.

Was I? The thought hit me suddenly. Was that the problem? Didn't I make it clear that I was off the market?

"You really love her," Alizee nearly sneered the statement, her face twisting into something unattractive. "Your Carrie."

"Yes," I said. I wasn't going to make any apologies for it. If anything, it was Carrie I owed an apology to, for not making sure people knew that there was no room for negotiation in our relationship. "I love her and I'm not going to do anything to hurt her."

"She would never have to know." Alizee gave me a seductive smile.

I shook my head. "I'm not going to betray her."

Alizee's mouth flattened and she took a step back. Even while being rejected, she was the picture of calm and collected. "It will cost you your deal."

"So be it." The words were easier to say than I thought they would be.

She laughed and shook her head in disbelief. "You will lose everything."

"If I have her, it'll be worth it. The idea of having everything, but losing her..." My heart twisted at the thought of a life without her. "She's all I need."

"How noble." Alizee rolled her eyes. "You are a fool."

"Maybe," I agreed. "But it doesn't change anything. Call Vincent and tell him you're killing the idea. Or I'll make the call if you want me to."

"I am not calling Vincent," she said. "Because I am not going to stop the project."

"You're not?" I refused to let myself hope. Alizee didn't strike me as the forgiving type. There was a catch here. I was sure of it.

"Of course not," she said scornfully. "Why would I do that? A sex club in Cannes will be quite beneficial for my own businesses. I fully intend to continue my support."

"Oh, well, all right then." I was pleasantly surprised. That had gone better than I could have expected.

"You, however." Her eyes narrowed and she gave me a look that was anything but friendly. "If you are not going to fuck me, you can get the hell off of my yacht."

I stared at her. I'd expected an ultimatum, where I would have to allow Vincent to buy out my part of the club. I hadn't expected her to kick me off the boat. I looked around. We were a good ways from the harbor.

"Go." She pointed.

"You want me to swim?"

Alizee reached behind her and unzipped her dress, letting it fall off her shoulders to reveal that she wasn't wearing anything underneath. "Swim or fuck. Your choice."

I took off my shoes, tied the laces to my belt and walked to the edge. Part of me wanted to look back at Alizee to see if she was going to relent, but judging by the sounds I was hearing behind me, she'd decided that if I wasn't going to get her off, she'd take care of it herself. I really didn't want to see that, so I bit the bullet and jumped.

The water was colder than it looked and my clothes weighed me down, but I didn't let any of that distract me. I began to swim, taking strong, even strokes that moved me steadily to the shore. I tried not to focus on the way my arms ached or how uncomfortable I was. Instead, I thought about what I was swimming toward.

I had a feeling it'd take me a while to find a cab that would take me back, wet as I'd be, but once I got back to the hotel, my plans were very simple. I was going to wrap my arms around Carrie and kiss her until I forgot what it had felt like to have Alizee's mouth on mine. Then, I was going to bend Carrie over the couch so I could see how red her ass was from last night and I was going to fuck her until she screamed. Once she did that, I'd take her to our bedroom and make her come until she passed out.

That should help me forget that this awful day had ever happened.

I kept those thoughts in my head as I swam and they helped warm me. There was only one downside. When I climbed out of the water, after thinking of all the ways I wanted to ravish my hot girlfriend, I had a massive erection despite the cold water. That, plus the way my pants were clinging to me now made for an embarrassing walk to catch a cab.

As I walked, I made a decision. I was going to call Vincent and tell him he could deal with Alizee from here on out. For the rest of the trip, I didn't want to be anywhere near her. Well, I'd make the call after fucking Carrie senseless. That was my top priority.

TWENTY-NINE

CARRIE

I'd been pacing ever since I'd gotten back from the docks, unable to sit down or even stop. I couldn't get the image out of my head, no matter how hard I tried. And, believe me, I tried.

Every time I closed my eyes, all I could see was Alizee and Gavin locked in an embrace. Then I'd opened my eyes and all I could see was the same thing. I tried focusing on the problem at hand, how I would be able to see Gavin and pretend everything was normal. The thought of seeing him and not saying anything tied a knot in my throat. Was I a good enough actress to pull it off?

I heard the sound of a key card in the lock and knew my time was up. Whatever came next, there wouldn't be any going back. Either I'd lie to him or I'd go off and have to deal with the fallout.

When the door opened, I turned and, for a few blissful moments, forgot about what had happened earlier. Gavin was dripping on the carpet. Every inch of him was wet. His clothes clung to him, showing off every dip and curve of his body. His hair was a mess, plastered to his face in some places and lank in others. He was a mess.

But his eyes were heated and I recognized the way he was walking toward me, the purpose in his step.

I froze, torn between several choices. I could forget everything I'd seen, remind myself of everything Gavin and I had been through and trust him to tell me what I needed to know. I could accept his kiss and let things progress to where I knew we both wanted it to go. No matter how pissed I was, my body always responded to him.

I could stay silent, but hold on to my anger, pushing him away without reason or excuse. I would see questions and pain in his eyes, and ignore them. I'd wait until after Pierre's story was done or after we were back in the US to confront him.

Or, I could forget about all the consequences and have it out with him right here. Demand to know why he lied and what he'd been doing with Alizee. See if he lied again. I could tell him everything, how he'd been blinded by a pretty face.

Before I could decide, Gavin's hands were cupping my face and the shock of cold from his skin went through me. Then his lips came down on mine. I shivered at the chill in them and then again because of the heat that followed. His tongue pushed past my lips, twisting around my tongue and drawing it into his mouth. I moaned as he sucked on my tongue, sending a bolt of desire straight through me.

Had he done that to Alizee?

The thought was like a bucket of ice water, far colder than Gavin's skin.

The hands that had been clutching at his wet shirt now pushed him away. His mouth tore away from mine and I saw the surprise in his eyes as he took a step back. I shoved him harder, putting some force into it this time.

"What the hell, Carrie?" He stared at me.

The anger his kiss had chased away came back with a vengeance. I wanted to scream at him, tell him I didn't want him kissing me after he'd just been doing the same to Alizee. I wanted to yell at him for lying to me, accuse him of sneaking around behind my back.

Then I heard Pierre's voice in the back of my head, warning me what would happen if I told. I thought about all the people who would suffer if we were right about Alizee. If she was able to hide her operation because I couldn't put others above my personal life, I'd never forgive myself.

I went with the first excuse I could think of. "I feel like shit," I snapped. "It hurts to sit or lay down because you spanked me yesterday."

Gavin flinched, his eyes filling with hurt. It cut my heart, but I couldn't take it back, not without spilling everything. Besides, the anger inside me needed to go somewhere.

"My nipples hurt and I have a fucking hickey on my neck like I'm some high school slut whose boyfriend couldn't control himself." I put my hand over the mark I hadn't bothered to use concealer on.

Even as I said it, I hated myself for lying. I loved that he'd claimed me, that he said I was his. True, my ass did sting and my nipples were chafing against my bra, but the sensations turned me on more than they hurt. They were reminders of last night and how Gavin had let himself go.

"Carrie?"

The expression on his face was one of shock and pain. The

way he said my name almost made me break, but then I remembered what it had felt like when I'd seen him kissing Alizee.

"I just need some space." I turned away before he could see the tears threatening to spill over. I was halfway to the room when I heard footsteps behind me. I turned, finally thinking to ask, "Why are you so wet?" But before I could ask the question, my phone rang.

I grabbed it out of my pocket, desperate for a distraction. I didn't even care if it was a sales call. I'd talk to anyone at the moment if it meant a few more minutes of not having to look at Gavin.

"Hello?" I answered without looking at the caller ID.

"Carrie?"

I instantly recognized Pierre's voice and a flare of annoyance went through me. Was he calling to check up on me?

"What?" I was definitely not in the mood to deal with him acting like I was some kid who needed to be handled.

"Did you tell him?"

"No. Now, what do you want?" As much as I hated to admit it, at least being pissed at him was a diversion, helping keep my mind off of the fact that I could feel Gavin's eyes on me.

"I have a file you need to see." Pierre didn't seem too concerned with my attitude. "Do you want to meet tomorrow?"

I saw my out and took it. "Now's better."

"Really?" Pierre sounded surprised, with a hint of amusement. "I had the impression you were quite cross with me."

"That's one way to put it," I said dryly. "But if it's that important to you, I'll come now."

"Shall we meet at your hotel?"

"No," I said. "The Jean Luc Pele La Table." I named one of the smaller restaurants I'd seen in Cannes.

"I will be there shortly."

I hung up the phone, took a shaky breath and turned to face Gavin again. One glance at his face, however, told me I wouldn't be able to look at him. He was pale and his hands were clenched into fists.

"I have to go."

"It's him, isn't it? That journalist." Gavin's voice was hard. "You're going to see him again?"

My lips flattened. Funny... him acting like it was a big deal that I wanted to go meet Pierre when he'd been lip-locking with Alizee not more than an hour ago.

"Is that what this is about?" he asked as I started toward the door. I found the jealousy in his voice ironic. "You don't want me to touch you because..." There was a pause, and then he continued. "Have you been... spending time with him?"

"While you were out with Vincent earlier?" I stressed the name as I opened the door. "There's an idea. Why don't you give your buddy a call? Maybe you can have another 'business meeting.'"

I slammed the door behind me as I stalked out into the hallway. I didn't run, but I hurried, afraid of what would happen if Gavin came after me. I wasn't sure I could handle going through that a second time. But I apparently shouldn't have worried. He didn't come after me. He let me go.

THIRTY

I walked to the restaurant, using the time to regain my composure. The day was just as bright and sunny as it had been earlier, but I wasn't in the mood to appreciate any of it. In fact, at the moment, I was thinking about how spring in the city might actually reflect my current mood better. I didn't like being angry and hurt while the sun was shining down from a bright blue sky. It made me feel petty.

Was I being petty?

I had to consider the question as I made my way down the street. Hadn't Gavin proven himself to me more than once? Shouldn't I give him the benefit of the doubt? When he'd shown up at the hotel, soaked to the skin, shouldn't that have been a clue that something was wrong? Why hadn't I asked him what had happened instead of lashing out at him?

Because, I realized, even after all of this, I was still insecure.

As I neared the restaurant, I pulled my curls up behind my head and twisted them into a knot that would keep them out of my face. I stopped, closed my eyes and took a slow, deep breath.

Whatever Pierre wanted to show me had to be important for him to have asked to meet twice in the same day, especially since he didn't want Gavin getting suspicious about what we were doing. As much as this was tearing me up, what Pierre and I were doing was bigger than the relationship between Gavin and me.

I didn't see Pierre at any of the outside tables, so I walked into Jean Luc Pele La Table and looked around. He wasn't there yet, but I wasn't going to stand around looking like the tourist I was. I walked over to the display case and looked at my choices. The young man at the counter spoke better English than some Americans so I placed my order, then took my food outside and found an out of the way place to sit.

I spotted Pierre before he saw me. His expression was serious and I didn't see even a hint of that charming smile until his eyes met mine. Even then, it was a shadow of what it was the first time I'd seen it. That alone told me he had something important.

He didn't bother going into the restaurant itself, but rather came straight to me. As he approached, I saw that he was holding a manila envelope. My curiosity piqued, I leaned forward, my partially eaten sandwich forgotten. All of this shit with Gavin would be worth it if we could get something real against Alizee. If Pierre and I could find enough for him to write an article and me to present the evidence to the local authorities, Alizee would be exposed and Gavin would see her for who she was. Who knew how many hundreds, if not thousands, of people we'd save from horrible fates. The time and effort it would take to patch things up with Gavin wouldn't seem so awful if I helped accomplish all of that.

"Thank you for coming so quickly," Pierre said as he slid into the seat next to me. His knee brushed against mine.

"You said you had something important to show me?" I started to scoot my chair to the side to put more distance between the two of us, then stopped. He wasn't flirting, so there was no need to establish boundaries. He was just sitting close so he could show me what he had without risking anyone else seeing.

"I have a... contact in the police," Pierre began. "When I first began investigating Alizee, I asked for him to pass along any information he saw about Alizee or any of the property she owns." He opened the envelope and pulled out two light tan folders. He handed them both to me without a word.

I hesitated, then took them. I was pretty sure I didn't want to see what was inside, but I opened the top one anyway.

And immediately regretted it.

I forced myself not to push it away. Doing the kind of work I'd done for the past year, I'd seen some pretty gruesome things, but it never got any easier. I had more than one person tell me that when it started getting easy, that's when it was time to get out. If this was the indication, then I was still good because the crime scene photo I was looking at made me regret having eaten.

"North Star," Pierre said. "Or, that is the name she used at work. There is no record of a real identity."

"Stripper?" I forced the word past the bile threatening to rise.

"At one of Alizee's clubs," he confirmed. "And rumor says she was paid for more than taking off her clothes."

"So she was a prostitute." I made it a statement. I flipped through the pictures, each one showing another brutal angle to the crime.

He nodded. "Three prior arrests for solicitation." He gestured toward the paper I was currently on. Her mug shot showed a once-pretty blonde who'd definitely lived a hard life. She looked decades older than her twenty-three years.

"The last page is the..." He frowned as he searched for the word. "Death report?"

"Autopsy report?" I asked as I turned to that page. He nodded, but I didn't need the confirmation. While it was written in French, I'd seen enough of these to recognize the similarities. I glanced at it and then looked to Pierre for translation.

"She was strangled," he said. "But the other injuries happened when she was alive."

I inhaled a slow, shaky breath. Whoever had done this had enjoyed it. I closed the first file and opened the second. Even though I was prepared this time, it didn't make things easier. Especially since half of the girl's face was missing. I managed to keep myself from being sick, but it was a close call.

"Daria Petrova. Sixteen-year-old runaway from Russia." Pierre said, leaning close enough that his arm brushed against mine. "Shot in the back of the head."

"Also a prostitute?" I asked the question even though I was pretty certain of the answer.

"Yes," he said. "Found beaten, raped and shot two days after North was found."

"Did she also work in one of Alizee's clubs?" I breathed a sigh of relief as I closed the file, even though I knew I'd never truly get those images out of my head.

"There is no record of her," he said.

"Which doesn't mean she wasn't working the same place North was," I reasoned.

Pierre nodded. "Both girls were last seen at the club where North worked and were found in the same alley."

"You think Alizee had something to do with this," I said, another statement, no question.

"I do," he admitted. "I believe North did, said or saw something she wasn't supposed to and Alizee killed her for it." He took both of the files and slid them back into the envelope. "I believe Daria saw the murder and was executed."

"Did you tell your police contact that?" I asked.

He frowned. "I did, but there is no evidence to support my claim. My contact will not present this theory without more than my word."

"What's the theory they're working with now?"

"They were prostitutes. Their lives were full of danger," he said. "It is to be expected that they would have a violent and young death."

"So they're not even going to look for the killer or killers?" I knew similar atrocities happened back home, a person's status prompting the intensity in which an investigation was done. It didn't make it any less wrong.

"They will look," he said. "But only if they have the time."

"And you're sure Alizee did this?"

"I'm certain she gave the orders," he said. "And I wish to see her in jail for it. Someone must speak for these girls."

I nodded in understanding. I had the same passion for my work. So many of these girls – and boys – were tossed aside like garbage, treated as if they didn't matter. They needed an advocate, someone to step up and say it wasn't okay to treat a human being this way. I felt a surge of warm admiration for Pierre and what he was trying to do.

"This is why I was so adamant that you not speak to Gavin about being at the docks," Pierre said.

My heart twisted as the pain returned. "I didn't say anything."

"If Alizee knows we suspect her of wrongdoing, she will go to any lengths to ensure she cannot be connected to these deaths, to cover her tracks. I need hard evidence that will force the authorities to pursue her as a suspect."

I put aside my own feelings for the greater good. "How can I help?"

He smiled at me. "I was hoping you would offer. I need you to spy on Alizee."

"Spy on her?" I echoed. "How am I supposed to do that?"

"Go to the meetings with your boyfriend. Try to get close with her, encourage her to confide in you."

"You think she's going to confess to me just because I make nice?" My nails bit into my palm and I had to force my hand to relax.

"No," he said. "That would be foolish. I believe she will provide you with information that may lead us to clues that will provide the evidence we need. It may be a confirmation of places she has gone, of people she knows."

I didn't say anything and he let the silence stand. I could tell he knew how difficult this decision was for me to make, especially after what I'd seen, but it wasn't just that. This whole thing brought back memories of Howard and everything I'd gone through a year ago. I didn't regret the decisions I made then, not for a moment, but it wasn't something I wanted to go through again. Now, I found myself in a similar situation, though I doubted I'd be in as much danger. Alizee might be a murderous bitch, but I'd already survived a lecherous sexual sadist. More importantly, I was an American citizen in a tourist city. If I went missing or turned up dead, Cannes would get negative press as well as international pressure to find the person responsible.

Small comfort since it'd still mean I was dead.

But that wasn't the point. I had to decide if I was willing to put my relationship with Gavin, as well as both of our lives, on the line to stop Alizee.

"Please," Pierre said softly. "Help me."

I reached out and put my hand over his. "All right," I said. I gave him a grim smile. "I'll help you."

He gave me that dazzling smile that made his dimples appear. "Then let us put that bitch behind bars."

I nodded as I chuckled. It was dark business we were doing, but at least we were doing something.

Carrie pushing me away when I kissed her had been a surprise, but I'd thought, for a moment, it was because I was wet and cold. Then I saw her face and it wasn't the swim that was making me cold. When she started in about the pain she was in because of the sex we'd had last night, it was like a punch in the gut. And then she'd taken a call from Pierre, that journalist she'd been spending time with while I was at business meetings. I wasn't sure which was stronger, the jealousy that surged through me at how easily she spoke to him after what she'd just said to me, or the pain her words had brought.

When she said she was meeting him, I couldn't stop myself from wondering if he was the reason Carrie was pulling away from me. Was it possible I freaked her out so badly last night that she'd turned to Pierre?

I was barely able to keep my voice steady when I asked the question. Then she said I should have another "business meeting" and stormed out. I stared at the door as it slammed shut. What had she meant by that? Was she angry I had another meeting with Vincent? I don't understand why she didn't tell me not to go this morning. I would've been happy to stay. There had to be something she wasn't telling me.

And I needed to know what it was so I could fix it.

That broke my paralysis and I went after her. The elevator doors were already closed by the time I stepped into the hallway, and I knew I'd be too late to catch her if I waited for it to come back up. I headed for the stairs.

I wasn't quite running, but I wasn't walking either. I had to catch her, tell her that whatever I had done, I'd make it right. If she wanted me to break my contract with Vincent, I'd do it. I'd give up the club here and back home if she didn't want me involved with any of it. I'd find another job. Anything to fix this.

I caught a glimpse of Carrie's hair shining in the sun as she pushed open the lobby doors and I hurried after her. I considered calling out to her, but didn't want to have this discussion in public. I heard her say the name of the restaurant where they were going to meet, so I wasn't worried about losing her. I knew she was meeting Pierre. I didn't know the guy, but I didn't like him.

I frowned as I walked, closing the distance. Somehow, I didn't think going off on Pierre would put me into Carrie's better graces. She seemed to like him. I just didn't know how much. I needed to know. I needed to know if what had happened between Carrie and me was because of Pierre. And this was the perfect time and place to find out.

I slowed down until my pace matched hers. I could still see her, but I wasn't getting any closer now. It wasn't about catching up to her now, not yet. I had a different plan. I'd wait until I had a better idea of what I was dealing with.

Carrie went inside and I situated myself so I could see the

patio without obstruction. If they ate inside, I wouldn't be able to see anything, but I was counting on Carrie wanting to be in the sunshine. A few minutes later, she came out and found a table.

A voice in my head said I was being unreasonable, that I should just walk over and talk to her. That was the smart thing to do. The right thing. We needed to talk about what had happened.

I tossed the voice away as I noticed a handsome man walking toward Carrie, carrying an envelope in his hand. I watched as they talked, their bodies only inches away from each other. He kept leaning closer to her, their arms brushing. She didn't make an attempt to pull away and I felt sick. She'd pushed me away and now she was letting this man touch her. When she smiled at him and put her hand over his, I turned away.

I couldn't watch. Part of me wanted to leave. Go back to the hotel and face Carrie when she returned.

Movement caught the corner of my eye and I looked up in reflex. Pierre was walking by, carrying the envelope and looking like he'd just achieved some sort of major accomplishment. Anger burned the pain and made it more manageable.

I needed to talk to him. Find out what the hell he was doing with the woman I loved. I stood, ready to follow and confront. I'd taken only a couple steps when my phone rang. I cursed, wanting to ignore it, but it was my business ringtone. It was probably Vincent, since Alizee wasn't likely to speak to me again anytime soon. I could only hope. After what had happened with her, I needed to talk to Vincent and see if things were still on track.

I swore again and pulled out my phone. I was starting to

regret having purchased a waterproof one. If my phone had been destroyed when Alizee made me swim to shore, it would've been a good excuse to not take the call. Since I didn't have that excuse, and I was too tired to lie, I answered.

"Yes?" It took all of my self-control not to snap at him.

"What the hell happened this morning, Gavin?" Vincent sounded mildly amused. "Alizee called me, said you weren't anything like she expected."

I scowled. "Did she tell you to kill the deal?"

"No." Now he sounded curious. "Why would she have done that?"

I didn't answer. This wasn't something I wanted to talk about over the phone.

"Meet me at La Femme en Bleu," he said, sensing my hesitation.

"A strip club at two in the afternoon?" I asked. I wasn't sure why that surprised me.

"It's never too early to watch beautiful women dance," he countered.

I sighed. "I'm on my way." When I hung up, I looked down the street, but Pierre was gone.

Dammit!

Now I had only two choices. Go talk to Carrie or meet with Vincent. Either way, I was going to have to talk about things I wanted to avoid. Maybe if I talked to Vincent and got that all taken care of, I'd be able to tell Carrie that work wouldn't interfere with us again.

I sighed and hailed a cab. Putting it off wasn't going to make this any easier. During the ride, I thought about how I would explain things to Vincent. Should I try to cushion it? Make it sound like Alizee hadn't been out of line? Leave out what she'd said after I'd turned her down? Or did I lay it all out for him, tell him everything exactly how it went down? No emotion, no inflection. Just the facts.

I still hadn't made up my mind which tact I would take when the cab pulled in front of the club. It was one more thing I didn't know how to handle, which only served to piss me off further. I walked into the club, barely glancing at the scantily-clad women walking by with trays of drinks, and only then because I was trying not to run into them. The doorman pointed me toward a corner booth and that's where I went now, fully expecting to see Vincent with a couple girls hanging all over him. Instead, he was sitting by himself, looking less than interested in the pair of girls on stage who were writhing all over each other. That was a little strange, but not enough to squash the anger I felt about everything that had happened today.

I sat down on the edge of the booth seat.

"So, Gavin, what happened?" Vincent turned toward me, his eyes narrowed. "You don't look very happy." His gaze went from top to bottom. "Or very dry."

"I'm not," I said. "Either one, actually."

He leaned his arms on the table. "What's going on?"

"Alizee came on to me," I said and ran my hand through my still-wet hair. "Fuck that. She full-on propositioned me and then kissed me. Threatened to kill the deal if I didn't fuck her." It all came out a bit harsher than I'd originally intended, but I didn't apologize.

"And?" he asked, his tone mild.

"And nothing," I snapped. "I'm not going to betray Carrie like that." I tried not to think about how Carrie might be betraying me.

"Even if it cost you the deal? The club here?" he asked.

I gave him a hard look. "Even if it cost me everything."

"Good." He beamed at me.

I stared at him. What the hell was that about? Why did he look so fucking happy? The anger I'd kept in check threatened to crack the surface.

"I'm glad you didn't give in to her," he said. "If you had, the deal would've been off and I would've been looking for a new partner."

Now I was really confused. What the fuck was going on? Vincent gave me a smile and I slammed my hand down on the table.

Before I could say anything though, Vincent spoke, "Do you know how I got my start?"

"I don't care," I said through gritted teeth. "Alizee threatened me, kissed me, then made me swim to shore when I turned her down. I've had a shitty day so far and I want to know why the hell you think this is funny."

"I'll get there, I promise." Vincent's expression sobered. "Trust me, Gavin. You're going to want to hear this."

I wasn't sure I agreed with him, but calmed down enough to nod for him to go on.

"I came from Corsica," he began. "I was poor, but I worked hard. I am a self-made businessman, a success story, though not our island's biggest one. That," he said, "is Alizee."

I remembered how they'd talked in a language I hadn't recognized. "You knew her?"

"In a way," he admitted. "Everyone on Corsica knows Alizee because she is a member of the biggest crime family on the island. Me, she did not recognize, but that was not a surprise."

"So you're, what, working with her because of some weird childhood jealousy thing?"

His face hardened and I instantly knew there was something more here, something much stronger than anything I held against Alizee.

"Self-made business man." There was bitterness in his voice. "Married my childhood sweetheart. Had a beautiful little girl who I gave everything she wanted. Had the perfect life."

I had a bad feeling I wasn't going to like what came next. As soon as he spoke, I found out I was right.

"Three years ago, when she was sixteen, my daughter became angry because I wouldn't let her go out with an older boy she liked. She ran away to Cannes with him, and it turned out he was a recruiter for one of Alizee's clubs." He looked down at the table, and then back up at me. "It took me a year but I finally tracked her here. I was too late. What I found was that she had been turned out, forced into prostitution and several months before I arrived in Cannes, her body was found in an alley. The police ruled it a suicide."

Damn. I didn't know what to say. I knew if my daughter had disappeared, been hurt, been murdered... I shook away the thought, unable to imagine it. Skylar was my world, the only person I cared about more than Carrie.

"I know Alizee was responsible for her death. Even if not directly, then indirectly. The police did not care, no matter how much pressure I put on them." Vincent's normally jovial voice was laced with anger and pain worse than anything I'd ever felt. "I have been trying to gather evidence, proof of what she's done."

"I'm truly sorry for your loss," I said. "But I don't understand what that has to do with Alizee hitting on me or why you're working with her."

"Because you turned her down, I know I can trust you," he said. "And I needed a partner I could trust to take Alizee down. You are that partner."

What he'd been telling me finally sunk in. Alizee wasn't just a flirt or a blackmailer. She was dangerous. A trafficker. Possibly a murderer. A murderer who was pissed at me.

Carrie.

Shit.

Alizee could go after Carrie because of what I'd done.

I pulled out my phone and hit her contact number.

Voicemail.

I left a message and then dialed again.

Dammit Carrie. My heart pounded. Pick up.

THIRTY-TWO

CARRIE

I was standing on the balcony, looking out at the ocean and trying to figure out how to handle this thing with Gavin when he called the first time. I let it go to voicemail. I didn't want to have this conversation over the phone. Hell, I didn't want to have it at all, but it needed to be done. The phone dinged to say he'd left a message and I sighed. It was probably just a 'call me, we need to talk' or 'where are you' message. I should've been the one asked where he was. I'd reluctantly come back to the room after Pierre left the restaurant, knowing I couldn't leave things with Gavin the way they'd been, but he'd been gone. No note, no indication of where he'd gone or when he'd be back. Of course, my thoughts had automatically gone a negative route.

My phone rang again. Gavin's ringtone. I frowned. He must've called back right after leaving the voicemail. That didn't seem like the kind of thing he'd do unless something was wrong. I wasn't quite sure I was ready to talk to him, but I did go to my voicemail.

"Babe, please call me."

I could hear the worry in Gavin's voice and immediately tensed.

"I'm with Vincent right now at La Femme en Bleu and I need you to call me. Please, Carrie."

I frowned at the phone. I was pretty sure the place Gavin mentioned was a strip club, but the fact that he'd told me his location spoke volumes. I wasn't stupid enough to think Gavin never took a business meeting at a strip club, but he also didn't generally offer the information.

I sent a quick text saying I was coming to him and waited for his response. If he said just to call him, I'd know it wasn't as urgent as he'd made it sound. Instead, I got a message that simply said, "Hurry."

It didn't matter how angry I'd been or where things had been left between us. I went. I'd never forgive myself if something happened to him.

The cab driver didn't even blink when I gave him the name of the club and I tried desperate to keep my mind off of all the possibilities that swirled in my head. By the time we reached the club, my nerves were frayed and I barely even glanced at the bills I gave to the driver.

The man at the door opened it for me and gave a polite nod as I walked by. The place was half-full of people I assumed were mostly tourists and half-naked waitresses who were barely wearing more than the women on stage. I found it strange that a country with topless beaches still had strip clubs that thrived. I supposed it was the difference between women just walking around and seeing them dance and grind.

I caught movement toward the back and looked up. Gavin was coming toward me, an expression of pure relief on his face. I started his way, now even more worried about what was going on. It couldn't have been just because I'd gone to see Pierre. That would've been a bit of an overreaction.

He pulled me into his arms without saying a word and, for a moment, I relaxed into his embrace. I let myself pretend everything was okay and then pulled back. Gavin didn't let me go far though. He slid his arm around my shoulders and led me back to the booth next to where Vincent was standing.

"Carrie." Vincent nodded.

"Vincent."

He glanced at Gavin and a silent message seemed to pass between the two of them. "I think I will leave you two alone to talk. You can speak freely here."

"Thanks, Vincent," Gavin said. He waited until Vincent started toward the front of the club before motioning for me to sit.

Now that it was just the two of us in a secluded booth I assumed was meant for private dances, all of the day's previous emotions came flooding back. I stayed on the opposite side of the table, my hands clenched on my lap, and waited for him to explain himself.

He raked his hand through his hair and I saw that it was still damp. "I'm not sure where to start."

I tried not to scowl as I leaned in so that I was sitting closer to him. The music was too loud for us to have an entire conversation sitting across from each other without leaning in. Probably why Vincent had said we were free to talk here.

"Just say it, Gavin," I said.

A flash of something crossed his face and then vanished. I recognized that look, the guarded expression, and I hated it.

"There are some things about Vincent and Alizee that you need to know."

I wasn't going to sit here and let him treat me like I was too stupid or naïve to know what was going on. "I know."

His eyes widened. "What do you mean you know? How?"

"I was there."

Now he looked confused. "I just found out what was going on not more than twenty minutes ago. I don't understand."

"Do I need to spell it out for you?" I snapped. "I was at the docks this morning and saw you on your little 'business trip.' You know, the one supposedly with Vincent. The one with your lips wrapped around Alizee on her yacht. Yeah. That one."

All the color drained from Gavin's face and I saw him putting pieces together.

"You – you were there?"

"Yes, Gavin, I was there. And I got quite the eyeful." I crossed my arms, digging my nails into my upper arms to keep myself from crying. I needed to channel my anger, not my hurt.

"Carrie, babe, that's not... I mean, it isn't..." He slammed his hand down on the table. "Dammit!" His eyes flashed. "Why didn't you just say something?"

"What was I supposed to say?" I avoided the question. "You lied to me about where you were going and who you were going to be with. Unless, of course, you didn't know you'd be hanging out on Alizee's yacht with her." I raised an eyebrow as he flushed. "That's what I thought."

He started to reach across the table as if he expected me to hold his hands, then he stopped and pulled back. "It's not what you think."

"Really? Because I think you didn't want me to know you were meeting her and not Vincent. And I think that's because..." I let my voice trail off as tears started to form in my eyes. I wasn't going to cry, not here. "It doesn't matter the reason. You lied and you kissed her."

"You must've missed the finale then," he snapped. "Where she made me swim back to shore because I refused to fuck her, even though she threatened to kill the deal."

My eyes went wide. That certainly explained why he'd been soaked when he'd gotten back to the hotel.

"And you're one to talk." He leaned toward me, his eyes flashing now. "I saw you with Pierre."

I frowned. "That's not the same thing. I told you I was going to meet him. And I sure as hell didn't kiss him!"

"You two looked awfully cozy."

"You followed me?" What was happening to us?

"And how did you see me with Alizee if you hadn't been following me?"

"I apparently had a reason to," I countered. "You lied about where you were going."

"Yes," he admitted. "I wasn't entirely honest about where I was going because I didn't want you to worry. I got the impression you didn't like Alizee very much."

I gave a snort of laughter. "How very observant of you. That's an understatement."

"I shouldn't have lied," he said. "Okay? It was a mistake. I should've just been honest and even invited you to come along." He started to say something else and then stopped.

"Spill it," I said. "We might as well get everything out in the open."

"Is what you saw... is that why you said those things earlier?"

There was a cautious hope in his eyes that reminded me of the pain I'd seen on his face back at the hotel.

"Because if what happened last night freaked you out or scared you," he continued. "And that's why you went to Pierre, we don't have to do any of that—"

"Wait," I cut him off. "You think I'm cheating on you with Pierre because of what we did last night?" The expression on his face said it all. "I'm not interested in Pierre. Not that way." I sighed and slid over so that we were side-by-side. "I'm sorry I made you feel like I didn't love every moment of last night. I loved you sharing that part of yourself with me." I reached up and brushed his hair back, letting my fingers linger on his cheek.

"Why did you say it then? Payback for what you thought was going on between Alizee and me?" He caught my hand in his and pressed his lips against the tips of my fingers.

I sighed and said a silent apology to Pierre. "It's complicated because I wasn't at the docks alone."

Gavin's eyes narrowed. "You were there with the journalist."

I nodded. "He's investigating Alizee and that's what we were doing when I saw you. Pierre said I couldn't talk to you about it because if Alizee knew he was looking into her, she'd bolt."

"And he wouldn't be able to expose her illegal activities," Gavin finished my thought.

I looked up at him, surprised.

"You know how I said I had to tell you some things about Vincent and Alizee?" he asked. "Well, that's part of it."

I leaned my head against his shoulder, the flood of relief going through me leaving me trembling. He put his arms around me and pulled me close. "I'm so sorry," I repeated. "I should've trusted you, and not just about the meeting, but also that you'd believe me when I said she was up to no good."

He kissed the top of my head. "And I'm sorry I lied to you about where I was going this morning and for following you to meet Pierre. I should've trusted you, too. Hearing you say those things about me spanking you..." His voice trailed off for a moment before he continued, "That's what I've been scared of, Carrie. This past year, a part of me has always been waiting for this. For you to realize you could do so much better than me. I thought that showing you what I really wanted was the last straw."

I laughed and felt him stiffen. I tilted my head back so I could look at him. "And here I've been worrying that you wanted Alizee because I didn't respond the way you wanted me to, that you'd finally realized you were way out of my league."

He looked startled for a moment and then cupped the side of my face. "Carrie, I don't want anyone except you." He ran his thumb along my bottom lip. "I don't know what I did to deserve you."

I slid my hand behind his neck and pulled his head down until his mouth met mine. I kept the kiss brief and chaste, aware that we were in public, but even that small contact was enough to send heat blazing through me. I closed my eyes, love for Gavin washing over me, chasing away all the negative.

"There are still things I need to tell you," he said, his voice low. "But I'm thinking they can wait a bit longer." He released me and stood, holding out his hand to me. "We come first."

I nodded and slid my hand into his. We would stop Alizee, and Vincent if he was involved. We would help Pierre write his story or whatever else we needed to do. But after. Saving the world could wait a little longer.

We took a cab back to the hotel, keeping our hands linked the entire way. In the backseat, I snuggled under his arm, my fingers tracing patterns across his flat stomach. Absently, I wondered what it must've been like to watch him walk out of the ocean, his clothes clinging to every dip and curve of his body.

My stomach tightened with desire.

He kissed the top of my head, then moved down to my temple. The brush of his lips against skin made me shiver.

"I love you," he breathed. "Do you have any idea how much I love you?"

I looked up at him. "About as much as I love you."

His mouth lightly touched mine. "There are so many things I'm looking forward to doing to you."

His eyes shone with desire, twisting things deep inside me. "And I can't wait to let you do them."

Impossibly, his eyes darkened even more. "Fuck, Carrie. I'm not going to be able to walk into that hotel without embarrassing myself."

I gave him a wicked grin and slid my hand down to the growing bulge at the front of his pants. He stifled a moan as I cupped his cock. "You've got nothing to be embarrassed about."

He lowered his head so that his mouth was against my ear. "Keep that up and I'm not going to care that we're in the back of a cab. I'm going to fuck you right here."

I took a shuddering breath at the image his words created. It wasn't something I'd actually want him to do, but I couldn't deny the thought wasn't arousing. I was really glad they hadn't chosen somewhere further from the hotel. A longer ride, and I wasn't entirely certain I wouldn't have told him to go for it anyway.

When the cab pulled up to the curb, Gavin shoved a wad of bills at the driver and practically dragged me out of the car. We went straight for the elevators, ignoring the surprised looks we received. I wasn't sure if it was because we were rushing or that Gavin looked a bit bedraggled now that his clothes had dried. It also might've been that his pants weren't doing anything to disguise his partial erection.

All I could think about, though, was getting that delicious piece of flesh out of his pants and into mine. Figuratively, of course. Literally, I wanted him in my mouth, and then between my legs. Pants would just get in the way.

The moment we stepped into the elevator, my control cracked. Gavin's thumb rubbed against the side of my hand, each pass making me think of how it felt when he did the same motion over my clit.

Fuck it.

I turned toward Gavin, pulling my hand from his and pushing him against the side wall. He looked down at me with a startled expression that quickly vanished when I reached over and pushed the stop button. I dropped to my knees even as he said my name. I smiled up at him and reached for his belt. He caught his breath, his hand brushing over my curls before settling on my head. I opened his pants and reached into his underwear, wrapping my fingers around him. His lips parted as I pulled his cock out, stroking it as it hardened.

"What do you want, Gavin?" I asked, my mouth close to his cock, but not touching it. It twitched as I breathed on his skin. I glanced up at him. "Tell me what you want."

"You," he said gruffly.

I smiled as I lightly ran my fingers over his cock. "Are you going to take what you want?"

"Are you teasing me?" His fingers dug into my hair. There was an edge to his voice that sent a thrill through me.

"And if I am?" I asked coyly.

He took a shaky breath, but his voice was steady when he spoke. "Open your mouth."

I did as I was told, butterflies fluttering in my stomach as Gavin drew my head toward him. His cock slid across my tongue and the taste of salt – skin and water – burst through my mouth. I wrapped my lips around him, letting him control how deep he went. It was the ultimate act of trust. Him trusting me not to use my teeth or panic. Me trusting him not to give more than I could take.

I put my hands on hips for balance, but didn't try to take control. He thrust slowly at first, his gaze on me as he gauged my reaction. When he saw whatever it was that he was looking for, his hand tightened and he began to move faster. His cock slid into the back of my mouth and I focused on relaxing my throat, giving Gavin whatever access he wanted.

Some women might feel that being on their knees, allowing

a man to fuck their mouth, was humiliating. I found it heady, powerful. The way I felt his cock swelling in my mouth. The moans coming from his mouth. How his fingers dug into my scalp.

He pushed deep, forcing his entire length into my mouth. He held me there and I fought the urge to pull back. I took slow breaths through my nose and worked on not gagging. Just when I thought it'd be too much, he released me and took a step back.

I coughed, but made sure I gave Gavin a watery smile. I wanted him to know I thoroughly enjoyed the start of what I hoped would be something even more fun.

He reached down and pulled me to my feet, his eyes blazing. He crushed me against him, his lips coming down on mine with bruising force. His tongue forced open my mouth, plundering every inch while his hands slid under my shirt, caressing bare skin.

I moaned, but took a step back. I wanted him so badly, but not here. An elevator quickie sounded exciting, but wasn't what I wanted right now. I reached behind me and hit the button to get us going again, then gestured toward Gavin's exposed cock.

"As much as I'm sure there are a lot of women – and men – who'd appreciate the view." I took a step toward him. "That's mine."

He grinned at me as he tucked himself into his pants and pulled his jacket around to hide his erection. He was just in time too. One floor up, the elevator stopped and a pair of gray-haired women climbed on. They glanced at me, then at Gavin, before turning back to me. The taller of the two winked, but the other was bolder.

"If I'd had him in here, I would've kept the elevator stopped for a lot longer."

A burst of laughter bubbled out of me and, after a moment, Gavin and the old women both joined in. We laughed until we reached our floor and then said good-bye to the two strangers. The good humor lasted until we entered the hotel room and then it shifted.

Gavin's arms wrapped around my waist and he lifted me up. I wrapped my legs around him and latched my mouth to his neck. He moaned as I lightly bit down before pressing my lips against his ear. "My turn to leave a mark." His hands flexed against me and I sucked his skin into my mouth again.

As he lowered me to the bed, I felt a stab of satisfaction when I saw the dark mark on his neck. Then his hands were on my clothes, pulling my shirt over my head and tossing it aside. He made a sound of pure desire and then went to work on my jeans. While he was busy with those, I got rid of the bra and then tugged at Gavin's shirt.

It didn't take us long to finish shedding our clothes and then he was stretching out on top of me, skin sliding against skin. His hands slid up my sides and then around to cup my breasts. He squeezed and I moaned. As my head fell back, his mouth made its way down my jaw and then to my neck.

My nipples throbbed as his fingers rolled and pulled at them. Jolts of pain shot through me, going straight to my pussy. It was sharper than it had been last night, intensified by my already-sore body. My back arched, silently begging for more. I moaned.

"Are you okay?" Gavin's voice was soft as his hands stilled. "Are you too sore for this?"

"No," I said. I shook my head. "It feels amazing. Please don't stop."

"I love you," he said as his mouth came down on mine.

His teeth closed on my bottom lip, worrying at it until I cried out, and then he soothed it with his tongue. His fingers slid between my legs and I opened wider, granting him access to my already soaking core. I dug my nails into his shoulders as his fingers slid inside me. When he curled them, pressing against my g-spot, I cried out, a shock of pleasure rocking through me.

"Come for me, baby," he growled the command against my neck. "Come for me."

His lips moved down further and latched around my nipple. As he sucked the hardened flesh into his mouth, his fingers rubbed against that spot inside me until I was panting, begging for release. The moment his teeth grazed the tip, I did as I was told.

"Yes!" I cried out as I writhed against him, my hips pushing down until the heel of his hand rubbed against my clit and I screamed his name.

"That's my girl." Gavin's fingers slipped out of me and I felt something thicker, harder, pushing against my pussy.

My eyes rolled back into my head as he surged forward, filling me. His pace was fast, almost brutal. Every thrust went deep, and still, I rose to meet him. I wanted more, all of him. Our bodies came together over and over again, two entities working toward becoming one.

I felt it coming, the pressure inside me building, and I knew Gavin felt it too. His voice was rough in my ear, endearments mixed with curses. Sounds of pleasure fell from both our lips and I urged him onward.

Then, an explosion, an inferno. Fire blazed over my skin, through my body. Electricity across my nerves.

I clung to Gavin as we came together. He emptied himself inside me as my pussy contracted around him, squeezing every last drop of pleasure for us both. Only after we were both spent did we collapse back onto the bed, limbs still entwined.

He pressed his lips against my sweaty temple. "I love you."

I gave a happy sigh. "Me too."

For a moment, everything was perfect.

We had twenty minutes. Twenty blissful minutes where Gavin and I basked in the afterglow of amazing sex. The air conditioning dried the sweat on our bodies and we listened to the sound of each other's breathing slowing, our heartbeats returning to normal.

And then his phone rang.

I sighed and looked over at him.

"Remember when I said there were things I needed to tell you?" Gavin said as he rolled over and reached for his pants. "I'm guessing the call is related. Once I'm off, we'll need to talk."

He picked up his phone. "Vincent." There was a long pause where I assumed Vincent was giving one of his lengthy monologues. "All right," he said. "We'll be there." When he hung up, he looked over at me. "You're really not going to like this."

I sat up, but didn't cover myself. I didn't feel as if I needed any protection. Whatever had been coming between us was gone now, and I had a good feeling it wasn't coming back. I might not like what he was going to say, but we were in it together.

"First, I have to fill you in on everything Vincent told me before you got to the club."

"The strip club?"

His head jerked up, but he relaxed as soon as he saw my grin. I'd seen him there. He hadn't looked at any of the half-naked or fully-naked women the entire time we'd been there.

"Yes." He smiled back as he sat down next to me.

I sighed. "Before you start, we should probably get dressed." He gave me a questioning look. "Or at least covered, because I won't be able to concentrate if you're naked."

He laughed, pulled the blanket over his lap and then started to tell me everything Vincent had told him. I had to admit, I hadn't seen any of that coming. I'd been sure Vincent was in on it too. The story would be easy enough to check. Gavin might've trusted his business partner, but I was still cynical, no matter how sad the story. A call back home would get things rolling, until then, I'd trust Gavin's judgment.

"All right," I said when he got to the end. "What am I not going to like?"

"Alizee is having a party tonight and wants us there."

He was wrong. I didn't just dislike the idea. I loathed it. Abhorred. Despised. But I'd do what needed to be done.

"Okay," I said. "I'm in." Gavin looked at me, surprised. "But you're going to owe me." I slid my hand under the blanket and wrapped my fingers around his cock.

"Oh, I'll enjoy paying you back." Gavin smiled as he pulled me on top of him. "With interest."

I laughed. We had some time before the party and I intended to take advantage of every minute of it.

THIRTY-FOUR
CARRIE

By the time we had to get up and get ready, we were both limp, boneless, and wishing we had nowhere to go. I could've laid in Gavin's arms for hours and been content. Based on the reluctance on his face, I felt safe assuming he was thinking along the same lines. We'd had sex twice more and I lost count the number of times I'd climaxed. We were in sync again and not just physically. There was an emotional and mental connection that had been hit or miss for months. It had been there each time we came together today and I felt more at ease than I had in a long time.

Still, we had work to do.

"Are we going to the yacht?" I couldn't resist asking the question as I rolled out of his embrace. He glared at me and I laughed. After a moment, he joined in.

"No, smart-ass," he retorted. "She has a place here. One of the rich neighborhoods. Her house is huge, so she's hosting the party there."

"And you'd know this how?" I asked as I headed for the bathroom.

"Oh, didn't I tell you? Vincent and I stopped by a couple times for the nightly orgy."

I threw a dirty look over my shoulder and stuck out my tongue for good measure before I disappeared into the bathroom. It was nice to be able to joke with him about this kind of thing instead of getting upset about it.

"Vincent's been there," Gavin called after me. "He filled me in on a lot of what Alizee owns. What she's bought with her earnings from exploiting people."

I could feel him getting back into the right frame of mind and I followed his example. Now that we were good, we needed to focus on helping Vincent and Pierre take down Alizee. I turned on the shower and waited a moment for the hot water to warm up. I'd wait until I was out of the shower to go over plans with Gavin. Between what Vincent had said and the pictures Pierre had shown me, we knew Alizee was dangerous. The fact that she'd come this far meant she was also very smart. The only way this was going to work would be if we had a plan in place. We needed to know what we were going to do as well as the where and when. And we needed to make sure we were prepared for any contingencies. Nothing could catch us off guard.

WHEN GAVIN CALLED Alizee's house large, it had been an understatement. At least comparatively. Her place was at least three times the size of the average homes I'd seen during my short stay. The gate across the driveway and the massive amount of security rivaled some of the pictures I'd seen from Krissy in LA.

We didn't have any problem getting in, but I still felt a bit out of place as Gavin and I walked toward the front door. The people walking around us weren't rich celebrities and businessmen like the ones we usually spent time with back home. No, these were old money. Old money that made prominent New York families look like second-class citizens. These were the kinds of people who could claim royal blood somewhere in their genealogy. Here, it wasn't money that mattered as much as it was the titles and the bloodlines.

Alizee was at the door, greeting guests as they came in and I felt Gavin stiffen next to me. Vincent wasn't anywhere to be seen, so we either had to act normal and go in on our own, or wait for Vincent and risk Alizee getting suspicious that something was going on.

"It's okay for things to be awkward," I whispered so that only Gavin could hear me. "She doesn't know what you have or haven't told me about your swim earlier today. For all she knows, you're acting uncomfortable because of that."

"Good point," Gavin said and relaxed a little. "Let's make sure she thinks that's what's going on."

I nodded. I didn't need him to tell me what he was thinking because I was thinking it too. I waited until Alizee looked right at us and then leaned into Gavin and slid my arm around his waist in a possessive gesture any woman would recognize instantly. I gave her a haughty smirk and then fixed a coldly polite smile on my face.

Gavin kept his arm around my shoulders as we approached, a stiff smile on his face.

"Alizee," he said politely.

"Gavin."

Her voice was warm as she looked at him and it was all I could do not to slap her into next week. Then she looked at me and a different kind of heat came into her eyes. She didn't bother to disguise her contempt of me anymore. At least not to me. I had no doubt the righteous mask would slip back on the second someone else approached.

"How nice of you both to come." She gestured for us to enter the house. "Please, make yourselves at home."

We stepped past and I breathed a sigh of relief. It was a fine line to walk, trying to convince her my dislike of her stemmed only from her obsession with Gavin and not because I knew about her disgusting side business. Or rather, the business that supported everything else she did. Sometimes the best disguise was distraction and misdirection.

Gavin and I went inside and began to mingle. Or, rather, Gavin mingled while I smiled and nodded, only understanding a word here and there half the time. Some of the people, when they discovered we were American, switched to English, but most didn't. I liked to think it was because they weren't comfortable conversing in another language and not because they thought they were too good to do it. I knew a lot of Europeans thought Americans were snobs because they thought everyone should speak English, but that wasn't the case with me. French just hadn't been the language I'd chosen to study in college. In New York, it was more beneficial to know Spanish than French.

After the first couple of introductions and subsequent conversations, I decided that if I wasn't able to be a part of talking to these people, the least I could do is observe my surroundings. We might be working with Vincent, but I was still loyal to what Pierre wanted too. There was no reason both couldn't be accomplished. Besides, if I could discover something that could help us, so much the better.

There were two floors, though it was clear that the upstairs were off limits. The burly men standing at the base of the staircase didn't look like the kind of people it'd be easy to slip one over on. Across the massive room I assumed was a parlor or entertaining room of some kind, were a pair of double doors. I couldn't see details, but the glimpse of shimmering blue told me a pool was out there. Judging by how far we'd driven and the direction we were facing, it was a safe bet that at least the second story had a beautiful ocean view.

The interior was full of expensive looking art work and sculptures I was pretty sure were worth ten times more than what Gavin and I had in our apartment back home. With each one, I wondered how many people she'd had to sell or how many tricks she'd had to force girls to turn just to get another painting for her fucking wall.

After my second glass of champagne, I excused myself to the restroom. I considered trying to sneak past the guards at the stairs or try to convince them to let me go upstairs, but I decided against it. It wasn't like Alizee would be keeping a couple of Russian prostitutes under the bed or in the linen closet. Knowing her expensive tastes was enough for me to make a mental note to tell Pierre to look into Alizee's finances.

I squeezed Gavin's arm and he gave me a warm smile before I walked away in search of a bathroom. I found it easily enough and shook my head at the opulence while I did my business. Once I was finished, I started back for the main room. Maybe Vincent would be here by now and he could let us know what we needed to do to get this ball rolling. I didn't want to pretend to be glad to be here any longer than necessary.

I'd barely made it two steps down the hallway when Alizee appeared, flanked by two men even bigger than the ones who'd been guarding the stairs. I stopped where I was, my instincts telling me something bad was about to go down.

One of the men tried to grab my purse and it fell to the floor. Along with it a bracelet I'd never seen before.

"I invite you into my house and you steal from me?" Alizee made a tsking sound as she picked up the bracelet. "That is not a nice thing to do."

"I didn't steal anything, Alizee." I kept my voice calm and even, as if I thought this was only a matter of mistaken identity or a misunderstanding. Inwardly, I was trying not to panic. Images of the two girls Pierre had shown me flashed through my mind.

"Really?" she asked. She held up the bracelet that sparkled in the hall light.

It was a diamond bracelet, and knowing what I did about her, I didn't doubt for a moment that it was real.

"How come this was in your purse," she continued. "My security will testify to that."

"I didn't take that, and you know it." My hands clenched into.

She shook her head, a wicked smile spreading across her face. "I think we need to put you somewhere while we wait for the police to come." She looked up at the darker of the two men and rattled something off in French before adding, for my benefit, "She will not cause you any trouble."

Like hell I wouldn't. I was already trying to figure out the best way kick while wearing a dress.

"If she does, I might be forced to think Gavin had something to do with this as well."

I scowled at her. "No one will believe you. It's your word against ours."

"You are correct that it will be your word against mine, but many will believe me. After all, you Americans are always coming in and taking what is not yours." She handed the diamond bracelet to the guard on her left. "Perhaps it is time someone did the same to you."

"I'm not the type of person you can make disappear," I said as the men took a step toward me. I chose my words carefully. "Gavin won't leave here without me and Vincent knows we're both here. People back in New York know we're here."

She shrugged. "Perhaps you will see the error of your ways and confess, though that would make it likely no one would believe you about any future accusations." She took a step toward me, a predatory gleam in her eyes.

"I wouldn't hold my breath," I said, standing firm.

"I would consider it, if I were you," she countered. "Because accidents do happen. And not just accidents. I'm sure there are many women who would kill their lover if they found him cheating. And some who would then turn their weapon on themselves." Her eyes narrowed. "I will give you time to think as I would prefer not to ruin my lovely party by calling the authorities about a murder suicide committed by an American woman who caught her lover with me."

I had to hand it to her. As far as blackmail went, that was a good threat, and I had no doubt she'd follow through with it.

She gestured toward me as she spoke. "My men will escort you to a room where you can think about my offer."

"And what are you going to do?" I didn't really want to know the answer.

"I am going to speak to Gavin in private." She smiled at me.

"I hope when we meet again later, we will both be satisfied with the conclusions that have been reached."

I hadn't thought I could hate someone as much as I hated Gavin's previous partner, Howard, but Alizee had managed to top him. I didn't resist as the guards approached me. No good would come from trying to fight them off. I had to be smart about this if I wanted to get Gavin and me out of here in one piece. I just hoped I was smart enough to outwit the bitch.

I tried to be subtle about looking around for Carrie, but I wasn't sure I fooled the old couple I was talking to. They were nice enough, but I was starting to get a bit worried. Carrie said she was going to the restroom, but unless there was a crazy long line, she'd been gone for too long. I caught a pause in the conversation and excused myself.

I headed toward the bathroom, but didn't get far before I saw Alizee walking my way. Her expression was serious and I felt a surge of concern for Carrie. Had something happened to her?

"Gavin, please come with me." Alizee gave me a sweet smile that didn't go to her eyes.

"Have you seen Carrie?" I didn't expect her to answer honestly, but I had to try, even if just to see what she said.

"I need to speak with you about your girlfriend."

That didn't sound good, which meant I wasn't sure what was going on. As much as I hated it, I knew I needed to hear what she had to say.

"Lead the way."

She walked away from the main room, taking a turn down an empty hallway. Halfway down the hall, she opened a door and went inside. She didn't say anything or even motioned for me to follow, but I did anyway. I hated knowing she expected it of me, but this wasn't really the time or place to be taking a stand, not when Carrie could be in trouble.

We were standing in a library. A fireplace on one wall, but it wasn't lit. All around it and lining the other walls were bookshelves filled with volume after volume of classics, most of which I assumed were first editions. This was the kind of library rich people had to show off how wealthy they were, not to store books for the pleasure of reading. These books probably never left the shelves.

"Where's Carrie?" I asked, sick of Alizee's games.

"I'm afraid your little lover is in some trouble," Alizee said. Her smile was more pleased than seductive, but I could see lust in it. "Seems she was caught trying to steal a diamond bracelet of mine. Naughty girl."

I glared at her. "What the hell have you done?"

"Nothing."

Such a worldly woman should not be able to speak in such an innocent tone.

"Alizee, if this is about what happened between us…"

"This is about just that," she said. She walked around me and closed the door. "Because I always get what I want, and you did not cooperate."

"So because I didn't fuck you, you're going to accuse my girl-friend of stealing a bracelet?" I stared at her. "Are you really that petty?"

"Petty?" She laughed as she moved closer, putting less than an inch between us. "I prefer to think of myself as creatively motivated."

"You know what, Alizee, I'm going to call your bluff," I said, exasperated. I'd had enough. "Whatever lies and threats you've told Carrie aren't going to work. She didn't take anything of yours."

"And she will be free to share that with the authorities," Alizee said. "Though I would not consider that a wise decision. After all, I do have a reputation in Cannes, and the police may be more likely to believe me over a stranger who is suffering from financial problems."

"We'll see about that," I said. "Especially since I don't think you're going to call the police anyway."

"And what would make you say that?" She ran her fingers down my arm and I was grateful I was wearing long sleeves. I didn't like her touching me, but I couldn't push her away, not when we were still doing this little dance.

"Because I don't think you'd want the cops snooping around here." I stayed cautious, but I saw an opportunity I wasn't going to pass up.

Her hands moved to my chest and pushed my suit jacket off my shoulders. "Is that so? Do you believe I do not have those in the department who will vouch for my honesty and integrity?"

"Oh, I think you do," I said, resisting the urge to push her hands away. There was something I needed more than I wanted her off of me. "But I also think you're involved in some things that even your buddies at the police station can't sweep under the rug."

Her face tightened. "You've been a busy boy."

I took the opportunity to take a step back and put more distance between the two of us. "I have," I admitted. "And I know more than you think."

"Such as?"

I knew I had to be careful here. "I know that your clubs have a bit of a reputation among customers who are looking for... companionship."

A slow smile spread across her face. "You are accusing me of supporting prostitution?"

I just raised an eyebrow and waited for her to say more on her own.

She sighed. "No, that's not it. Prostitution is not something one would care so much about."

"You're right," I admitted. "Not if it was working women doing it on their own."

"You own – I am sorry, owned – a sex club. This is part of the business," she said.

"It does tend to be," I said.

"And, of course," she continued. "Supply must always meet the demand. When it does not, we must be willing to go to lengths to provide for our client's needs."

"And what lengths are those?" I wondered if I could actually get her to say it.

She ran her index finger across her bottom lip in a gesture I assumed was supposed to be seductive. "I only choose those whom no one will miss. Ones who would have ended up working the streets anyway. And if you wish, I will share with you."

I felt sick, but didn't let it show. She'd confessed and now I had to wait for an opportunity to get out of here and find Vincent.

"Now that we have that out of the way," she said. "Shall we get back to discussing the terms of me not having Carrie arrested for theft?" She took a step into my personal space again, the intent in her eyes clear.

A deep primal part of me wanted to go completely drama queen and start pounding on the door, screaming for someone to let me out. I almost laughed at myself for it, but the situation was too serious to find much humor in it. Instead, when the two men with no necks and even less of a sense of humor than I had at the moment closed the door, I stood in the center of the room and took a slow, deep breath. I closed my eyes and repeated it, trying to calm myself. This was far from the worst situation I'd ever been in, and I'd always made it out okay.

I opened my eyes. I needed to keep my head. I looked around. They'd put me in what looked like a spare room, just like Alizee had told them to. Compared to the rest of the house, it was plain, but still nicer than most places.

That didn't matter though. I wasn't here to admire Alizee's interior decorating. I needed to find something that would help me get out of here. I glanced at the window. If I'd been here by myself, it would've been simple. Unlock the window and climb out. Awkward in my tight, fancy dress, but definitely doable since I was still on the ground floor. The problem was, I wasn't here by myself.

I couldn't run, not with Gavin still here. I would've called him, but I hadn't my phone. It was still in my purse, somewhere on the floor in the main hall unless one of the guards had picked it up.

I frowned. Well, the easy way wasn't going to work for me. I supposed that meant I was looking for the hard way.

And I had a bad feeling that way was going to involve a weapon of some kind. I began to look for something I could use. The problem was, I didn't need the weapon against Alizee. I could take her, I was sure. The two massive guys outside the door, however...

I'd need something big.

There was plenty of furniture in the room, but it was the heavy, antique kind of wood I wasn't strong enough to break. Great for a spare room. Sucked for needing a weapon.

I started toward one of the other two doors in the room. One would be a closet, the other a bathroom. I doubted I'd find anything there, but I had to at least look. I couldn't just sit here and do nothing.

I'd only made it a few feet when I heard noise from outside. Not party noise. Other noise. Bad, fighting kind of noise.

I wasn't sure if that was a good or bad thing, but I hoped a fight meant Gavin had figured out what happened and was coming for me. I just couldn't figure out a way he could take down both of those guys on his own. I loved the guy and he was tough, but those two were dangerous.

I tensed as the door opened, not knowing who I was going to see. The person walking in was just about the last person I expected to see.

"Fancy meeting you here." Pierre flashed a dimple.

"Pierre, oh my God. How did you find me? What are you doing here?" Relief flooded through me as I looked into his friendly face.

He grinned again. "What is the phrase?" he asked. "Rescuing a damsel in distress?"

I was still in shock and searched my brain for a decent response. I just couldn't wrap my mind around it. Pierre was here! How?

"How did you know I was here?" I finally found my voice enough to ask.

"I have my ways." He turned toward the door and looked both ways. "What reason did she give for locking you in here?"

"She claimed I stole from her," I said and started toward the door. "I need to find Gavin. She could be hurting him."

He held up his hand and I froze, suddenly frightened as to who may be coming from the hallway. He placed a finger against his lips to hush me. I didn't dare breathing, just listened intently.

Finally, after endless minutes, he whispered, "Can you prove you are innocent?"

"She said I took a bracelet of her. My prints won't be on it," I whispered back, wondering if was safe to try again. Now that I felt a spark of hope, I feel desperate to get to Gavin.

Pierre opened the door again to peek out, and I began to say we should climb out the windows when I saw them, the two security guards slumped on the ground.

For a moment, I didn't think anything of it, I'd seen unconscious bodies before. It made perfect sense that Pierre would have needed to overtake them to get to me. Then, I realized there was blood, a lot of it and realized Pierre had killed the men, not only knocked them unconscious as I'd first supposed.

Slowly, my brain began to process everything happening around me and I gasped, it all beginning to make horrific sense.

I looked at the guard's again.

The wide eyes.

A gaping wound across their throats.

I looked at Pierre, trying to understand. The gooseflesh that crept up my skin was evidence I already knew.

He sighed and eased the door closed again, trapping me with him in the spare room. "I wish you had not seen them, that you would have trusted me to lead you out of here without witnessing things you shouldn't."

"It was self-defense, right?" My lawyer's brain scrambled for an explanation that would get me out of here in one piece. "You saw that they were holding me against my will. You tried to talk them into releasing me and they attacked. You had no choice."

He gave me an appraising look. "You truly are a skilled lawyer."

"Thank you." I slowly backed away. The window was definitely looking like my best bet right now. I had to get away from Pierre before I could worry about where Gavin was.

"And I like you, Carrie," he continued.

This was not going a good way.

"But you are an honest person. You will have to tell what you saw, and I cannot allow that. My employers cannot allow that."

"Your employers?" I asked. I wasn't stupid. The moment I'd seen the bodies I knew Pierre wasn't a journalist, but I asked for confirmation anyway. Part of me wanted to know so, if I got out of here, I'd have information. Most of it, however, was because I needed to keep him talking.

"Let us say that my... family is not fond of hers. In Corsica, we are what you would call rivals." Pierre reached down and pulled a knife from his boot. It still had blood on it.

A thought hit me. "Those pictures you showed me, the files... were they real?"

"Yes," he said. "I needed for you to believe me so that you would testify to the authorities about the things Alizee had done. Your word would have weight."

"So she killed those girls?" Even as I said it, I knew what the answer would be.

"Unfortunately," Pierre said. "Alizee is not so sloppy. She does not leave evidence. I was forced to create my own."

I felt sick. I'd trusted this man, believed that our goals were the same. I couldn't afford to think about that now though. I had to keep him talking.

"If you're from some rival family, why didn't you just kill her? You obviously don't have a problem killing people, and getting to Alizee isn't too difficult."

"You are much smarter than I thought," Pierre said. There was admiration in his voice, as if he hadn't expected me to come up with such a good question. "If I killed her, my family would be the first suspect. It could cause war between our families and that would result in death. If she is arrested or discredited, we cannot be blamed."

"And everyone else is just collateral damage?" My heel hit the wall and I knew I was there. The window was to my left, a desk to my right. If I was going to do this, I needed to do it fast.

"I truly am sorry," Pierre said. "This is just business."

And then he lunged.

Just as Pierre started to make his move and my brain began to work on some sort of gibberish I suppose had something to do with fight or flight, the door opened.

Vincent let out what I assumed was a string of curse words in his native tongue and Pierre turned.

Maybe it was a reaction to what Howard had done, maybe it was instinct. Most likely, it was my self-defense classes kicking it. Whatever triggered it, I reacted.

My hand closed around something solid and heavy and I swung it at Pierre's head.

I had one of those moments where things seemed to go into slow motion.

I watched Pierre start to turn his head as the statue arced toward him. There was a moment of surprise in his eyes, followed by the realization that, no matter how fast he moved, he couldn't get away. The head of the statue slammed into the side of his face with a hollow-sounding thunk and the momentum spun him around. His eyes rolled back in his head and his body dropped. Blood sprayed from his mouth and I was pretty sure there were a couple pieces of teeth in it too.

As he collapsed to the ground, sound and speed came back into the world. My mouth hung open in shock and I could hear my blood rushing in my ears. Sure, I'd had a face-off with Howard that had been violent and physical, but I'd at least known Howard had been a sleaze before he tried to rape and sell me. I'd thought Pierre had been my friend. The swiftness he'd gone from being savior to killer took my breath and was more than a little shock to my system.

"Carrie?" Vincent said my name, his tone cautious.

I turned toward him and he took a step back, his eyes flicking down. I followed his gaze and saw him staring at the statue still clutched in my hand. One side of it was smeared with blood.

"Fuck!" I dropped the statue. I looked at Vincent and I could feel the horror on my face.

"Gavin told you I am on your side?" Vincent's voice was cautious.

I nodded. "I'm sorry about your daughter," I said automatically.

"Thank you," Vincent said hurriedly. He glanced behind him into the hallway and then down at the two men on the floor. He frowned. "I don't understand. Why would the man Alizee sent to kill you also kill her security guards?"

"He didn't work for Alizee," I said. "He said he was from a rival family in Corsica."

Vincent's eyebrows shot up and he came closer, this time looking at Pierre rather than me. "He said that?"

"He was supposed to discredit Alizee or something..." My short-circuiting brain finally remembered how to work enough to communicate what I should've been doing instead of standing here talking to Vincent. "Shit! Gavin!"

"Where is he?" Vincent asked.

"I don't know," I said. "But wherever he is, he's with Alizee and that can't be good, especially if she's telling him she's going to have me arrested."

Vincent looked confused, but I didn't want to waste more time by trying to explain, especially not when I'd already let myself waste time freaking out.

"Find something to tie him up with." I gestured toward Pierre. "And call the cops. We might not have enough to take down Alizee right now, but Pierre's killed four people I know of and tried to kill me."

"And you are going to...?"

"Find Gavin," I said as I leaned down toward Pierre. I'd spotted something useful. "And if Alizee has done anything at all to him, I'm going to kick her scrawny ass back to Corsica."

I was pretty sure there were a lot of men who would've loved to have a woman as beautiful as Alizee try to seduce them, and more than a few who wouldn't mind if she was a complete psychopath, but I wasn't one of them. And I probably wouldn't have been one of them even if she hadn't been threatening to arrest my girlfriend.

"It's very simple," she said as she pressed her body against mine. "You give me what I want and things in France do not become complicated for you and your lover." Her hands were at my waist, tugging my shirt from my pants.

My hands curled into fists. I didn't know how to get her away from me without having to physically manhandle her, and I knew that wasn't a good idea. She was already accusing Carrie of a crime she hadn't committed. If did anything she didn't like, I had no doubt the next set of false charges would be against me. Vincent might be able to help, but it might cost him everything.

"I promise," she continued as her fingers skimmed over a

strip of bare skin at my waist, "you will enjoy it." She smiled at me. "So much so that you may ask for more."

I put my hands on her shoulders as one of her hands dropped to the front of my pants, cupping my still soft cock. Her mouth twisted into a scowl when she realized I wasn't enjoying her ministrations. I seized the opportunity to move her away enough that I could step out from between her and the wall, putting distance between us even though she was still between me and the door.

"It's not going to happen, Alizee," I said firmly. "I am not going to have sex with you. Carrie is innocent and I'll make sure everyone knows it. I don't care how many officials you buy off, you're not going to pin some theft on my girlfriend just because I can't get hard enough to fuck you."

"I believe I will," she said. "I may even find more items she stole to ensure she enjoys the hospitality of a French jail for a while."

I bit back the insult on the tip of my tongue and focused on trying to find a way to get out of here and look for Carrie. I had no doubt Alizee had security guards all over and they could easily take me down. Even if it was just me, I wasn't sure I could get out. But it wasn't just me. Carrie was here somewhere and I knew Alizee would call the cops on Carrie if I ran.

"Alizee, think about this." I decided to try to reason with her. "If I don't want to have sex with you, it's going to be difficult for me to... perform. It won't be satisfying for either of us."

She laughed. "Come now, Gavin, do not play coy with me." She took a step toward me, making sure she was still positioned between me and the exit. "I am quite a skilled lover. I have no doubt I can... persuade you to be an active participant."

Apparently I was being too subtle. I glanced down at my

jacket. There was one thing I could say that would definitely get my point across. I hadn't wanted to put it quite this bluntly, but she wasn't really leaving me any choice. "You know that black-mailing someone into sex is rape, right? And what you just said, you're taking about non-consensual sex, Alizee. That's illegal. So how about you just take a step back, let me and Carrie leave, and we can pretend like none of this happened."

"Rape?" She raised an eyebrow. "Americans have funny notions about sex. A woman cannot rape a man who is able to perform."

I made a disgusted sound. "Unfortunately, there are Americans who would agree with you about that." I started to edge toward my jacket. "But I don't think I'll have a problem proving it."

"I do not understand." She scowled at me. "This is not a betrayal of your precious lover." The words dripped with scorn. "You would do this to protect her. Is that not a, as you Americans would say, a free pass? You are being given the chance to fuck me without repercussion from Carrie. She cannot claim you cheated and there would be no guilt as your reasons would be noble."

"You don't get it," I said. "I don't want a 'free pass,' Carrie is the only woman I want."

I was within arm's reach of my jacket. I didn't want to grab it now, not when I still didn't have a clear line to the door. I could knock Alizee down if I had to, but if she had some of those massive men within shouting distance, I wouldn't get very far. I would need a better head-start.

"Very well," Alizee said.

She reached toward the fireplace and picked up the poker. From the look of it, it was iron and while the point wasn't knife sharp, I had no doubt it could be used to kill. She pointed it at me.

"If that is your final word, then you will wait here while I have my men bring Carrie to us."

Her obvious threat told me she wasn't bringing Carrie here so she could let us both go together. Well, that and the fact that I'd see how vindictive she could be.

"I am going to hurt her while you watch. And then I will have my guards hurt her."

Alizee and Howard would've been a match made in heaven, I thought. I remembered what it had been like to see Carrie tied up and know that Howard wanted to rape her. I'd never forgotten the expression of fear and pain on her face. I couldn't put her through that again. No matter what it meant for me.

My shoulders slumped and I gave a weary sigh. I didn't have a choice. Well, I did, but it was a shit choice. I could keep telling Alizee no and then watch her torture Carrie because I didn't want to do something I found distasteful. Or I could do what needed to be done and protect the woman I loved. Sleeping with Alizee would hurt Carrie, I knew, but I trusted she would understand why I did it.

I had to make a decision and it came down to which was the lesser of two evils, which would hurt Carrie less. When I thought about it that way, it wasn't difficult to know which was best. Knowing it and having the guts to follow through with it were two totally different things, however.

"Okay," I said. I kept my voice flat, not wanting Alizee to know how much this was costing me. "I'll do it." The words were sour in my mouth. "I'll fuck you."

It wasn't as hard as I thought it'd be to find where Alizee was stashing Gavin. I couldn't really take super-sleuth credit though. I just spotted the security guard standing in front of a hallway that didn't have any people in it. If he'd only been looking out toward the party like he was trying to keep people from going down the hallway, I wouldn't have thought anything of it, but the way he kept glancing behind him told me there was someone back there.

I kept near the wall as I made my way along the edge of the crowd toward the guard. As I grew closer, I could see him shift his weight from one foot to the other as if he was nervous. A thin sheen of sweat coated his forehead.

He turned as I approached. He rattled something off in French and held up a hand so there was no mistaking his meaning.

"Look." I pitched my voice low so no one else could hear me. "I've been watching you for a while. You're so hot. Have you ever had sex with an American woman?"

"American?" His English was heavy accented, but understandable. "You think you are better than a French woman?" He laughed.

I grabbed his crotch and leaned in closely to whisper in his ear, "If you've never tried, how would you know? Are you willing to take the chance you'll miss out on something amazing? I'll blow you mind, among other things."

He didn't reply, but I could feel him getting harder. That was answer enough.

"I tell you what. Meet me in that room and I'll show you what a real woman can do to a hot, strong stud like you." I nodded in the direction of one of the rooms behind him.

He waited for a moment, then nodded and turned aside to let me pass.

"Give me five minutes to get ready, hun." I winked as I walked into the hallway. I could feel his eyes on me.

Inside, I thought I'd have to try every room in the hall, but I quickly noticed that only one of the first four doors were closed. I doubted Alizee would've stationed the guard so far up in the hall if she was down at the other end. She and Gavin had to be behind the closed door.

A locked door, I was sure. I glanced toward the guard, but he'd vanished. Probably just to the bathroom to prepare himself for what he thought was going to be the time of his life. I looked at the door again. I'd seen enough brothel raids to know I could either try to slam into it with my shoulder or I could try to kick it in. I slipped off my high heels as I weighed my choices.

I wasn't tiny, but I was far from a large, muscular person. I wasn't sure my shoulder would have enough force behind it to break the lock. I'd had a cop once explain the best spot to kick on a door to get the right angle to break the lock. I knew I could put a lot of force behind it and that I could hit the right spot. The problem was my dress. It was far too tight for me to get my leg up where it needed to be.

Dammit! I grabbed the slit in the side and pulled. After a moment, the seams gave and, with a tearing sound, the slit ran all the way to my waist. I was flashing my panties every time I moved, but that wasn't my concern at the moment. I had only one chance to get this right. If I didn't break the door down in a single kick, Alizee would know I was out here and that would be bad.

I closed my eyes and took a slow breath to steady myself. "Here goes nothing," I muttered.

The jolt that went up my leg as my foot connected was painful, but it barely registered. I was too focused on the now open door. I raised the gun I'd stolen from Pierre and entered quickly, sweeping from side to side like I'd seen the cops do when they went after a trafficking ring.

Alizee stood frozen, her hands inside Gavin's open shirt while his hands gripped the edge of the table behind him, as if her touch was painful.

"Get the hell away from him!" I ordered.

Gavin was staring at me, but I didn't look at him. I kept my eyes on Alizee. She glared at me, but slowly backed away.

"First you steal from me and now you threaten me with a gun?" Alizee eyes were flashing. "You are putting yourself into worse trouble."

"Shut up," I snapped. "We both know I didn't steal anything, which means you detaining me was kidnapping."

"But you are carrying a firearm," Alizee countered.

"I took it off of the man who killed the guards you had outside my door." I sidled around, never taking my gun off her.

"Seems you have enemies in Corsica who're willing to kill to see you discredited."

Shock rippled across her face and, then, was gone. She hadn't known and it had thrown her off balance. That was good. I wanted her off her game.

"I know about the human trafficking," I said. Vincent might not like it, but it was time to put all the cards on the table. At least, our cards, I wouldn't share his secrets. Once Alizee was in custody, if Vincent wanted to accuse Alizee of killing his daughter, that was his business.

"You know nothing," Alize said scornfully.

"I know you use your clubs as fronts where your clients, if they have the money, can buy sex or even a person. I know you take frequent trips on your yacht and that you have the resources and connections to make sure it's not thoroughly inspected." I was just a few feet from Gavin now.

"You can prove none of this," she said, waving a dismissive hand. "My government will not take kindly to Americans accusing a citizen of such things."

"But we're not your only accusers," I said. "Even so, you held both of us against our will and, the way it looked when I came in, were about to engage in sexual assault."

She gave me a smile meant to provoke. "He was enjoying it. In fact, he agreed to fuck me. You interrupted."

"Carrie, I–" Gavin started.

"I know," I interrupted. "Either she's lying or she threatened to kill me unless you had sex with her. I know you'd never cheat on me." I wasn't saying it for Alizee's benefit or because this wasn't the time for this kind of discussion. I said it because it was true. I trusted that Gavin wouldn't willingly allow Alizee to touch him.

"Foolish," Alizee hissed. "If you had given me what I wanted, you would have your club, money, a place in Cannes. To succeed in this business, you must be willing to do whatever it takes."

"No," I disagreed. "There are lines, and you crossed them. All of them. And, right now, a friend is calling the cops. You're finished, Alizee."

She stared at me for a second, her face frozen. Then she let out an inarticulate cry of rage and grabbed something from where it had been leaning against a wall. I had a split second to register that it was a fireplace poker, and then she was running toward Gavin, her arm up and ready to strike.

"Stop!" I shouted, even though I knew it would do no good. I had to give her the chance. When she didn't take it, I pulled the trigger.

The bullet slammed into her shoulder, spinning her around. She cried out in pain, dropped the poker and then fell to the floor. I hurried over and kicked the poker away. Gavin loosened his tie, pulled it off and tied Alizee's hands together. She let out a stream of curses in several languages, but we ignored her. Gavin fastened the end of the tie to the table leg and then went in search of something to use for her legs. I kept the gun trained on her, looking up only when I heard someone at the door. It was the guard I'd talked to. He looked down at Alizee then back up at me as I now pointed the gun at him. He slowly raised his hands over his head.

Gavin returned, grabbed the guard and tied them both securely with what looked like a curtain tie. Once that was done, he looked at me. The adrenalin rush was making my hands shake.

He gently took the gun out of my hands. He stashed it in his belt and then wrapped his arms around me. I pressed my face against his bare chest, breathing in the scent of him.

"I love you," he whispered.

Before I could respond, his mouth covered mine. Oblivious to the guard, Alizee or the sirens in the distance, he kissed me slowly, thoroughly. His tongue explored every inch of my mouth as if trying to memorize it. I responded with equal enthusiasm, wanting nothing more than to forget what had happened and lose myself in the man I loved. I'd come too close to losing him too many times. Never again, I promised myself. Never again.

FORTY

CARRIE

We were still kissing when the cops showed up, but both of us refused to be embarrassed about it. It was Vincent who'd alerted them and I knew he had explained things when I saw the understanding look on one of the officer's faces.

As much as I wanted to just leave everything for them to sort out while Gavin and I went back to our hotel, more explanations had to be given. I found a cop who spoke English and quickly gave my statement, as well as directions to the spare room where Pierre was still being guarded by Vincent.

While I was talking to one cop, Gavin was talking to another, explaining in French what happened on his end. A paramedic and a cop were crouched on either side of Alizee and she was rattling away in French, her eyes throwing daggers at Gavin and I the entire time. I hated not knowing what she was saying. I promised myself that if we really did end up with a club in Cannes, I'd learn French.

By the time Gavin and I were both cleared by the paramedics, Vincent had arrived. He walked past Alizee, not even looking at her as he approached Gavin and me. He embraced Gavin first and then me. Unlike before, I accepted the hug without reservation.

"I wanted to see you both before you returned to your hotel," he said. "I had to thank you for what you did. Thanks to you, my daughter will have her justice. I may not be able to see Alizee convicted of killing my girl, but she will at least have to stand trial for her crimes."

"I'm pretty sure she's going to spend the rest of her life in prison," Gavin said. "Even if it's not for what she did to your daughter. She confessed that she was engaged in human trafficking and prostitution. She also attempted to set up Carrie for theft, tried to blackmail me into having sex with her and that she didn't care if I consented or not."

"So you will testify?" Vincent said.

"I'm guessing we're not going to have to." Gavin patted the pocket of his jacket and looked quite pleased with himself. "I recorded all of it."

"Thank you," Vincent said again. His eyes were shining and I knew he was trying not to cry. "Go back to your hotel now. I will speak with you tomorrow about our plans for the club as well as a gift of gratitude for what you did."

"We don't need anything," I protested.

Vincent held up a hand. "But you will receive it none-theless. Go, sleep. Rest. We will talk again later."

I looked at Gavin and he nodded. He said something to one of the cops. I assumed he was asking if we were free to go because when the officer nodded, Gavin reached over and took my hand, leading me out of the library and back through the house where the party-goers had become gawkers. It wasn't until then that I remembered the side of my dress was ripped nearly to my waist.

"Um, jacket?"

Gavin glanced down at me, puzzled until he saw the full length of leg and partial panties I was exposing. His eyes darkened and he immediately handed over the jacket. As I tied it around my waist, he spoke quietly, "Since it's already torn, does that mean I can rip it off of you?"

A shiver of pleasure went through me. Everything we'd been through had my body flooded with chemicals and I needed a release. That sounded like an amazing way to start.

"Yes please," I responded.

Gavin growled in the back of his throat and put his hand on the small of my back, guiding me the rest of the way out of the house. "We need to get back in our room before I decide it's a good idea to get things going in the cab."

I was pretty sure he was only half serious, but I wasn't going to take any chances. I flagged down a cab and we promised the driver a big tip if he made short work of the trip. We got there in record time and Gavin gave the driver enough to make the man smile. We barely acknowledged it as we hurried into the hotel, ignoring the looks people threw my way, and took the agonizingly slow elevator ride to our room. I was sure I would explode before we got there, but I somehow managed to hold it together until we got through the door.

Gavin kicked the door closed even as he pulled his jacket off me and then it became a race to see who could get the other's clothes off the quickest. He won, of course, because he did as he promised. With a loud ripping sound, my dress became little more than a rag and was unceremoniously dropped to the floor, joining our shoes and his shirt. Even as we pulled off the rest of the clothes separating us, Gavin wrapped his arm around my waist and lowered me to the floor. We were still just a few feet inside the room, but it seemed like the best place at the moment. I didn't want to wait even the few seconds it took to get to the couch.

"Have I told you how much I love you?" Gavin murmured as he pushed my hair back from my face.

I nodded and pulled him down on top of me. "Now show me."

His hand twisted in my curls and he pulled my head to the side. I ran my hands up his sides as he began to kiss down my neck. Wet, open kisses that quickly became teeth worrying at skin, nips that sent little pinpricks dancing over my skin. I moaned as his mouth moved lower to lavish attention first on one breast and then on the other.

I slid my hand between us, my fingers teasing the tip of his cock, mimicking the wonderful things his tongue was doing to my nipples. When his teeth scraped over the sensitive flesh, I ran my nails lightly over the head of his cock.

"Fuck," he groaned. His eyes were almost black when he looked at me. "You keep touching me like that and this is going to be over too fast."

He pushed himself up and moved his cock out of my reach. Before I could complain, he spread my legs and settled between them. I cried out his name as he ran his tongue between my folds, teasing and dancing across my flesh. When he took my clit into his mouth, I moaned, then swore as he slid a finger inside.

"Yes!" My back arched as he curled his finger inside me. He lightly touched my clit with his teeth and I yelped. It hadn't hurt, but it had definitely been unexpected. Then he did it again, a little harder, and fireworks exploded inside me.

Even as I was coming, he slid a second finger into my pussy, coaxing me higher, holding me there until it was almost too much. Then he stood and picked me up. I felt cool wood under my ass as he set me on the table, but then he was pushing inside me and that was all I could feel.

My head fell forward against his shoulder as my entire body shuddered. Despite his earlier haste, he moved slowly, sliding into me an inch at a time.

"I love watching your face when I enter you." His voice was low, husky. "Fast or slow, it doesn't matter. If I could, I'd record your expression just so I could watch it over and over."

A thrill went through me and I shivered. "Yes," I moaned.

"And it's not just now," Gavin said. "I love the look on your face when you come. When I pinch your nipples." He nipped at my earlobe. "When I spank you. You are so fucking hot, do you know that?"

He held me tight as he came to rest fully sheathed inside me. I wrapped my legs around his waist, crossing my ankles just beneath his ass. The front of our bodies were pressed together, no space between us. Neither of us spoke as we held each other, joined as intimately as two people could be.

"Never again," he said softly. "I'm never going to do anything that puts you in danger."

I looked at him and brushed my lips across his. "I don't care about that. As long as we're together. All I want is you."

"You've got me," he said with a smile. He rested his forehead against mine and began to move.

His thrusts were hard and deep, drawing a cry from me with each one. I moved with him, meeting him with enough force to make him swear. My arms were wrapped around his neck, giving me the leverage I needed and I tugged on his hair, pulling his head back so that I could look him in the eyes.

"I want everything you have to give me." My voice was breathless and I could feel the pressure inside me growing. "I want you to show me every part of your world. Pain and pleasure. Dominance and submission. I want to be your everything."

"You are." His fingers dug into my hips.

"Promise me," I said. "Promise me you won't back down again. That you won't shy away from what you want."

"I promise." His eyes were clear and I could see the weight that had lifted from him. "And I promise to take you places you've never been."

He moved one hand between us and rubbed his thumb across my clit, pressing hard. My body stiffened as I came and still he kept the steady pressure, sending wave after wave of nearly painful pleasure crashing over me. A cross between a whimper and a moan came out of me and the sound seemed to undo him. He crushed me against his chest and came, his hips jerking as he emptied himself inside me.

We stayed there for several minutes as our bodies cooled and our breathing slowed. I caught my breath when he finally pulled out of me, my pussy throbbing at the sudden loss. Before I could climb down, he picked me up again. "I fully intend to make love to you all night," he said as he nuzzled the space below my ear. "But first, I want to try out that huge tub."

I laughed and leaned my head on his shoulder. I meant what I'd said. I didn't care where he took me; only that we were together. I had to admit though, a hot bath together did sound like exactly what we needed after everything we'd been through.

"Can we have bubbles?" I asked as he carried me to the bathroom.

"Bubbles?" He raised an eyebrow. "I'm a man. I don't do bubble baths."

I ran my teeth over his nipple. "I promise I'll make it worth your while."

He made a sound low in his throat. "Fuck. Just nothing floral, okay?"

I grinned. He was going to smell like roses by the time we were done. And if that meant he had to punish me again, well – my pussy throbbed in anticipation – so be it.

THE END

Krissy's story continues in *Finding Perfection (Club Prive Book 6)*, available now.

When Vincent said he wanted to give us something as a thank you for what we'd done, I thought he'd do something like buy us dinner out or something like that. I didn't expect our trip home from Cannes to be in Vincent's private jet, and I certainly didn't expect a detour to Paris.

He had a limo waiting for us and it took us straight to the Four Seasons where we were informed that we had an "All About the Chocolate" spa treatment scheduled later that afternoon. I wasn't entirely sure what that was, but I felt pretty confident that Carrie would like it. After all, it was chocolate.

The best part though was, as unexpected as the surprise was, Vincent had perfect timing. The last couple days we'd been in Cannes, Carrie and I had done some sight-seeing as well as meeting with Vincent to continue planning our joint project. But in the back of my head, I'd had something else brewing. I just hadn't known when the best time was to do it. I'd known from the moment I'd seen her that I'd wanted her. It hadn't taken me much longer to realize I wouldn't ever want anyone else. This trip had done a lot of things, not the least of which was make me admit that it was time for a change.

When Vincent told us about his gift to us, I'd taken it as a sign. Before we got out of the limo at the hotel, I asked the driver if he'd wait and take us somewhere. In flawless English, he told me he'd been hired to take us wherever we wished to go over the duration of our trip. When I mentioned a place I'd seen my last time here, he'd immediately nodded and said he'd wait while we got settled in.

Now, as we rode, Carrie stared out the window, exclaiming over all the sights. We'd be going to the Eiffel Tower tonight for dinner thanks to reservations Vincent had made, and we'd have plenty of time to see the other landmarks tomorrow, but this afternoon, there was a place I wanted to show her first. I'd purposefully been cryptic when I said we were going to go somewhere, but I didn't think she suspected anything more than another site seeing tour.

I'd been to Paris a couple times over the years, but had rarely taken the time to look around. One of the places I had been, however, was the Square Jehan Rictus. And that was where we went now. I held out my hand and helped Carrie from the back. She gave me a puzzled look as I led her up the sidewalk, but didn't say anything. She simply threaded her fingers between mine and let me lead her.

"A few years ago, I was up late and couldn't sleep. Jet lag or something. So I went out for a walk." I stopped in front of a large black tile wall and gestured toward it. Carrie turned, her eyes widening. "I ended up here."

"This is beautiful," she breathed as she took a step closer.

On the black tile was written, in various languages and myriad scripts, dozens of different versions of "I love you." It was called the "I Love You Wall." I meant to do some research on it, find out how it came to be, but I kept forgetting. I made a mental note to try to remember this time.

"I must've stared at this wall for a good twenty minutes," I continued with my story. "I've been to some of the biggest museums and art galleries in the world, seen the most famous paintings and sculptures done by the masters, but something about this spoke to me." I squeezed Carrie's hand and she turned to look at me. "When Camille died, I never thought I'd find love again and seeing this wall just made that all the more real. Then I met you."

She smiled and I knew she thought she knew what was coming next. A declaration of love. A kiss.

But she was wrong.

"I could tell you how I feel about you in every language I know, every language that's written here." I gestured toward the wall. "But it'd never be enough. I could make love to you every minute of every hour of every day, but it'd never be enough to show you how I feel."

I saw her catch her breath and knew it was time.

I dropped down onto one knee, even as I reached into my pocket with my free hand and pulled out the small box I'd purchased just before we'd left. The same woman who designed Carrie's necklace had made the ring too. I opened the box and watched Carrie's jaw drop.

"All I can do is promise to love you and to spend every waking moment of the rest of my life trying to prove to you just how much you mean to me." My voice caught in my throat. I thought this would be easy, that since I knew Carrie loved me, it was just a matter of making it official. Only now did it occur to me that I wasn't sure what I would do if she said no. There was no way to know unless I asked. "Will you marry me?"

For one heart-stopping moment, I thought she was going to turn me down, but then I saw that she was just trying to control her emotions. Finally, she nodded, her eyes shining with tears.

"Yes!" She bent down and pressed her lips to mine. "Yes, Gavin."

I slid the ring onto her finger and stood, wrapping my arms around her and pulling her to me. I took her mouth, this time kissing with more enthusiasm. Our tongues twisted around each other and I felt my body start to respond. It wasn't until I heard applause that I remembered we were in public.

I pulled back and caught a glimpse of Carrie's flushed face before I turned to see an audience of a half dozen people grinning at us and clapping. I smiled back and wrapped my arm around Carrie's waist.

"Can we go back now?" she said softly.

I looked down at her, concerned that something was wrong. Then I saw the lust in her eyes.

"We have a couple hours before that spa treatment and I think we should celebrate." She gave me a slow smile. "And I have something I want to give you too."

My cock stirred and I nodded, not trusting myself to give a publicly appropriate response. I followed her back toward the limo, my eyes constantly drawn down to our linked hands and the ring that was now sparkling on Carrie's finger. I never wanted to see it off. My stomach clenched at the thought of seeing it when we made love. Maybe we wouldn't do much sight-seeing during our time here. I'd be okay with that.

EPILOGUE

CARRIE

Officially, we'd been engaged for two months and all of the people important to us knew, but tonight was the night we were making the public announcement. It was also the night we were re-opening Club Privé.

And not as a dance club.

The day Gavin had asked me to marry him, I told him I wanted to give him something too. I'd been considering it for days and figured Vincent's surprise trip would be the best time to share. He'd been shocked, but it hadn't taken much to convince him I was serious.

When we'd gotten back to the states, we'd worked together on a truly joint venture. A sex club for consenting adults only, with no professionals allowed. All entertainment was carefully screened and we had set up an agreement with the local authorities to ensure there would be nothing illegal going on. Before we even opened our doors, we made sure we had a reputation for everything being above board. We knew that it might cost us some business, but that was a price we were willing to pay.

Tonight, it looked like that was going to pay off.

I'd purposefully chosen a tiny, dark blue dress with spaghetti straps, a v-neck and a short hemline to wear tonight and the moment I saw Gavin's eyes light up, I knew he remembered I'd been wearing something similar the first time I'd gone to his club. The first night we'd slept together. It wasn't the same dress since that one had been borrowed from my best friend, but it was close enough.

Speaking of Krissy...

I turned as I heard her call my name over the pulse-pounding music. I threw my arms around her. I was happy she was doing so well in LA, but I missed her so much. Standing slightly behind her and looking much more relaxed than I'd seen him before was Krissy's boyfriend DeVon. He was hot – not as hot as Gavin, in my opinion – and there were more than a few heads turning to check him out. Or they might've been looking at Krissy since she was wearing a tight, barely-there dress that almost made me look like a nun.

Behind her came our other two friends, Dena and Leslie, each dressed in different, but equally sexy dresses. Dena's was a shimmery silver that made her pale gray eyes shine and made her, with her pixie cut and petite body, look like some sort of fantastical creature. Leslie, however, was in a bright emerald green that complimented her thick red curls and showed off every inch of her curves.

Krissy and DeVon weren't the only ones getting admiring looks from our customers.

After about an hour or so, Gavin went on stage and thanked everyone for coming. He set out the official rules without sounding legalistic and then introduced me as his business partner and his fiancée. Once the cheers died down, he told everyone to have fun and led me off the stage.

My friends, after telling us both how well we'd done, went off to the dance floor. Gavin looked down at me and I knew he was wondering if I wanted to dance. I shook my head and glanced toward the door at the back of the club. His eyes darkened and he pulled me through the crowd after him as he headed for the door.

The sound died down as we left the main floor and neither of us broke it. I wondered if, like me, Gavin was remembering the first time we'd walked down the hallway toward that door. This time, however, I was going into that room knowing exactly what was there and that I was going in with the man I loved and would be spending the rest of my life with.

Over the past two months, Gavin had been teaching me about the things he enjoyed and we'd established a not-quite Dom / Sub relationship. I wasn't sure how we differed from other couples, but I didn't care. It worked for us and that's what was important. Tonight, however, would be the first time we'd use this room for what it was designed for.

As soon as the door closed behind us, shutting out the last of the sound from downstairs, it was like nothing existed except Gavin and me. I looked at him and waited for his instruction.

"Take off your dress." His voice had taken on that authoritative note that meant good things were in store for me.

I kept my eyes locked with his as I slowly lowered the zipper and shimmied out of the tight garment. Gavin's eyes widened, then narrowed as he saw my little contribution to making tonight exciting.

Once I stepped out of the dress, the only thing I still wore were a pair of six-inch stilettos. My nipples started to harden at the chill in the room, but my pussy had been wet from the moment I'd stepped outside without my panties.

Gavin walked toward me, the expression on his face making me even wetter. "You were out there with nothing on under your dress?"

I gave him a coy smile. "I thought you liked it when I didn't wear panties."

"Bend over the bed." He pulled his shirt over his head, revealing every inch of golden skin and hard muscles. "You need to be punished."

"Yes, Sir." I walked to the bed, putting a little extra swing in my step. I felt his eyes on me as I went and knew I'd pay for the teasing. My pussy throbbed at the thought.

I put my hands on the bed and my ass in the air. A moment later, I heard Gavin walking toward me. I tensed in anticipation, waiting to feel his hand on my skin, but it didn't come. Instead, I heard a drawer open and looked over.

"Face forward," he snapped. There was no anger in his voice and I obeyed immediately.

A moment later, I felt the brush of soft leather and knew what he'd gotten. More than once, he'd said he wanted to use a flogger on me. It looked like tonight was going to be the night.

"Let yourself feel," he said as he ran the strips down my spine.

I nodded, letting him know I was ready.

I heard the crack a split second before I felt the leather snap against my flesh. I gasped. This was nothing like it had been with his hand. That had been solid, a spreading of warmth across my skin. This was sharper, more intense. It wasn't more painful, just different. Smaller points of pressure. He flicked his wrist again and I cried out. My head felt forward, my hair falling in curtains around my face. I squeezed my eyes closed.

"When we go back out," Gavin said. "I want to know that you're going to feel every moment of this. Your dress rubbing against your ass, chafing the sensitive skin."

I shivered, then yelped as the flogger struck me again.

"The next time you decide to forgo panties without my permission, I won't just use this on your ass," he continued, his voice low. "I'll make you stand like this, legs apart, and spread your cheeks. Or maybe I'll have you lay down on the bed and stretch your legs as wide as you can. I'll flog your pussy until your clit is swollen and you're begging me to stop, then soothe it with my mouth until you're pleading for more."

I whimpered. I was torn, unsure if I was turned on by what he was saying or dreading it. I was leaning toward the first one. Every single thing Gavin had introduced me to, I'd enjoyed, no matter how kinky or strange it had seemed at first. I trusted him.

Two quick snaps made my body jerk and then Gavin's hands were on me, sliding over my burning ass and up my sides. He cupped my breasts, squeezing them tightly until I cried out. His fingers started to work on my nipples, pulling and tugging on them until my arms were shaking as pleasure and pain mingled until I couldn't tell where one stopped and the other began.

"I'm going to fuck you." Gavin's mouth was right at my ear. "And you're going to keep pinching and twisting your nipples until I come. When you put that dress back on, your ass isn't the only thing I want throbbing."

"Fuck," I whispered.

"You're not allowed to touch your clit," he continued. "I'm

not going to touch it either." He nipped the side of my neck. "And I'm not going to come until you do."

I swore again.

He pulled me upright, resting my back against his bare chest. At some point, he'd removed his pants and I felt his cock hard and heavy against my hip.

"Put your hands on your breasts." Gavin's hands dropped and mine took their place.

My nipples were already getting sore, but I did as he told me to and began to pinch and twist the sensitive flesh. My fingers tightened involuntarily as he buried himself inside me with one quick thrust. I wailed, grateful the walls were soundproof. Pain shot through me, down from my nipples and up from where he was stretching me without any preparation. Tears filled my eyes as I danced that line between straight pain and that edge that my body craved. Over these past few weeks, Gavin tapped into an even deeper, primal part of me than I realized existed. Now, he was pushing me further than before.

His hands settled on my hips as he began to thrust into me, each stroke pushing me onto my toes, driving me further and further up that line.

"Keep working those pretty little nipples." Gavin panted.

My head fell against his shoulder, my eyes closed. My muscles were shaking, trembling, as the sensations threatened to overwhelm me.

"Open your eyes," Gavin commanded.

I did and realized for the first time that he'd positioned us in front of a mirror. I couldn't believe what I saw. The erotic image of watching Gavin's body move into mine sliding in and out between my legs. The way my pussy opened around him, welcoming him as if he were a part of me. My skin flushed and glistening with sweat. My fingers on my swollen nipples. Gavin's eyes, nearly black. The muscles on his neck and arms stood out as he pounded into me.

"Come for me." Gavin sucked on my neck, then bit down.

I tried to scream his name as I came, but nothing came out. My hands dropped, my entire body going limp. My legs buckled, but Gavin continued to thrust into me, his arms wrapping around my waist, holding me upright. Once, twice, and then on the third stroke, he growled my name, his arms tightening around me until I could barely breath. He dropped to his knees, driving his cock so deep inside me I saw stars.

He pressed his face against the side of my neck, his breath caressing my skin. "I love you, Carrie."

"I love you, too." I shifted until I was curled on his lap, my head resting on his shoulder. I looked at my hand, the jewels on my engagement ring sparkling. "And I'm looking forward to a lifetime of this."

He chuckled. "Me too." He kissed my temple. "But how about we shower first?"

"Sounds good to me," I said. "But maybe we can play with a couple other toys first?"

He growled, low in his throat and I felt his cock stir inside me. "I would like that very much."

THE END
Club Prive continues in *Finding Perfection (Club Prive Book 6)*, available now. Turn the page for a free preview.

ABOUT THE AUTHOR

M. S. Parker is a USA Today Bestselling author and the author of the Erotic Romance series, Club Privè and Chasing Perfection.

Living in Las Vegas, she enjoys sitting by the pool with her laptop writing on her next spicy romance.

Growing up all she wanted to be was a dancer, actor or author. So far only the latter has come true but M. S. Parker hasn't retired her dancing shoes just yet. She is still waiting for the call for her to appear on Dancing With The Stars.

When M. S. isn't writing, she can usually be found reading– oops, scratch that! She is always writing.

For more information:
www.msparker.com
msparkerbooks@gmail.com

 facebook.com/msparkerauthor

PREVIEW: FINDING PERFECTION (CLUB PRIVE 6)

ONE
KRISSY

It seemed like more than a year since I'd been in New York, not a little less than one. For six years, this city had been my home. The three women I'd met here had become more of a family to me than my own mother and father. Dena and Leslie stood with me now as we waited for the fourth member of our group to appear. Carrie and her fiancé, Gavin, were the reason my own boyfriend, DeVon, and I had flown in from LA. Not only were Carrie and Gavin officially announcing their engagement, but it was also the re-opening of their club, the place where they'd had their first date. Well, sort of. The story of their relationship was the only one I knew that was even crazier than how DeVon and I had come together. The two of them had been through a lot and they deserved this celebration.

"There." DeVon's voice sent a shiver through me even though there wasn't anything sexual about the word or his intensions. His hand on my back sent heat through me that had nothing to do with the press of bodies all around us.

I followed where he pointed and saw the person I'd been

looking for. I grinned and shouted her name as I made my way through the crowd towards my friend. When I'd first met her at Columbia, she'd been much quieter and definitely less well-dressed. She was always beautiful, but her time with Gavin had given her the confidence to show the person I'd always known her to be.

We'd been roommates since freshman year and being apart for this long hadn't been easy. Of course, we'd both made new friends and found the paths our lives were meant to take, but that didn't mean we hadn't missed each other. The thing about being so close, the two of us picked up right where we'd left off. After a while, Dena and Leslie chose partners from their many admirers and moved off to dance. Gavin and Carrie headed off somewhere – I assumed to visit the private room she'd told me about the club having. And I definitely didn't blame her. If I had a hot guy and a private sex playroom, I'd spend as much time in there as possible. Well, at least I had one half of that equation here.

I looked up at DeVon. "Shall we dance?" I held out my hand.

He smiled at me, a slow, sensual smile that tightened things low inside me. That was the kind of smile I'd learned held the promise of great things to come. When DeVon and I had first been doing this little back-and-forth thing where we tried to deny how we felt about each other, he'd said that he didn't dance. When asked why by one of our mutual friends, he'd said it was because he'd never found the right partner.

He slid his hand into mine and the two of us moved onto the dance floor. His hand slid up my bare arm and then down to the small of my back. He pulled me tight against him until our bodies were pressed together intimately. If we'd been at a normal dance club, it might've been almost obscene, the way we began to move together, but here, everything was a precursor to sex. Well, except for the actual sex that I assumed was happening in the more dimly lit parts of the club.

"That dress looks amazing." DeVon pressed his mouth against my ear. The hand on my back moved down to my ass. "But I don't like it."

I turned my head enough to give him a puzzled look.

"Too many men in here are wondering if you could possibly look as good without it as you do with it." His hand slid lower and the tips of his fingers brushed against the tops of my thighs.

I'd specifically chosen this dress because it wasn't one I could wear to a function back home – when had I started referring to LA as home instead of New York? – and the re-opening of a sex club had seemed like the perfect fit for it. It was simple in the sense that it was plain white, without any fancy stitching or cuts, but no one would describe the dress as boring. At least not the way I was wearing it. Carrie would've called the dress one of my "barely there" outfits.

"There are just as many women looking at you," I countered. And it wasn't just women. I saw more than a few men looking our way who weren't checking me out.

"Well, if people are looking…" DeVon's Italian accent thickened the way it always did when he was angry or aroused. "Maybe we should give them something to look at."

I was wearing my favorite heels, which put me close enough to DeVon's over-six-feet frame that all I had to do was tilt my head for our faces to be only an inch apart. I saw the heat in his eyes and then his mouth was coming down on mine. Electricity zinged through me as his tongue darted into my mouth, tasting of the champagne we'd been drinking. I wrapped my arms around his neck and buried my fingers in his wavy, black hair. He slid his hand under my dress, squeezing my ass even as his action pushed the hem up enough to flash some flesh at the people around us. The idea that men were ogling my ass as DeVon fondled it made me writhe against him, less of a dance now than something even more primal.

I bit down on DeVon's bottom lip, then sucked it into my mouth, reveling in the growl I felt reverberating through his chest. His mouth moved down my jaw even as his free hand tangled in the hair I'd left down to cascade over my shoulders. With a tug that sent a jolt straight through me, he yanked my head to the side and kissed his way down my neck.

I dug my nails into his shoulders as he sucked the tender skin of my throat into his mouth. Ever since we'd gone public with our relationship, he'd been enjoying leaving hickeys and bite marks in visible places. My neck. Collarbone. The tops of my breasts. My eyelids fluttered as DeVon sucked on my neck, each pull making me even more wet.

He slid his hand down my leg and pulled it up, hooking it around his hip. I ignored the fact that my skirt was gathering up around my waist and flashing my white thong. All I cared about was the way DeVon's cock was now rubbing against me just right.

"Do you think you can get off like this?" DeVon asked as he sucked my earlobe into his mouth. He ground his pelvis against me and I moaned. "Dancing with all these people around us, knowing that all they have to do is look and they'll see your firm ass in those tiny little panties."

It hit me then. He wasn't going to let this go until I came. A thrill ran through me. I wasn't an exhibitionist. Not in a true sense where I'd want people watching me have sex, like on a stage or someone in my room, but this was different. Aside from the fact that I was actually clothed, the club wasn't brightly lit. People would see mostly shadows, the suggestion of what we were doing. If they were paying attention to us in the first place. People were probably more interested in their own partners.

Still, it turned me on, knowing people could watch at least a bit while DeVon and I danced.

He covered my mouth with his, the kiss hard and demanding. All of the desire I could feel in his body, the tension in his arms, how hard his cock was as it pressed against me, he poured all of it into that kiss. His tongue thrust into my mouth, exploring every inch of it. I moaned as I writhed against him, the fabric providing exquisite friction against my clit. We'd been together for almost a year and it was still fireworks every time we touched.

His fingers tightened in my hair, sending little pinpricks of pain and pleasure into my scalp. He tore his mouth away from mine and our eyes met. The love and desire that burned there only made me want to come more. I loved being able to do what he asked. What he commanded. I loved the expression on his face when I obeyed.

"Come, Ms. Jensen."

I smiled as I remembered how our first time together, he'd used my last name rather than my first, as if it could put a distance between us. It hadn't worked even then.

"Come for me, baby." His hand tightened on my hip, fingers digging into flesh, the extra pressure exactly what I needed.

I groaned, biting my bottom lip to hold back the cry that wanted to escape. I shuddered as I came and DeVon released my leg. I put my foot on the floor, but it was DeVon's arms that held me steady, kept us moving to the music until the strength returned to my legs. Once I could stand on my own, I reached down and took his hand, moving us off of the dance floor. I waved at Dena and Leslie as we passed, but I didn't stop. I'd spend time with them tomorrow. As for Carrie and Gavin, I wasn't going to waste my time looking for them. I knew they were busy. And once DeVon and I got back to our hotel, I intended to be just as busy.

TWO
KRISSY

"You packed the handcuffs?" I raised an eyebrow. I wasn't sure why I was surprised. I'd been on several trips with DeVon in the time we'd been together and he believed in the Boy Scout motto of always being prepared. I just doubted whoever had come up with that motto had been thinking of sex toys at the time.

DeVon and I had been all over each other from the moment we'd gotten into the town car Gavin had commissioned for us for the weekend. Before we'd gone more than a couple yards, DeVon had me stretched out on the seat and was pulling off my panties. I'd spared a moment to glance at the tinted window between us and the driver, but then DeVon had pushed my legs up so that my feet were flat on the seat – or at least as flat as they could be in heels – and I'd known what was coming next.

"Shh," DeVon cautioned. "I don't know how soundproofed it is back here."

I'd considered glaring at him, but then he'd pressed his mouth against the inside of my thigh, sucking and nipping at the tender skin there until I'd been fighting back moans. The first time he'd ever marked me, it had been in that same spot, a place where no one from work would've been able to see it since Mirage had strict no-fraternization policies at the time. Things had changed since DeVon and I had started dating.

"I wonder how many times I can make you come before we get to the hotel?" he'd asked just before burying his face between my legs.

Thanks to some traffic, the answer had turned out to be three times. Before I'd met DeVon, that would've been a record for a whole night with a lover. Since we'd gotten together, the four orgasms I'd had so far tonight had become about average. And I'd gotten the impression that tonight wasn't going to be average.

He'd had to help me walk into the hotel and I'd been pretty sure the people we'd passed had thought I was drunk. I hadn't cared what they thought, as long as they hadn't realized that my panties had been in DeVon's pocket and that, despite DeVon's very attentive tongue, the insides of my thighs had been dripping.

Now, we were in our room, standing next to our king-sized bed, and DeVon was holding up a pair of handcuffs and giving me that wicked grin of his that said I was going to be sore tomorrow. I held out my hands in the universal sign for 'cuff me, Officer. I've been naughty.'

"Strip." His voice held that authoritative note that had always twisted something inside me.

First went the shoes. Then, I grabbed the hem of my dress and pulled it over my head in one quick gesture, leaving me in just a strapless bra, the same white lace as the panties in his pocket. I gave him a moment to appreciate the view and then tossed the bra on the floor, too. With a sly grin, I ran my hands up my sides and cupped my breasts. They weren't overly large, but they weren't small either, just a bit above average. DeVon's eyes narrowed as I caressed my breasts, my fingers making circles around my nipples until they hardened into little bullet points.

"Did I say you could touch yourself?" He took a step towards me and I shivered in anticipation.

When I'd first met DeVon, I'd thought he'd been a control freak, wanting nothing more than to boss women around into pleasuring him. I'd ended up realizing that hadn't been the case. He enjoyed domination and I definitely enjoyed submitting to him, but what made us work was that I wasn't the traditional definition of a Sub. Not in the BDSM world. I liked pushing back...and he liked it when I did. What made us so good for each other was that we understood the other's needs and knew exactly how to fill them.

"No, Sir." I gave my nipples a light pinch and watched DeVon's eyes darken to almost black.

He reached out and took one of my wrists. Cool metal brushed my skin as he clicked one side of the handcuffs into place. Immediately, I knew that these weren't the flimsy trick ones that magicians used on their assistants. These were the real thing. Only one way out and that was the key DeVon set on the table next to the bed before reaching for my other hand.

He paused for a moment, a thoughtful expression on his face. I didn't say anything, letting him make whatever decision it was he was making. After a moment, he locked my hands in front of me and then took a step back. Slowly, he peeled off the fitted t-shirt he was wearing, revealing a long, lean torso with defined muscles beneath tanned skin. He was tall, with broad shoulders, but not quite as muscular as, say, Gavin. But like my friend's fiancé, DeVon had a strength and power to him that went beyond build. He was physically intimidating, but it was truly his charisma and personality that made people listen to him.

He unbuttoned his jeans and pulled the zipper down, but didn't take them off. He left them open, revealing a thin trail of black curls that ran from his belly button down to disappear between the folds of fabric.

I realized, with a jolt of desire, that he wasn't wearing anything under his jeans. I bit my lip. If I'd known that, I would've had my hand down his pants and around his cock back at the club.

He reached into the bag he'd taken the handcuffs out of and what came out next made my mouth go dry.

The leather belt was wide, definitely too wide to be fashionable. Not that DeVon really wore belts unless he had something like this in mind. Those were all stylish, and much thinner, which meant they hurt more. Wide belts were more like hands, spreading the sensations over a distance.

This was something that I hadn't known before I'd met him.

"Turn around."

I stayed where I was for a moment, holding his gaze, and then I did as I was told. I spread my legs shoulder-width apart, but stayed straight, not knowing how else he wanted me positioned. Over the past few months, he'd spanked me with his hand and used a crop on me. The belt had been a recent addition, though he still only kept to my ass. I knew some women – including former lovers of his – had wanted him to whip their backs and breasts. Some had even wanted their pussies whipped. I'd always liked things a bit rough, but he was still easing me into a lot of the kinkier things he enjoyed. My ass throbbed at the memory of the first time he'd taken me there. I'd slept with my fair share of men and I'd never been close to a prude, but DeVon had been my first for quite a few things.

"Hands on the bed."

It was a bit awkward with the handcuffs, but I balanced myself on my hands and waited.

The first blow was across both cheeks, barely enough to sting. The second was harder, heat spreading across my skin. Three and four came quick together and I gasped. The fifth made me cry out as it caught me across the lower part of my ass, the leather almost, but not quite, brushing against my pussy

"Move to your elbows."

I hesitated and leather cracked against my skin again. I did as I was told, suddenly aware of how much this position exposed my pussy as well as my ass.

The belt came down again, this time, curling around my hips, the center of it lightly connecting with my lower lips. My entire body jerked. It hadn't hurt. Not exactly. It was a sharp sensation, unlike anything I'd felt there before. When he repeated the same strike, I made a strangled sound that I wasn't sure was a protest, but I didn't know if it was a plea to continue, either. My brain scrambled to make sense of everything I was feeling.

When my legs were trembling and my body was torn between pain and pleasure, only then did he finally stop. My ass felt like it was on fire. He hadn't quite taken me to the bruising point, but sitting tomorrow was going to be a real bitch.

"That's my girl." He leaned over me and pressed his lips against my spine.

I sighed as his mouth began to make its way down my back, his tongue tracing patterns across my skin. When his hands slid over my ass, I whimpered, a shudder running through my entire body. His touch was gentle, but my skin was so sensitive that even the slightest touch was felt. Then his tongue was soothing my pussy.

I moaned as his mouth moved up. Another new thing I'd been on the giving and receiving end of recently. When we'd gotten ready for tonight, DeVon had given me a suggestion that I was now glad I'd followed. The tip of his tongue teased at my asshole, lightly moving over it even as he slid a finger into my pussy. The duel sensations began to pull me towards yet another climax. When he pushed a second finger into me, I squeezed my eyes shut as the first ripple of orgasmic pleasure washed over me. He twisted his fingers, his knuckles rubbing against my g-spot.

As I began to come, he pulled his mouth away, focusing on pumping his fingers into me, forcing my climax harder and higher. My knees bent and I writhed on his hand, unsure if I was trying to get away or get more of him inside me. Then his hand was gone and my legs almost gave out.

The smell of mint filled the air and I heard liquid being spat into the trashcan. A moment later, DeVon used my hair to pull me upright and turn my face towards him. I could taste mouthwash as he kissed me. It was teeth and tongue, as rough as his previous treatment had been, and my pussy dripped with my arousal.

"I was going to fuck your ass from behind," he said as he pulled away.

I shivered, remembering how intense that first experience had been, the way he'd stretched me, filled me. I could only imagine how it would feel combined with his hips slapping against my overheated and already sore skin.

"But I changed my mind." He released me so suddenly that I almost fell.

By the time I regained my balance, he was already on the bed, his long body stretched out, cock jutting up in the air, thick and swollen.

"I want to watch those beautiful tits of yours bounce while you ride me." He crooked his finger at me and motioned me forward. "And you're going to make yourself come at least one more time before I do."

I climbed onto the bed, waiting for the rest. He never gave me something so easy. My entire body was like a live wire, every nerve burning. It wouldn't take much for me to get off again.

"But you can't touch your clit."

Damn him.

I glared at him as I awkwardly swung a leg over his waist. I put my hands on his stomach, flexing my fingers until my nails dug into his skin. He hissed, his hands moving to grip my thighs. He pulled me forward until his cock bumped against my pussy. I reached beneath me to position him at my entrance, but I didn't lower myself onto him. Not yet. I slid just the head inside, teasing him with the tight heat he knew was waiting for him.

"Do you think you're in charge, Ms. Jensen?" His question was half-teasing. It had been what he'd asked me the first time we'd slept together, letting me know in no uncertain terms who was in control.

"I don't know, Mr. Ricci," I teased right back. "From where I'm sitting, it sure seems like it."

His hands moved up to my breasts. I gasped as he squeezed them, then cried out when his fingers began to work on my nipples. I kept my hands on his stomach as I struggled to stay upright. He twisted and pulled, doing all of the wonderful things I'd discovered I didn't just enjoy, but that I actually craved.

He sat up suddenly, his mouth coming down on my breast as his hands went to my waist. He worried at the flesh with his teeth and lips until I knew I'd be covered with marks. Then he took my nipple into his mouth and I swore.

"Cheater," I breathed as he sucked and bit until my nipple was swollen and throbbing. When he started on the other one, my stomach tightened and I knew I was close to coming. I was torn. On one hand, if I started riding him now, I'd come in seconds, but that meant I'd be giving in. My stubbornness won out.

He looked up at me, my nipple caught between his teeth. He pulled his head back, stretching my flesh until I cried out. My hands were trapped between us, folded against our stomachs.

"Are you in charge?" he asked his question again.

I started to nod, but everything disappeared in a wail when he did two things at once. The hands on my waist pushed me down as his hips snapped up, impaling me in one almost-brutal thrust that instantly made me come.

My head fell back as he held me against him, using his position to continue moving both of us. Each time I came down, I was met with his hips coming up, driving him deep. He gave me no respite, forcing one orgasm into another until I couldn't tell where one ended and the other began, and still he kept going. My arms and legs were limp, unable to process any commands I gave them – if I could've formed a coherent thought. At the moment, I was reduced to sounds of pleasure mixed with the occasional word or phrase.

"Yes! Please. Please. DeVon, yes."

Then he was biting down on the side of my throat and a new explosion went through me. I felt him coming inside me even as everything started to go gray. As consciousness began to fall away, I heard him say my name and I tucked my body against his, trusting him to take care of me. And then I let myself slip under.

THREE

DEVON

I looked down at the beautiful woman curled up against me and wondered, not for the first time, how I'd gotten so lucky.

I'd always considered myself the poster boy for the American dream. I'd come over from Italy when I was just eighteen with barely twenty dollars to my name and a scholarship to Berkley. Now, fifteen years later, I was the CEO of one of the biggest talent agencies in Hollywood and had more money than I knew what to do with. I'd paid my dues, worked my ass off. I'd had my heart broken and my trust betrayed, but I'd told myself that it had been good for me because it had made me see how people really were.

I'd slept with hundreds of women, indulging in fantasies most men could never hope to make real. Threesomes. Foursomes. Kinks that had run from a little bondage to out-and-out S&M. I'd never had relationships, only women I'd fucked. I'd never kept one around longer than a few weeks, not as a steady 'partner.' There'd been a couple that most people would've called fuck buddies, women who I'd been able to call any time, but who hadn't had any expectations. Whenever a woman had started to think she meant something to me other than a good fuck, it had been time to say good-bye.

Everything about my life, from the outside, had looked perfect. Hell, even I had thought it had been perfect. And then Krissy Jensen had walked into Mirage for a job interview. She'd been like no one I'd ever met before. Everything I'd thrown at her, she hadn't brushed off. She'd fought back. She hadn't cared who I was or how much money I had. Very few men had ever gone toe-to-toe with me. Krissy was the only woman who'd ever held her own with me. I had a feeling her friend Carrie might've been able to get close, maybe those other two women Krissy was friends with, but I doubted it. Krissy was the strongest person I knew, male or female, and it was one of the things I loved the most about her.

People who knew my sexual proclivities might've assumed that I'd want some submissive little mouse, the kind of woman who'd say, "Yes, Master," and take everything I gave her. Before, I'd liked that, but back then, sex hadn't meant the same. It had been about power and control. I'd always pleased my partners, never did anything they didn't just agree to but that they enjoyed. But it hadn't been about me wanting them to be happy. It had been selfish, me stroking my pride at how good a lover I was. It had taken me a long time, but I'd finally come to grips with the fact that because of what had happened between my ex-fiancée and my former best friend, I had the need to prove that she hadn't chosen him because I was bad in bed.

I brushed a few strands of silky hair back from Krissy's face, letting my fingers linger on her forehead before sliding down her cheek. A surge of love went through me. Admitting how I felt about her hadn't been easy. It had taken me months to actually say the words, "I love you," but she'd known that when I'd said them, they had been the truth, not something to say because it had been expected.

I'd always laughed at people when they'd talked about meeting their other half, or their soul mate. Even when I'd been with Haley and had thought that had been love, I hadn't believed in any of that shit. Meeting Krissy had turned everything upside down. She wasn't just my other half. She was what I'd have been if I'd been a woman. Smart. Strong. Fiery. She'd defied the expectations of her socialite mother and made her own way. Moved to New York City and then out to Los Angeles because she wanted to make something of herself. Not to prove anything to anyone, but because that had been what she'd wanted.

She was ambitious, but not ruthless in a typical Hollywood way. She'd do what needed to be done, but only if it didn't hurt the people she cared about. She worked hard, but money wasn't everything to her. She was compassionate to those who deserved it and brutal towards those who hurt the innocent.

I'd once seen her decimate a director who'd fired and then assaulted a thirteen-year-old client of ours because the boy had refused to have sex with him. There hadn't been enough evidence for official charges, but Krissy had taken it on anyway. I'd seen a lot of careers hit rock bottom and then rise to the top again. It wouldn't happen with Rudolph Delfire. He wasn't just through in Hollywood. Pretty much anyone with an internet connection knew what he'd been accused of and the kind of public humiliation they'd be subject to if they defended him.

I'd never seen anyone so driven. Except me, of course. She was everything I'd never known I wanted.

She was damn near perfect.

I kissed the top of her head and looked out the window at the clear blue skies. I knew she loved her adopted hometown of New York, especially since that's where her friends were, but I'd always prefer the West Coast. It was the beginning of July and the city had been brutally hot, but overcast half the time. At least if it was hot in LA, the sun would be out. Granted, there was always the smog to take into account, but we only had to deal with that when we were at the apartment in the city itself. Our house didn't get much smog.

Our house. Our apartment. Even though we'd been living together for a couple months, I was still getting used to the idea. Surprisingly, not in a bad way. After Haley, I'd never thought I'd ever want to live with someone. That was too much of a commitment, too much of a risk of being hurt. Krissy'd originally signed a six-month lease when she'd moved to LA and when she'd mentioned that she was debating looking for a nicer place when her lease was up, asking her to move in with me had just felt like the right thing to do. I'd been more nervous than I'd admitted, but it hadn't taken me long to realize that I loved living with her. That I didn't ever want her to not be there. Sure, she wasn't exactly the neatest person in the world, but she made the places looked lived in. Besides, I paid the cleaning crew well.

As it had been more frequently over the last few months, my gaze was drawn to Krissy's hand. Her left hand. My heart started to pound. I never wanted to lose Krissy and I never wanted to be with anyone else, but I wasn't sure where I stood on marriage. I'd proposed to Haley and, two days later, had caught her fucking my best friend. I knew Krissy would never do anything like that, but it was hard to shake the anxiety that came whenever I thought of making what I felt official. Fortunately, Krissy seemed content with where we were.

"Attention, passengers. This is your captain speaking. We'll be making our approach to LAX shortly."

I sighed. I hated to wake her, but we'd be landing soon. She hadn't gotten much sleep last night and it hadn't been my fault. We'd spent the Fourth of July with her friends, and then she and the other three women had decided they wanted to spend the entire night talking. Well, I wasn't sure if it was a conscious decision or not, but that's what had ended up happening, and Krissy had fallen asleep almost immediately after we'd boarded our flight back home.

"Krissy," I said softly. I gave her a little shake. "Babe, we're back."

She made a frustrated sound that brought a smile to my face. Even waking up, her hair a mess, her eyes full of sleep, she was beautiful. I kissed her forehead and handed her a bottle of water.

"I figured you would want a chance to wake up a bit before we landed."

She gave me a sleepy smile and rubbed her eyes.

I had the sudden urge to make a joke about Sleeping Beauty, but I knew Krissy. She'd most likely flip me off for the comment. My smile widened. We may not have been some Disney Princess and Prince Charming, but I would take our story over a fairy tale any day. We were making our own happy ending.

We made small talk as the two of us waited for our flight to land and then there was the usual hustle and bustle to get bags and catch taxis, though we were lucky enough not to have to deal with the latter. One of the benefits of having money meant we had a town car waiting for us. The driver was one we'd had before and he gave us both a smile as he opened the back door for us.

Once we were settled, I pulled out my phone and switched it off of airplane mode. It buzzed as a missed call came through, followed by a voicemail. I recognized the number even without the Caller ID. It was the agency. An extension didn't show, but since they'd left a message, I assumed it was important. Well, there was that and the fact that I'd given everyone the day off even though it was Monday. People in our line of work tended to spend quite a bit of time drinking on certain holidays, the Fourth being one of them. I had a feeling there were a lot my employees nursing hangovers today.

The message was brief, but I instantly recognized Melissa's voice. That made sense. My assistant would've gone in today, at least for a couple hours, even though I'd told her to take the day off, too. The only days she ever listened to me about were Christmas and Thanksgiving. Today, I was glad she hadn't stayed away.

I frowned as I hung up.

"What's wrong?" Krissy's voice was concerned.

"We have to head into the office," I said. I looked down at her. "Melissa called. Something's happened."

End of preview.
Club Prive continues in *Finding Perfection (Club Prive Book 6)*, available now.

ACKNOWLEDGMENTS

First, I would like to thank all of my readers. Without you, my books would not exist. I truly appreciate each and every one of you.

A big "thanks" goes out to all the Facebook fans, street team, beta readers, and advanced reviewers. You are a HUGE part of the success of all my series.

I have to thank my PA, Shannon Hunt. Without you my life would be a complete and utter mess. Also a big thank you goes out to my editor Lynette and my wonderful cover designer, Sinisa. You make my ideas and writing look so good.

Made in the USA
Middletown, DE
22 December 2019

81687291R00189